Mental Ward:
ECHOES OF THE PAST

Sirens Call Publications

Mental Ward:
Echoes of the Past

Copyright © 2013 Sirens Call Publications
www.sirenscallpublications.com
Print Edition

Edited by Gloria Bobrowicz

Artwork © Dark Angel Photography
Cover Design © Sirens Call Publications

ISBN-13: 978-0615890494 (Sirens Call Publications)
ISBN-10: 0615890490

MENTAL WARD:
ECHOES OF THE PAST

3 **Maintenance** *K. Trap Jones* ✓

21 **Wake** *Jason Cordova* ✓

45 **Where the Dead Things Have Gone** ✓
Sharon L. Higa

79 **The Blue Girl** *Lindsey Beth Goddard* ✓

101 **Room 309** *Chad P. Brown*

121 **Brother Keepers** *Lockett Hollis* ✓

149 **Eternal Asylum** *Sarah Cass* ✓

177 **Screams** *Alex Chase*

215 **Sleepover at St. Mary's Hospital** ✓
Kimberly Lay

241 **The Castle on the Hill** *Joseph A. Lapin* ✓

267 **Corridors** *Brent Abell*

283 **Rose Wing** *Denzell Cooper* ✓

319 **About the Authors**

Sirens Call Publications

MAINTENANCE

K. Trap Jones

I have seen many things during my tenure at Bay Pines, but none of that would matter; none of that could have prepared me for what I saw that night. It was just a job, something to pay the bills. I did not envision the level of torment and sheer frustration that would bombard me. My emotions became entangled in a dismal display of self-pity, one that I am having difficulty unwinding. I found myself praying each night for the rise of the sun, as I fully believed that everything would return back to the level of sanity that I was accustomed to.

A handy man; a maintenance man, whatever the job description listed was what I intended to be. I always had a keen eye for fixing broken things; from appliances to automobiles, it didn't matter. I could pretty much repair anything. Even as a child, I would break things on purpose just to fix it a few minutes later. Maintenance is not a wealthy career choice and it is extremely underrated, but it's what I liked to do. Following the dream carried me aimlessly throughout several apartment complexes, local businesses and whatnot, but the level of pay was never there; not until I saw the posting at Bay Pines. I fit the job description as if I had written it myself. The large asylum on the outskirts of town was well established and well known amongst the city. The vastness of the property and the amount of maintenance required would be a dream job for a person like me.

With high confidence, I answered the job opening and with resume in hand I walked up the steps of the asylum. I felt as if I was in full control over my destiny. The position was a fate that I wanted to conquer. The dealer had handed out all of the cards and I was going all in. The warden greeted me in the foyer. A delightful, elderly man, he was overly gracious in his demeanor. It took a bit of time for me to get accustomed to his over the top excitement, but I adjusted accordingly. Following him through the halls towards his office, we passed several patients dressed in the typical white gown hospital attire. I thought nothing of their involuntary trembling or the scraping of the walls with their nails. I had to keep my eye on the prize of employment.

"I appreciate the prompt response to the open position," he stated, walking quickly towards his office door.

"The position certainly caught my eye. I have a great deal of maintenance experience," I replied, trying not to over indulge in my skill level.

As the warden rattled his keys in order to fit one inside the door of his office, a screaming patient barreled through the hall, chased by two guards. I observed the woman being tackled by the guards. Restraining her, the guards kept her from self-inflicting harm. Mumbling in tongues, her face shook horribly as her eyes revealed a sea of white. My throat clamored, my lips became dry, but my mind remained focused on the task at hand.

"Good, good. We require immediate fulfillment of the position. In a place like this, the mind is not the only thing that breaks," he continued, chuckling at his own words.

The office was nothing special; in fact it appeared much like a closet with no windows. Full book shelves stood floor to ceiling and a modest little desk was being suffocated by file folders and papers.

"Let's take a look at your resume," the warden said, sitting back into a squeaky chair.

Without hesitation, I handed over my work history and took control of the conversation.

"As you can clearly see, my qualifications are all there. Maintenance and repairing broken items is my specialty. With over twenty years of experience, I am fully confident that I can tend to the needs of your company and the employees, and of course, patients," my tone was dead on, full of confidence and pride in my previous work experiences.

"Good, good," the warden answered, barely glimpsing at my resume, "we need a new maintenance man that matches your qualifications."

I felt like a piece of meat; a hollowed shell of a candidate. He was distracted by something. His attention was not what I was used to during a job interview, but I chose not to dwell in the notion.

"If you don't mind me asking, what happened to the other maintenance man?" I asked, not sure why, but at the moment it felt like a good conversational piece.

"Our previous maintenance man did not work well under the pressures of the asylum, but I am sure that you will meet the challenge at hand," he replied, shuffling through several files. "The asylum has a life of its own, some accept it; others do not."

I wasn't exactly sure as to what he was talking about, but I nodded in agreement just to show that I was listening.

"When do you need to fill the position?" I asked, pretty sure I already knew the answer.

"Immediately, the list of broken items is compounding as we speak."

I waited for the job offer, but instead was greeted with an eerie silence as he continued his search for something upon his desk. He was hard to read, was the offer assumed or was the interview over? I couldn't tell. To break the silence, I threw out another useless question.

"How many patients does Bay Pines have?"

"Nine hundred and ninety five, to be exact," he answered. "How are you around death?"

His rebuttal question caught me off guard, forcing my mind to clamor for words.

"I, I, I am good with death," I responded, thinking that I had just lost the job with my word choice.

"Tolerance of death is an important requirement for the position. Within the walls of the asylum, death is patient #996," he explained, sliding over a piece of paper to me along with a pen. "Sign here and the job is yours."

I glanced over the small texted paper; my excitement over achieving the job overshadowed the words that I should have read. My eyes went straight for the vacant line that awaited my signature. The warden noticed me quickly scanning the words as I signed.

"Just a formality; there are many visions within the halls that will greet your eyes. This is just insurance that those visions are kept within and not shared with the outside world. Mental rehabilitation is often misunderstood. We like to try our best to avoid any potential confusion."

"Understood," I promptly answered, not completely understanding what he stated. Handing the pen and form back to him, I gloated internally about my new job. Excitement swelled my eyes and moistened my tongue.

"As part of the position, we do offer quarters with a bed as well as three meals per day. Little perks to help along the way," he proclaimed with a smile, handing me a work list of broken items. "Pay is bi-weekly. I'll have someone show you to your room."

After shaking his hand and exiting the office, I was greeted by a large, burly man extending his hand.

"Welcome aboard," the man kindly said. "Name is Tyler; head guard here at Bay Pines. Congratulations on the new job. Good, honest maintenance men with mental stamina are hard to come across. Let's first get you a uniform."

Tyler led me down the hallway where our conversation continued.

"How long have you been here?" I asked, probing for information about the asylum.

"Oh, about five years or so."

"How many employees does Bay Pines have?"

"It fluctuates. At any given time, the number could be as high as fifty or as low as twenty-five," Tyler continued, walking through the hall. "Our turnover rate serves as a thorn in the side of the asylum."

"Is the leaving voluntary?"

Tyler smiles.

"Since my stay here, you are the tenth maintenance man I have met."

"Why do you think that is?"

"This place is unlike anything you have seen; the sights and sounds can torment you if you allow it. This is no place for a weak minded socialite seeking stability. The mental decay is often times difficult to deal with. Those who stick around have come to terms with their state of mental strength. Avoidance of drama and turmoil will lead to tenure free of dismay and disorder."

Opening a cabinet, Tyler handed me a tightly folded shirt and pants similar to his attire.

"Your name badge will arrive after you show you have the ability to stay," he says with a grin. "No reason in wasting resources on something that may not last."

My gleaming eyes met his challenge without words. I would wear that uniform with pride, proving my worth amongst the staff.

"Your room is down the hall to the right," he announced, gesturing through the crowd of patients. "I'll check in with you from time to time to see how you are adjusting. For now, I must tend to my chores."

I watched as his white shirt blended effortlessly through the sea of patients crowding the hallway. Gripping my uniform tightly, I waded through the patients trying hard not to make eye contact with any of them. The varying demeanors made the hallway come alive with ramblings and shrieks of terror. I maintained my composure as I felt hands gripping my shirt. Calmly grabbing the wrist, I pulled the fingers away as I continued towards my room.

With the door shut behind me, I took a deep breath to inhale the solitude of being alone, but the disgusting environment of the abode siphoned any such relief. The darkened room had no windows. A lone finicky light bulb hung from the ceiling, providing the only light. The ceiling was stained with water damage as excess water dripped to the floor, pooling upon the concrete. A rusty cot awaited me, which sat directly across from a decaying toilet. I knew the room smelled, but I chose to not breathe through my nose. Quick short breaths funneled past my lips in order to soothe my disapproving heart. I kept telling myself that it is a good paying job as I undressed and buttoned up my uniform.

A loud bang sounded on the door and rattled my senses. The sharpness of the noise tightened every muscle in my body. Pulling open the door, I saw the eyes of a woman. Her lips curled, revealing her non-hygienic teeth.

"They're coming; they always do," she mumbled uncontrollably, her eyes appearing distant.

Without responding, I shut the door, but could still hear her speaking. I had to get a grip on my emotions. Staring at my reflection within a cracked mirror hanging on the wall, I was able to pacify my racing heart. It was only a job and it had not even started. With my work list in hand, I opened the door and was immediately greeted by several patients pleading with me for mercy. A thick skin was what I required. The warden was correct; I needed to overlook the stench of death and the visions of decay in order to succeed. Pushing my way through the crowd, I felt myself becoming mentally stronger, focusing on the first item on the list. I was there to repair things, not get emotionally entangled with the patients.

The kitchen served as the starting point. A leaky gas pipe on a stove proved not to be a challenge, but my eyes needed to learn to stay focused on the task at hand. While replacing the tubing, my mind wandered around the kitchen and observed the thickened grime painting the walls a dark hue. Insects swarmed freely through the air, feasting on remnants of leftover food. Three meals a day? I was hoping that they did not get prepared within that particular kitchen.

A worn out fuse within the boiler room was next on the list. The furnace burned brightly, casting a red haze within the lower level of the asylum. The ash stained the walls and ceiling, forging a blackened pit. Hiding my nose and mouth within the shirt collar, I protected my lungs from ingesting the thickened black air. After replacing the fuse, I turned to climb the stairs, but was startled at the sight of a male patient huddled within the shadows of the room. Fear climbed up my spine as my tools fell to the ground. I had to once again focus on my breathing patterns in order to calm my racing heart rate.

I couldn't leave him down there; he appeared lost and confused. I placed my hand upon his shoulder to try to offer some sort of comfort, but he leapt up, pushing me back against the wall, gripping my throat. His tired, blood stained eyes had not slept in days. His face was covered in black ash, highlighting the abundant wrinkles within his skin.

"We have to get out; we must escape," he blurted out, drool streaming from the corners of his mouth. "The night must not come."

Keeping my composure, as I was legally an employee of the asylum, I thought it best to not go with my initial response of burying the claws of the hammer deep within his skull. Instead, I tried using words to ease his discomfort.

"It's ok, it's ok, I'll take you out of here," I said in a calm manner. His smile indicated that he understood me, but I think that he thought my words meant that I would take him out of the asylum. I just wanted to get him back upstairs with the others.

After leading him up the stairs, he filtered back within the sea of patients. I was particularly happy never to see him again. Third on the list was a leaky faucet within room #451. I took the rear stairs and as I exited into the hallway I was greeted with something very surprising; no patients. It was quite calm and satisfying to not have to twist through outreaching hands. However, the brutal screams echoing through the hallway snapped me back to reality. I followed the screams passing door #425. They got louder and more painful the further down I went. Door #431 swung open as I stopped walking. Tyler exited the room, shutting the door behind him. His uniform shirt was drenched in red. Wiping excess blood from his hands, he caught my eye.

"All in a day's work," he smiled, walking towards me.

I knew I needed to mind my own business, so I ignored the blood and screams.

"Do the patients roam freely all the time?" I asked, trying to change the subject and minimize the duration of the awkward situation.

"Yes, we're an asylum not a prison. Social encounters are necessary in order to correct a troubled mind, but occasionally one will go rogue," he continued, nodding towards the door he came out of. "When that happens, I get the call to...how should I say, get the mind back on track."

I had nothing else to add to the conversation; I didn't want to know any more than what he had already enlightened me about. Walking passed me, Tyler added one more statement.

"Lock down in thirty minutes."

I assumed he meant that all of the patients had to be in their rooms for the night. Quickly walking to room #451, I pushed open the door as the light from the hallway poured into the darkened room, splitting apart the shadows. I was relieved that the tenant was not there. Being alone was very gratifying as I repaired the leaky faucet by tightening the pipes and resealing the outside joints. It must have taken me a full thirty minutes to finish the task as a loud bell echoed throughout the room and hallway. The silence of the hall was destroyed by the wave of patients ascending the stairs seeking shelter within their rooms. Like a fish swimming upstream, I made my way back to the stairs and down to the lower level. An honest day's work, an honest day's pay.

The sun sank down; remnants of the bright rays faded through the windows of the first floor. Making my way to my room, I saw the warden leaving.

"How was your first day?" he asked, buttoning his coat.

"Great, I got a lot accomplished," I replied, not mentioning any of my encounters with patients.

"Good to hear, so I will hopefully see you in the morning."

"You don't stay on the grounds?" I asked, curious as to why he was rushing.

"No, no, no, I am only here when the sun is shining brightly. With the patients all asleep, the asylum needs no overseer," he replied with a stern voice. "Like I said, I hope to see you in the morning."

I stood alone in the foyer as the warden locked the door behind him. The sun crept further as the shadows pushed the light out of the asylum. Everything was quiet; everything was at peace. There was no more chaos within the halls; no more turmoil butchering the atmosphere. I was alone; it was quite relaxing.

Walking down the long hallway towards my room, I felt a presence, an inclination that I was being followed. Upon glancing backwards, I reassured myself that no one was there. Reaching for the door knob, I felt it again. Disturbances within a calm demeanor as if someone was standing right next me, invading my personal space. I was physically alone, but that did not stop my mind from trying to decipher the events. My eyes presented me visions that I could not comprehend. Looking down the hallway, I saw them, ghostly patients prying themselves from the stone walls. Hundreds of them moaned in agony as they scraped walls, desperately seeking release. I felt my hand trembling as it tried to grip the door knob. I was fixated on the walls and what I was witnessing. The hallway had come alive with the dead. The river of souls flowed towards me. Panic set in as my forearm muscles tightened, turning the knob. I could hear the moans spilling into my room from underneath the door. They were out there and I did not want to lay my eyes upon them anymore.

Silence again fell within the asylum. Thinking that I was hallucinating, I decided to rest my tired eyes. The rusty springs of the cot only offered partial comfort, but my aching bones desired more attention. Falling asleep, I felt a cool breeze brushing my face. Soothing at first, the breeze went back and forth as if someone was fanning me. Opening my eyes, I saw the soles of a pair of shoes swinging before me. Startled, I rolled out of bed and saw the vision of an asylum worker who had hung himself. With a tightened noose around his neck, he swayed ever so slightly above my bed. Dressed in a uniform, his mouth was gaped open, his eyes widened in fear. Any belief in ghosts I had was immediately escalated at that particular moment.

Behind me was another vision of a worker, his wrists cut to the bone. His body was slumped upon the floor within puddles of blood. As I backed towards the door, I kept staring at the visions. In a sadistic repeat of history, I watched as the first worker strung the rope and clenched it around his neck before stepping off of the bed. His neck snapped instantly as his body involuntarily twitched. The other man carved a razor blade deep into his flesh as blood spurted from his wounds. I could feel their pain and agony; I could understand their torment and suffering. Their emotions filled the room. Like clockwork, they repeated their deaths again.

With chaotic thoughts battering my insanity, I exited the room, but the hallway welcomed me with an abundance of death patterns, each unique in their own twisted ways. The ghosts paid no attention to me as I walked in a dazed state. Skulls were being smashed into walls; throats were being severed right before my eyes. Like a skipping vinyl record, the patterns repeated themselves over and over again. I was the only live person in the hallway, but that did not stop the asylum from feeling overcrowded with the dead.

The torment spewing from the walls was overwhelming. I felt insanity hopping on my back for a free ride. Within the foyer, the death continued up the staircases throughout the entire building. There was death around every corner, behind every door; it was unavoidable. Ghosts tossed themselves from the second landing, smashing into the ground. A ghost armed with a knife slaughtered three victims, butchering them to death. Gunfire rang out from near the front door as I watched a man enter the asylum. He opened fire at whoever was unfortunate enough to be in the foyer at the time. Bullets shattered the heads of patients. With one bullet left, the man swallowed the barrel and fired.

Further down the hallway leading to the kitchen, I saw a man dressed in a bloody apron wielding two cleavers. Madly swinging the blades, the man created ribbons of blood with every slice. I witnessed a guard getting attacked by several patients. They twisted his head until his neck gave way. Smashed in the back of their heads by an unknown object, the attackers collapsed and died alongside their victim.

There was so much death; so much pain. My mind could not decipher it all. It tried, but failed. An overwhelming fear clouded my judgment and shielded my eyes. I felt dizzy and sought stability by sitting upon the floor. The solid foundation provided me with much needed support. The feeling of the cool concrete reassured me that I was still sane. I felt that I was being challenged; attacked from all sides. Cowering on the floor, I sunk into the fetal position, tears squeezing through my sealed eyes. The serpent of torment pulled me into a deep slumber.

Jolted awake by Tyler, I shielded my eyes against the brightness of the sun leaking through the windows.

"You know you have a room, right?" he stated with a smile.

I quickly looked around after remembering the deadly visions that surrounded me. No ghosts; only patients laughing and smiling at my discomfort.

"Welcome to Bay Pines," Tyler stated behind a grin.

Through the front door, the warden walked in, keys in hand.

"What a beautiful morning, gentlemen," he said, walking towards us. "I see the new maintenance man is still here. I kept the flyer just in case."

"There were, there," I stuttered, not exactly sure as to what I was trying to say.

"No reason to explain. The question is, are you capable of fulfilling the position? Do you have the flexibility and the willingness to adapt to change? Others have tried, but I can see that your mind is intact. It is capable of seeing through the madness, concentrating on the task at hand. These are important traits that I am seeking within the maintenance position."

"Does this happen every night?"

"Yes," Tyler interjected.

"As the sun falls, the asylum awakens the souls of the dead. Those who lost their lives are embedded within the walls; mortar between the stones that construct this place. It is the essence of lunacy that highlights the production. Sometimes history is not meant to be unraveled and deciphered; we cannot understand everything, so why try?"

"The question is, are you capable of maintaining sanity?" Tyler asked, wearing the same blood stained shirt.

"I believe so," I responded with hesitation in my voice.

"Belief is a warped sense of reality; belief is fiction without boundaries. It is not a question of believing, it is a question of achieving. Are you capable of achieving success within the asylum with the knowledge that you have gained?" the warden explained. "Let us see how you react. Here is a new work list. If you complete the tasks, then your actions will speak for you."

I accepted the challenge in the warmth of the sun's rays, but knew that I would probably regret my decision with the rise of the moon. The warden smiled as I walked down the hallway, I could hear his voice following behind me.

"Remember, the asylum requires properly functioning machinery in order to prosper. That includes all employees and patients. Like I said, death is patient #996."

WAKE

Jason Cordova

I looked up at the Superintendent, confused. I had missed the last part of his introductory speech while lost in memories of a time past. It must have been evident upon my face for he frowned, sighed and repeated himself.

"It gets a little strange around here, young man. The usual creaks and groans of an old building that should have been replaced years ago, the patients who think they are being chased by demons, devils and who knows what else... The weirdness of it all makes you see – and hear – things that you thought are impossible. Don't let your imagination get the best of you. Stay focused and on task and you'll do fine."

"Sir, if I may?" I asked tentatively, speaking for the first time since I was ushered into his Spartan office. Aside from a picture of what I assumed were his children and a dying peace lily covered in dust, his desk was bare. The walls were naked as well and the carpet was an industrial gray. Much like the rest of the institution, it was worn, old and badly in need of a fresh face.

"Go ahead," he said, folding his hands on his desk.

"You said that the patients can be... restless," I tried, unable to find the proper word. "Wouldn't a, uh, sedative near the time they go to bed help them rest?"

"Good thinking," the Superintendent nodded. "However, our resident senior psychologist – Doctor Bartholomew, who you probably won't see since he works days – prefers a more alternative form of therapy for our patients. He believes that masking the symptoms doesn't help them deal with their overall problems, or something like that. In any case, I listen to the board certified doctor and deal with the craziness that comes with running a mental ward full of men and women who can be a danger to themselves. Or worse, others. So no, we don't sedate them."

"I was just wondering, sir."

"It's not a problem at all. I think I've answered that question a few dozen times in the past six months from new hires."

I glanced down, the beginnings of a question niggling away at the back of my mind. I decided not to ask, since I didn't want to risk this job. I was broke, living at home with my parents, and the proud owner of a creative writing degree from the local liberal arts college. Since I detested the food service industry, my options of employment after graduation had been limited. This was the first offer I had received, and with the state of the economy, I doubted I would see another one with as generous of a hiring package as this one.

Plus, I reminded myself as the Superintendent pulled the W-2 forms from his desk for me to sign, *the job is supposedly cake. Just make sure nobody tries to get out during the night and that they don't hurt themselves or others.* That was it. No fuss, no worries about feeding them or anything. The day staff handled the minute-to-minute interactions with the patients, leaving me alone with my laptop. I would have all the time in the world to write my novel, at long last.

I quickly filled out the forms, which promised that I would be taxed, taxed again and might get some back at some point in the future, and then signed the confidentiality agreement regarding patient information. That was tantamount to being hired, since patient privacy was the latest call to arms by rights advocacy groups. It was annoying, but necessary. If the patients didn't have any hope of privacy, why would they seek treatment?

"All right, here's your master key for all the outer doors," the Superintendent slid a silver key across his desk to me. I picked it up and pocketed it, making a mental note to get a ring for it later. "You shouldn't need to use it, though, since Maurice is in charge of locking up at night." He then pulled a different key from his desk and, with a moment's hesitation, slid it across to me as well. "This is our inner master key, which gives you access to everything in the institution. Be careful with it. I only have four copies."

I picked up the key and whistled softly. It was an ancient-looking skeleton key, a heavy iron piece with a large bit. Key wards were carved into the bit, grooves which allowed the key to open the locks. I inspected the large bow on the end and saw the initials *B.K.M.* engraved in the dark metal. I was fascinated by the key. *Stories could be written about this beast*, I thought. It was a weighty thing, and I decided that a bigger ring would be in order. I slid it into my breast pocket and looked at the Superintendent.

"Well, let's get you out onto the floor and acquaint you with the other two night staff. Boyko and Maurice have been begging for a third person for days now, complaining about how their rummy game was all screwed up with only two players."

"Ah," I muttered. I hated gin rummy. My grandmother played it religiously up to the day she died.

After picking up my briefcase from the floor, we left the office and walked out into the dimly lit hallway. Most of the patients were already in their rooms for the night, with the remaining day shifters guiding their docile wards to their respective rooms. The day shift people looked me over curiously as we passed, their eyes heavy on my back. *Judging me, perhaps?* I wasn't sure, but I figured if it bothered me too much I could always ask Maurice or Boyko – *what a strange name*, I thought – about it.

We turned left and walked down another long hallway. I spent some time looking around, gathering my bearings so I wouldn't get lost later if I had to wander around after everyone else had left. The yellow paint on the walls was cracked and peeling, and the tiled floor looked like it could use a good waxing. Despite the wear and tear of the ward, however, it appeared to be relatively clean.

We stopped at a small nurses station where two men, both elderly and not in the best of shape, were hunched over a table with a stack of playing cards before them. They were intent on their game and didn't see us approach.

"Gentlemen," the Superintendent coughed slightly. The two older men looked up, mild confusion in their eyes before they recognized him. "This is Kevin. He's our new hire, and I'm starting him out on thirds. Kevin, this guy on the right is Boyko, the old curmudgeon on the left is Maurice."

"I ain't no curmudgeon," Maurice grumbled as he stuck out his hand in my general direction. I shook it and was surprised. I tried not to wince; the old guy had one hell of a grip. Maurice let me go and jerked his thumb at the other man. "Boyko's the curmudgeon."

I looked over the other man. They could have passed for brothers if not for the differing color of skin. While Maurice was the color of night – I could detect a hint of Hispanic in his accent, which was odd–Boyko was a sickly, pasty white that I long associated with men who didn't see a lot of daylight. Both men were bald, clean shaven and wore glasses. Their button down blue shirts were identical, and for a moment I wondered if they shopped together.

"We don't have a uniform for the night crew," the Superintendent informed me. "But we do have a dress code. Collared shirts, slacks or khakis, comfortable shoes."

I nodded. "Good thing I guessed right."

"It wouldn't matter for your first week, really. Once you received a paycheck, I'd start to ask some rather pointed questions about your clothing. But since you seem to have everything already, I'm not going to worry about it.

Now, my wife's at home and dinner is waiting for me. I'll leave you in the tender graces of these two men. Boyko, try not the scare off the help. It's hard to find someone willing to work nights here."

Boyko made a non-committal grunt, which I took to be an assenting one. The Superintendent patted me on the back and glanced down at the briefcase I held in my hand. He nodded at it, acknowledging what I carried for the first time.

"We don't have Wi-Fi. I hope that's okay."

"Less distraction for me," I admitted. "I hope to get some writing done."

"An excellent way to stay awake, if you ask me," he chuckled dryly. "I think of myself as a bit of a writer as well."

"Oh? That's pretty cool," I said. Inwardly I rolled my eyes. With my degree – or because of it, I was never certain – someone else being a writer was something I heard all the time.

"Damn it, Soop. You hired a guy who don't play gin rummy," Maurice groused.

"Sorry boys. Well, I'm off. Hope your first night here goes smoothly," he said and walked away. I watched him go for a moment before looking at the elderly men who were technically my superiors. After a minute of silently watching them, waiting for something, I coughed.

"Got a cold?" Boyko grumbled, speaking for the first time. His voice was harsh, grating. I could tell in an instant that he wasn't going to like me much.

"No. I was just wondering what I should be doing."

"Lights out is at nine," Maurice began as he fiddled with the deck of cards. "Day shift leaves at nine-thirty, morning people come in around six. We're here from nine to six usually. You get one hour lunch break but the cafeteria is locked up after dinner. I'd recommend bringing a lunch box. I do a check on all outer doors around ten-ish, and you do a bed check at two. Just peek in their windows to see if they're in the room or not. I don't care if they're sleeping or jerking off, so long as they're in their room. We have four wings we're responsible for, with four more empty for now. There's a chart of all the occupied beds on that clipboard hanging on the wall over there. Use it. It has a map as well. Other than that, you can use the nurse's station up near the D Ward for your writing. Wall plugs over there. The fuses on this side are old and you could blow them out if you try to pull too much juice out of 'em. Any questions?"

"Uh, no?"

"Good. I'm forty in the hole on this bastard right now, and once I do a door check I'm making it all back. Anything comes up, come get us. Just remember the two o'clock bed check."

"You're not gettin' anything back," Boyko grumbled and looked up at me with icy blue eyes. "Take the bed chart, newbie. It'll help."

"Okay. Thanks," I said with feeling.

"*De nada*," Maurice waved his hand dismissively. I took that for the signal for me to leave. I reached over, grabbed the bed chart from the wall and proceeded to follow the map to the station near the D Ward.

After a wrong turn and a helpful young staff member I found the nurse's station. Maurice had been true to his word, as the desk had a comfortable chair with multiple outlets for me to plug into. I set my briefcase down, pulled out my laptop and cranked it to life. The station was mostly bare, though a large clock dominated the wall to my left. The entire ward was silent, sleeping, despite the early hour. I smiled for the first time that evening.

This job is going to be a piece of cake.

***

Two hours later I was thoroughly into the prologue of my book, a story about a young boy fighting dragons, when I decided I needed to stretch my legs a bit. I glanced at the large clock on the wall and saw that it was only ten, meaning I had four more hours until bed check. The D Ward was silent, sparsely populated. The wing could easily hold over one hundred patients, but fifteen currently called it home. I leaned back in my chair and grabbed the clipboard, flipping through the pages until I came to D Ward. I scanned the names and saw that the occupants were all women. I looked down the hall and decided I would do a bed check now on my ward, then hit the others later at the scheduled time. None of the doors of the ward could open without me noticing, and there was no way I could miss anyone approaching the station. I hit "save" on the file on my laptop and stood, feeling my knees scream in protest after being idle for so long. Bed chart in hand, I began to walk down the hall to the first series of rooms.

I peeked into the first room and saw the occupant lying still in her bed. A thin sliver of light from the outside allowed me to have a good view of the room. The walls were plain, padded for comfort and safety, though the upper walls were mildly dirty. The window, which had protective mesh covering it, was even dirtier. However, the sheets were clean and the floor looked okay. My earlier impression of the institution had been correct: worn, old and in need of some care, but a safe place nonetheless. I could see her breathing, so I checked her name off on the chart and moved on.

Room after room, the same situation repeated itself. A few of the woman were sleeping under their beds, their blankets pulled tightly around them, but that seemed harmless enough, so I let them remain there. I checked them off as I passed, and before long I was at the last occupied bed of the wing. I checked the name, looked inside the room, and saw the occupant sitting up in bed, staring at me.

I blinked, surprised. I hadn't expected anyone to be awake, though intellectually I should have known better. I watched her for a second, her gaze level as she met my eyes. I smiled, feeling a bit awkward, and she smiled back. I shook myself and turned away, feeling a bit odd. She was beautiful, not the normal stressed-out appearance that the majority of the women in the wing wore. Her eyes were bright, unafraid, and not cowed or spacey. They had a hint of sadness in them which touched my heart. Even her hair looked as though it had been washed and brushed recently. She was the absolute picture of what I termed "not crazy".

I walked back to my station, the patient's face burning in my mind. It was her smile, I decided after some thought. She had been happy to see me, which I hadn't expected. I thought that at a place like this everyone would be there against their will. Not for the first time was I forced to check my preconceived notions at the door.

I sat back down in my chair and looked at the screen. The story, which had been flowing easily minutes before, seemed unimportant to me now. The hero wasn't as interesting as he'd originally been, and the story seemed too quaint and predictable. I frowned, deleted a paragraph and stared at the monitor. It wasn't good enough. I started typing, stopped, and cursed. I suddenly realized that my hero was becoming nothing more than a common fantasy trope, and I hated being predictable.

I leaned back and closed my eyes, my mind on the book. *Was there a way to make him more original, something not straight out of every other book I'd read recently? How could I make him different than others?*

I heard a soft noise from down the hall and my eyes snapped open. The hallway seemed slightly darker, and my monitor had gone to screensaver mode. I glanced at the clock on the wall and groaned in horror. It was after midnight. Somehow I had fallen asleep, the comfortable chair lulling me into relaxing too much. My first night and I had fallen asleep on watch.

The noise returned, fainter than before. I struggled to identify it for a second before I recognized it as someone crying. I pulled myself out of the chair and grabbed my clipboard. I slowly walked down the hall, realizing instantly that the source of the sound was from the last room I had checked, the woman with the sad eyes. I approached it, uncertain as to what I should do. I knew that if there was a disturbance, I should go and get Boyko or Maurice. But... was this a disturbance? I was almost certain that crying in the dead of night was not too much of a disturbance, but I didn't want to be wrong. Not on my first night.

I reached her door and looked in the small window. She sat there, looking back at me. Her eyes were still sad, but something was wrong. I glanced around her room but saw nothing out of the ordinary. I looked back at her beautiful face and realized that her eyes were dry. She was looking at me, watching me. I opened my mouth to speak but stopped, unsure. Was I supposed to talk to them? Somehow, the Superintendent had left that part out during my admittedly brief orientation meeting.

I decided against it. I had no idea what her deal was, or why she was even in the institution. She could be some whack-job killer or something. I didn't want to antagonize a potentially violent patient, no matter how pretty she was. I turned away.

"Wait," she said. I stopped and looked back at her. She hadn't moved, hadn't changed her expression.

"Yeah?" I asked, my throat dry.

"What's your name?"

"Uh, Kevin. Kevin James," I replied, feeling foolish.

"Thank you."

"Uh, welcome?" I waited for a moment longer but she seemed content. I hurried back to my desk and sat down. I felt a slight chill run down to the base of my spine. As beautiful as she was, there was something decidedly weird about her. I leaned back and frowned, bothered. Then it suddenly hit me. If she hadn't been the one crying, then who had?

I stood back up, confused. The noise returned, louder than before, closer. It was in the D Ward, I was almost certain. Other than that, though, I had no idea who it was or where it was coming from. I scowled, my first night quickly turning into a pain in the ass. I grabbed my clipboard and started making rounds once more.

Every occupant was asleep, unmoving, except for the woman at the end. She was still sitting there, still staring at me. It was beginning to creep me out a little, so I decided to ignore her as best as I could. I looked down the hallway where the rest of the empty rooms were. Perhaps a window was open and the breeze outside was making the crying noise? I figured it was a long shot but, without anything to pin it down on, I had to check. If I still couldn't find it, I'd go get Maurice. I figured I didn't want to deal with Boyko that often.

I wandered down the hall and looked in the abandoned rooms. One by one I checked, the rooms haunting with their emptiness. As I moved further along, the quality of the rooms began to degrade. Some rooms were missing patches of padding, while others had water stains on the ceilings and dark, unidentifiable stains near the floor. The stainless steel cots were barren of mattresses, and the floors were covered in filth and waste. Trash was cluttered in the corner of one room, and something dark and unidentifiable was smeared all across the floor. I wiped my forehead, surprised to find myself sweating in spite of the cool night air.

The rooms were secure, though, with no windows broken and no noise coming from them. I scowled, thoroughly pissed off, and turned back to head to my desk. I froze and felt a wave of icy terror run through my veins. *Oh God, no*, I thought, horrified. One of the doors was wide open.

"Fuck me," I whispered and walked quickly back towards the room. I consulted my clipboard and saw that is was a middle-aged woman named Nancy Alvarez. I carefully approached the door, uncertain as to what I would find. I swallowed, steeled myself and peeked in.

"Nancy?" I asked, my voice hoarse. No reply. I looked at the bed and saw the still form of the woman lying in bed. I looked up and saw that her window was wedged open slightly, allowing for a small breeze. I blinked and almost laughed at myself. One of the day people had undoubtedly forgotten to secure her door and the wind had pushed it open. I fished my skeleton key out of my breast pocket and closed the door, securing the latch. The lock clicked and I pocketed the key, satisfied. My heart rate slowed down as my natural calm returned.

"Jesus," I muttered as I sat back down in my chair. The Superintendent had been right about the old place being spooky. My imagination as a writer was far more dangerous to me than I had anticipated, especially in a setting such as this. I checked the clock again and saw that it was closing in on one o'clock. I rubbed my eyes and yawned. Staying awake the first night was definitely going to be a challenge.

I tapped my keyboard and the laptop rumbled to life. I scratched my chin as I stared back down the hallway, wondering if the creepy/beautiful woman was still awake. Something about the way she stared at me both drew me to her and scared the piss out of me as well. I made a mental note to not go down there again unless it was a matter of life or death.

I looked at the screen and stopped cold. My heart lurched in my chest and my mouth was filled with ash. My story, the prologue which I had worked on for so long, wasn't there. Instead, my monitor was filled with gibberish.

The waking eyes of night are filled with sadness and delights.
The waking eyes of night are filled with sadness and delights.
The waking eyes of night are filled with sadness and delights.
The waking eyes of night are filled with sadness and delights.

"What the fuck?" I closed the word program and reopened the last saved version of it. The novel opened back up, the prologue on the screen, the words I had written hours before returned. I looked around the ward, suspicious. Was this Boyko or Maurice, messing with the new guy? I was becoming annoyed. I understood a little bit of hazing might be in order, but messing with my property was going too far. I closed the laptop and grabbed my clipboard. I would make my rounds now, then go talk to

Maurice to see if they were really messing with me. If I was lucky, I'd catch them plotting how they were going to mess with me next.

I walked quickly through the other three wings, doing my bed checks quickly. Most of the patients were asleep, though a few were sitting on their floors, rocking back and forth. However, none of them were attempting to hurt themselves, so I left them alone.

After the last bed, I looked at my map. Boyko and Maurice were down the next hall, followed by a right turn. I followed the directions and in no time at all found the two curmudgeonly old men, still arguing about their game of cards. It appeared that Boyko was getting the upper hand in the game.

"You cheatin', Boyko?" Maurice asked as I rounded the corner. The two men looked up at me and waved, their attitudes cheerful and good natured. Apparently Boyko was one of those guys who needed to be awake for a few hours before he was in any other mood than "horribly pissed off".

"How's it going, Newbie?" Boyko asked me.

"It's... okay, I guess," I admitted after a moment's thought. "The D Ward is creepy."

"Yeah, they stick them crazy bitches down there," Maurice informed me. "Half of them are here because they went sixteen different ways of crazy and killed someone. I heard one of them actually cut her man's pecker off and used it in their dinner. Fucking crazies."

"Damn," I whistled. I decided right then to not mention the open door to them. It'd probably cost me my job. "I did a bed check already because I was, ah, having problems staying awake."

"Yeah, it takes some gettin' used to," Maurice chuckled. He waved his hand for me to join them. "It's why me and Boyko here play cards all night. Keeps us awake. Join us and lose some money?"

"No thanks, I'm good," I smiled. "Wait, how do you lose money at gin rummy? You know, never mind. I just wanted to stop in and let you know that I'm still here."

"Well, since you already did a bed check, we'll swing on by around five-thirty or so and check on you. Daytimers roll in at about fifteen till six, so we need to be functional when they do get here."

I grinned. "So be awake, basically."

"Yep. Be 'wake and everything'll be okay," Boyko nodded.

I said thanks and went back to the D Ward, my mind wandering. It was obvious that neither man had left the station in quite a while, so they weren't messing with me. But *something* weird was going on in my ward. I thought back to the noise, the crying, the door being opened. I frowned and wondered if, perhaps, some vengeful spirit was at work or, worse still, a patient was out and completely screwing with my head.

"No, stop it," I growled. The Superintendent had warned me about letting my imagination get the better of me. The institution was old, dating back to the early twenties. Any building like this one was bound to have some weird noises or spooky crap going on at any random time. It was just the nature of places which were very old with some darker history. Combined with a man who had an overactive imagination and it added up to a badly written TV episode on cable.

The ward was silent when I returned. The wind had died down outside and the patients were still quietly resting. I did another bed check, just in case, though I avoided the last bed at the end of the hall. I knew she was still awake, somehow. I didn't want to deal with her creepiness. Besides, what if *she* had been the one who had fed her family her husband's...?

That was such a pleasant thought. Admittedly, a tiny part of me *was* morbidly curious to figure out which one of my wards had done such a deed.

I sat back down and my screen saver disappeared. The words to my novel were still there, though I had only written fifteen pages or so. Nothing fishy or strange had happened, which led me to believe that I had simply been half-asleep and typed out some crazy gibberish. I was still writing the prologue, with scene notes written in the margins just for safekeeping. Still, it wasn't a bad start, considering that I was writing while at work. I cracked my neck, settled in, and began to type again.

"Help," a voice floated down the hall, interrupting my progress. My head snapped up and my eyes narrowed. It had come from the last bed of the ward. Perfect. The pecker-hacker wanted my attention again. I growled in my throat and looked back down at my screen, ignoring the soft voice. I had only managed to add twelve words before the interruption. I grumbled and began to type again. Once more, her ethereal voice floated down the hall. "Help."

"Damn it,' I muttered and stood up. I picked up the clipboard and looked at the chart for her name. Somehow, in all the oddness of the night, I had missed what her name was. I scrolled down until I found her name: Sarah. I walked around the desk and towards her room, intent on giving her a piece of my mind.

As I walked, each step seemed to drag. The hallway was very long, very narrow, and created more shadows than I remembered from before. Each of the patient's doorways seemed deeper than normal, dark portals to faraway and long-forgotten hells. Every heartbeat echoed loudly in my ears, and every breath was more painful than the last. I rubbed my eyes and inhaled sharply. I was exhausted, I wasn't used to the place and I was growing impatient.

As I reached Sarah's room I noticed a peculiar smell which seemed to emanate from her doorway. It was faint, almost coppery and somewhat familiar. I looked in the window.

"What do you want, Sarah?" I asked grumpily. I didn't mean to sound that way, but my lack of sleep was beginning to take a toll upon me.

No reply. I realized after a moment that she had moved and was no longer sitting on the bed. She was now sitting in the corner, facing away, her arms wrapped around her knees. Her dark hair fell limply on her shoulders and her gown was stained horribly in the back. I was surprised at her ragged appearance. It had only been a few hours since I had marveled at how well-kept she had been. Now, though... now she was the epitome of crazy.

"Sarah?" I tried again.

"*The waking eyes of night are filled with sadness and delights*," she called out in a sing-song voice, her tone echoing from the corner. My blood turned cold as I recognized the words that I had somehow typed on my screen earlier.

"What did you say?" I asked.

"*The mourning light blooms and takes away the sights*," she continued. I tapped on the window to get her attention.

"Sarah? What's wrong?"

"*The Dark One guides me to the path that He made*," she sang, her voice growing louder with each passing note. "*Feed Him the souls that I have sworn, my debt is paid.*"

"Feed Him!" she screamed suddenly and burst from her seated position, charging the door. I yelped and jumped backwards as she slammed into the doorway, her tiny figure shaking the heavy door by the frame. Her tiny fists pounded on the glass, though she had no hope of breaking the thick, shatter-proof glass. "Feed Him! Feed Him!"

"Feed Him!" another woman cried out from a different room. One by one the women of the ward began to take up the chant. "Feed Him! Feed Him!"

"Y'all need to *shut the fuck up!*" I screamed, sweat pouring down my back and making my shirt cling to my skin. I looked down the long, dark hall of the ward, half-expecting every door to open and the crazy women to pour forth to kill me, or worse. My neck felt cold, clammy. I was beginning to be seriously freaked out.

The chanting cut off abruptly. Every hair on the back of my neck stood up as an electric charged surged through the air. I started shivering.

"Isn't the cold wonderful?" Sarah asked suddenly, her face pressed against the glass. A thin trickle of blood ran freely from her nose. She smiled, her teeth stained from the bleeding, her lips cracked. "It takes me home. My home. Do you have a home?"

"No," I whispered, my mouth answering before I could even begin to process the question.

"How sad. Home is where the heart is."

"I know."

"He gives me a home. A respite. Away from here."

"Sounds perfect."

"It is. He has such a gentle hand. All He asks is for one thing."

"What's that?"

"Sacrifice."

I stepped back, fully in control of myself once more. Sarah continued to press her face against the glass, though she no longer seemed to be trying to escape. Her lips smeared blood upon the window. Her eyes watched me, judging me, waiting to see what I would do next.

Truth be told, I had no idea what I would do next. Her blue eyes were piercing, cold yet inviting. I took another step back and tried to look away. To look at something other than her, to keep myself from drowning in her eyes. I stared at the wall, the door, the frame, but every second which passed drew my eyes back to hers. I cried out softly, the soft moan passing through my lips, unbidden.

"Help Him."

"I don't know how," I whispered in reply.

"Yes, you do."

I *did* know. I looked down at my bare hands, small but suited for the task at hand. There were fourteen offerings in the hall. Fourteen ways to honor Him, fourteen different ways to offer them up. I pictured every death in my mind, each more gruesome than the last. It would be perfect, well suited to the cold which He sought. The warmth of the bodies would eventually fade, which is what He wanted.

I looked down the hall. Every door was open, every woman were strewn out in their doorway. The bodies were old, worn, decomposed. Flies buzzed loudly in my ears, filling the void with the sound of death. The overwhelming stench of rot filled my nostrils. Blood pooled from beneath each of the women. It sickened me.

"No," I protested, my voice weak. "I don't want this."

"You don't?" a soft voice asked from over my shoulder. Her small, gentle hand took mine. Her fingers were cold, dry. Her skin was papery and flaked off in my hand. "You have done wondrous things in your life, Kevin, but none as wondrous as this."

The buzzing in my ears grew louder. I let go of Sarah's hand and covered my ears.

"No," I said again, stronger this time. I tore my gaze away from the dead women in the hallway. "No!"

I turned and pushed Sarah away. Her body, rotted like the others, stumbled backwards from the force of the shove. Her eyes, milky white and filled with death, looked betrayed. Her mouth, with blackened lips and broken teeth, turned into a frown. She hissed through those horrible teeth.

" *Traitor.*"

"No!" I shouted in defiance and turned to run. "I didn't do this! I didn't! I swear that I didn't want this!"

A heavy hand grabbed my shoulder, stopping me. I screamed like a little girl and nearly wet myself.

"Damn, boy," Maurice laughed as I bolted upright in the chair. "You done fell asleep, didn't you?"

"The fuck?!" I exploded, looking around the ward. None of the doors were open, the filth and blood gone. The bodies were missing, and the horrible buzzing from flies circling no longer filled my ears. The lights of the ward were still dimmed, though I could see the barest traces of sunrise beginning to creep in from the outside. Daylight was coming, my long first night at my new job was about over. I swore again and wiped my sweaty palms on my trousers.

"Heh," Maurice grunted. "First time Boyko fell asleep I smeared his ass with honey and poured feathers on it. Old coot bitched about it for months. Call him 'chicken ass' sometime and watch the fun. Heh. I took it easy on you, kid. Yeah, you're welcome."

I rubbed my eyes. "Damn. I didn't mean to... I mean, how... well, damn."

"Had a nightmare? This place does that to you."

"No. Well, yeah. Damn it, I wanted to get some more writing done."

Maurice leaned over my shoulder and looked at my monitor.

"Hell, you need more time to write? Looks like you wrote a goddamned book here."

"Huh?" I muttered and looked at the screen. I blinked and gasped, shocked.

Somehow, during the crazy night, I had written over three hundred pages. Instead of my fantasy novel, however, I had written a horror novel. I read it, engrossed in the words. The book was written in my voice, and yet... there was something darker, subtly dangerous in the pitch. I frowned, confused, before I slowly began to smile. Whatever had happened to me during the night, this shit was *good*. The pacing was fast and the plot – from what I had gleaned from the first few pages – was solid. My professors would have been impressed with the effort. I said as much to Maurice, who chuckled.

"Guess we found the perfect job for you then, right?"

I saved the file and closed the laptop. I shook my head in wonder and put the laptop inside my briefcase. I didn't know where it had come from, but my father always said to not look a gift horse in the mouth. I really had no idea what it meant, but it sounded good. I zipped it closed and looked back at the old man.

"We need to clock out or anything?"

"Naw, just write it on a sheet of paper and turn it in to the Soop at the end of the week."

"Cool."

"I'll meet you over at our station," Maurice said and wandered off, whistling softly as he went. I watched him go before I looked around at the D Ward for a final time.

Whatever the hell had happened, it was just a dream. I had been writing and somehow my brain had transposed what I was dreaming onto the pages. That was all. I'd heard of people doing that before, though up until now had never believed it. I shrugged mentally and grabbed my briefcase's handle.

Something warm and sticky filled my hand. *Fucking Maurice*, I grumbled as I set the briefcase down on the desk. The old man *had* gotten me, though not as good, evidently, as he had Boyko. I grimaced and looked down.

A bright red streak of blood was smeared across the palm of my hand.

WHERE THE DEAD HAVE GONE

Sharon L. Hilga

"Geeezus Ceeeerist, will you look at that?!" Tony's voice cracked at the end of his sentence, his words seeming to follow the upward arc of his flashlight. The wall seemed to stretch for eternity, disappearing into the darkness above, into the clouds obscuring the moon.

Rich played his flashlight along the length of the building, trying to gauge its width and also find a possible opening in the chain-linked barbed wire fencing surrounding the massive, crumbling structure. "Man," he mused, "Can you imagine what this place looked like in its heyday?"

Shawn struggled up beside him, dropping the big black case he was lugging at Rich's feet with a muffled thump. Straightening up and placing his hands to the small of his back, he groaned.

"Yeah, from the photos I saw in the Library, it was scary enough when it was a functioning facility." He looked at the spots visible in the beams of his friends' flashlights. He took a deep breath. "Now, it's just terrifying."

Tony looked over his shoulder and flashed the beam of his light into Shawn's face. "C'mon man, don't tell me your pussyin' out. We've come here to prove that the stories surrounding this place are pure bullshit – made up by old folks to keep young folks out, and made up by our so-called peers because of overactive imaginations and too many drugs done before comin' out to this place to do some real partyin'."

Rich cocked an eyebrow at his friend. He knew that Tony was the "Dyed-in-the-wool" skeptic among them – someone who truly did not believe unless he could actually see- and then he would spend whatever time it took to debunk what he had seen. He smiled at Shawn and gave him a 'Thumbs up' behind Tony's back. That is exactly the attitude they needed to round out their original team of two. They had done some 'small' stuff, but this was going to be the feather in their cap – would make them the envy of their school and give the actual proof to everyone in the town about the old McCane Therapeutic Sanitarium.

Shawn squinted ahead of Rich and nudged him to point the flashlight in a particular direction. "Flash the light there, bro. I think I see a way in."

Tony and Rich combined their lights and saw a piece of the chain-link fence sticking up a bit from the weed choked ground. Leaving Shawn to grab the case, the two boys walked over to the corner of the post.

"Hold this, will ya?" Tony thrust his flashlight at Rich before he could say anything. He bent over and grasped the corner of the chain-link. With a huge heave, Tony pulled the fence up and sideways. It gave way with almost eerie ease, jerking up to the middle height of the metal post it had been attached to, leaving enough room for all three of the guys and the case to fit.

After Rich and Shawn ducked under, Tony limboed in and pulled the fence back down, bending and shaping it to look as it had before they'd gone through. Satisfied with the result, he nodded and turned to face the others, dusting dirt and rust off his hands onto the front of his jeans.

All three stood still, getting their bearings to any kind of opening to the building. After a couple of minutes, Shawn pointed to their left. "There. As I recall from the pictures, there should be a staff entrance along the wall, down a couple of steps." Tony and Rich looked at him. He shifted a little, uncomfortable at their silent stares. "Well, dammit, it's a good place to start, right?"

Tony mock bowed and with an exaggerated motion, stepped aside. "Lead the way, B'wana."

Gritting his teeth, Shawn grabbed up the case and started across the dry, crackling grass. "Get up here and hold the flashlight for me, smart asses," he growled over his shoulder. "Should've given me a flashlight if you wanted me to lead the way," he muttered, just loud enough for the guys behind him to hear. Tony and Rich trotted up alongside him, Tony holding his light to the ground, Rich shining up ahead at the projected entrance.

They reached the stairs and Shawn leaned against the wall to catch his breath. With a startled hiss and a snap back, he jerked his hand away, shaking his fingers. "What the Hell...?" his voice trailed off as he glanced at the spot then back at his hand.

Rich and Tony stared at him. Rich leaned forward and touched the red brick. Tentatively at first, but then he laid his whole palm against it and kept it there.

"Don't you feel it?" Shawn's voice rose a little. Tony moved his light next to Rich and reached forward to touch the wall as well. With their hands still on the crumbling brick, they looked at Shawn. "Man, what did you feel?" Rich quietly asked.

Shawn looked at them with disbelief. "The cold, man! Don't you feel the intense cold? I thought I had frostbite!" He held his fingers out to the beam of the flashlight. The pads of his fingers and the thumb of his right hand were a mixture of red and white discoloration.

Rich bent down and slipped the catches on the case. He pulled out their digital camera and adjusted the night vision lens. Gesturing to Shawn he said, "Hold your hand out, dude. We need to get physical evidence of this."

Tony waited until Rich had taken three shots. He grabbed Shawn's hand and started examining it, turning the palm up and back down, looking for any other marks. Letting go, he turned back to the wall - ran his own hands across a four foot wide section, attempting to find any kind of temperature change around the wall itself. No such luck.

Shaking his head while rubbing his hands together he stepped back. "Beats the shit outta me, guys. I don't feel anything but a light coolness." He looked around and up. "I know its fall, but the weather hasn't been bad enough to get the brick that cold in such a short time." He looked at his watch. "It's only one a.m., man. I just don't get it."

Placing the digital camera back in the case, Rich reached in and pulled out a notebook. Grabbing a pen from inside his jacket, he notated the incident, date and time in the log. With a final jig of the pen, he closed the book and offered it to Shawn. "Great beginning huh? And we haven't even made it inside, yet!"

Tony laid his hand on the railing that ran alongside the steps. The rust and moisture felt like it was going to permanently stain his palm. He turned, flashing his light down and around, seeing where the steps were. "Found it!" he called out, moving to the beginning of the concrete platform. He flashed the light down, following the angle, until he spied the bottom frame of the door. He moved the light up, looking for the door knob. The knob was actually an old fashioned bolt with a huge, rusted padlock hooked through.

The scraping and crunching of their movements down the stairs announced the other boys' arrival. Shawn bumped into his back and muttered, "Sorry." Rich wedged himself next to Shawn and behind Tony, peering around his side. Tony nodded towards the door, at the same time holding the beam on the padlocked latch.

"Crap on toast," Shawn mumbled, but Tony only smiled over his shoulder at Rich and said, "Ready?"

A grin spread across Rich's face. Moving forward and nudging Shawn out of the way, Rich stage whispered, "Stand aside, Shawn. Let me n' the big guy handle this."

Without another word, both boys backed up about five paces then simultaneously threw themselves at the door. It snapped open with such ease the boys sprawled forward, thrown off balance, tripping over each other and ending up face first on the dank, musty, dust covered floor.

Shawn leaned forward and surveyed his two friends, splay legged and coughing in the dust they stirred up with their fall.

"Well, that was pretty easy," he said, turning to inspect the bolt and padlock. Both were rusted through, the entire wooden door jamb also rotted all the way up and across. Shawn reached up and picked at the wood. One section of the frame came off with a brittle crack right in his hand.

Standing up, clearing out their throats and spitting, Rich and Tony could only glare at their friend standing in the doorway with such a smug expression on his face. Finally Tony was able to stop coughing long enough to flip him the bird, which seemed to satisfy Rich that it conveyed how they both felt at the current moment.

Shawn bent down and grabbed the case. He stepped over the threshold and moved past his friends, who were now leaning against the wall of the corridor. He panned his flashlight down the narrow walkway until he found what he was looking for. Motioning to them he said, "In here, guys. This will be our base camp."

Tony and Rich pushed themselves off the wall and walked up to where Shawn was shining his light. Tony pulled his flashlight out of his back pocket and turned it on. What seemed to be an empty, black hole now appeared to be a vast, open locker room. Old hooks still hung at odd angles off one side wall and three benches, turned sideways and leaning against a bank of rusted metal lockers, came into view with the combined lights.

Rich focused his light on two of the benches, which still seemed in ok enough shape to hold their gear and themselves when they needed a break. "Must've been one of the Staff locker rooms, cause from what I read, the patients weren't treated to anything this nice."

Shawn stepped sideways while Tony stuffed his light in a back pocket, quickly moving towards one of the benches leaning crosswise against a locker. Rich looked up and pulled a chain hanging from the ceiling. The whole light socket as well as some plaster came down on his head and face. "What the h...." was all he got out of his mouth before they heard the sound. Shuffling, scuffling strides were coming from further down the hall. Holding their breath, they waited to see who would show up at the doorway.

Two minutes went by, three, and still no sign of anyone. Tony placed his finger to his lips and as quietly as he could, moved to the entrance. In one swift motion, he whirled around the doorjamb and faced left, shining his light full force down the way they thought the sounds had come from. Swinging his body and light around, he did a one eighty and yelled "Hey!" at the same time. Nothing stirred.

He looked back at Shawn and Rich in the room and shrugged his shoulders. "Well, wasn't that special. An invisible 'Welcoming Committee'." He stepped into the room as Shawn swung the case up and laid it on its back on one of the now upright benches. He snapped the catches and raised the lid. Tony peered in over the top of the lid. Rich sat down, dusting the remaining plaster out of his hair.

Pulling out an EMF Meter, Shawn handed it to Rich, explaining, "This will measure any electro-magnetic fields within the building. In other words, it reads any type of electricity within the location it's aimed at."

Rich flipped the hand held machine on. "What we'll do is take a base line reading from every area we enter. Shawn'll notate the reading in the book and we can compare them to any abnormal spikes or rises as we move around." He aimed the device at the hole in the ceiling where the light socket had been. The meter held steady at '0'.

"As you can see, man, there is no electricity in this place whatsoever. It was completely shut off in 1914, after the massacre." Tony looked over Rich's shoulder at the meter in his hand. "So, that means what to us?"

"It means," Shawn grunted as he pulled out a bigger object from the case and placed it in Tony's hands, "That if we get any kind of spike at all, any kind of rise, we may actually be in the presence of a ghost or possibly a residual haunting."

Tony was studying the machine. It looked like a camcorder from some alien planet. He glanced over at Rich holding the smaller EMF Meter. "No shit? Well, that's cool for him, but what does this thing do?"

Shawn smiled, "Well, since you're the muscles of our group and the token skeptic, I thought I'd give you the Thermal Detector."

"Say what?" The confusion on Tony's face was hilarious. Shawn bit the inside of his cheek to keep from laughing out loud.

"The Thermal Detector registers hot and cold spots. Here, let me show you." Shawn stepped behind Tony and grasped the hand holding the detector. Aiming the lens at Rich, he hit the on/record switch and within the viewing screen Rich came out in colors of red, yellow and orange, while the areas around him showed blues and purples. Rich shuffled his feet and pretended to pick his nose. Tony laughed out loud. "Cool man! Rich, I saw everything you did just now, without a flashlight!"

Shawn stepped back and nodded. "All ya gotta do, Tony, is aim it wherever we go. The Detector will do the rest." He reached into the case one more time and pulled out a Digital Recorder as well as the small digital camera, which found its home in his jacket pocket. Loading his cargo pants pockets with batteries for all three pieces of equipment, he flipped on his light and motioned towards the door.

"If we get separated, the main thing to do is don't panic. If we can't find each other within ten minutes, head back here to base camp. Don't," he turned and faced the other two, "go off on your own at all. This place is a maze in the daylight; there's all kinds of dangerous junk left here. In the dark, it's even worse. We don't want to drag anyone out here for help, get it?"

Tony grunted his agreement and Rich murmured "Yeah." All three stepped out of the room and turned to the left. Shawn shined his light on the walls. As they progressed down the hall, they were able to see stations as well as arrows painted in dull, but still legible day glow-white paint. The hall they were in was marked 'Staff Locker Rooms' with an arrow below the words pointing back the way they had just come from.

"See?" Shawn said. "Every corner is marked this way, telling you where we're at. You may have to rub the dust off or put the light right up to it, but if you keep your head, you won't get lost." He took a deep breath. "Alright, guys, let's catch us some ghosts."

They had been moving down the corridors for a while, taking left and right turns, trying to head towards the main lobby. They'd been focused on getting to their objective, so no one had done any talking. Tony finally decided it was time.

He whispered in mock exaggeration, "So Rich, what's the story on this place, huh? I mean, I've heard the rumors and old folk's tales, but what actually happened here, dude?"

Glancing down at his meter, Rich saw that the needle was still leveled at '0'. He told Shawn the reading then looked at him. Shawn nodded. "Go ahead. Now's as good a time as any." Rich dropped back to walk alongside Tony.

"Ok, here it is in a nutshell." He took a deep breath and all three slowed down so they could focus on the story.

"The 'McCane Therapeutic Sanitarium', as it was called, was built by a Dr. Bertrand McCane, who believed his ideas of treating the mentally ill were revolutionary and would enlighten the world. He invested all of his money into building this place. His family came from old money in England, and he had, throughout the years, added to the vast fortune, so an undertaking of this size was no problem for him. The construction started in the year eighteen eighty and was completed at the end of eighteen eighty five. The people around here thought he was Manna from Heaven."

Rich couldn't hide the sarcasm in his voice, even at the whispered level, "He brought jobs and prosperity back to this county with the construction and by hiring locals in the surrounding areas. People began bringing their family members to him by the droves, either to hopefully find a cure for their mental illnesses, keep them in circumstances that were far better than what they could do for them at home, or simply because that particular family member was considered a nuisance or shame on the family name."

Tony interrupted with a snort of derision. "How white of 'em."

Rich sighed. "Yeah, but it gets worse." Tony had looked down at the Thermal Imager screen but glanced up sharply when Rich made that comment. He went on, wanting to finish the story as quickly as possible.

"Somewhere along the way, Dr. McCane became mentally unbalanced himself. His Ice Water Bath Treatments and Sensory Deprivation Chambers, as well as physical restraints as punishment for bad behavior and getting fed for good behavior, were some of the tamer treatments he ordered used on the patients. Everyone who signed a family member into the Sanitarium also signed a contract stating that they could never come for visits or check on their progress. Doc McCane insisted that these types of visits could actually 'reverse' his advancements with these patients. The unsuspecting public believed the good doctor. So, once someone was signed in here, they were never seen again. Even after the event of their death." Rich stopped to take a breath. This part of the history of the place actually sickened him to repeat, but the facts were the facts. He continued.

"When we get to the back of this building, you can look out any window and see where the 'Cemetery' is. There are at least thirty rows of crosses with names and dates on them, but not one grave holds a corpse. Not one." Rich stopped for a brief minute to let this sink in to Tony's brain.

"Doc McCane did not want anyone taking a close look at his patients or how they died, so he opted to bury them, free of charge to the families. They could come to the graveside service, but the bodies were already placed, supposedly, in the pine coffins and the lids nailed shut. Some family members came to these services, others didn't even bother, but either way, it wouldn't have mattered. All that was being buried was a coffin filled with bags of dirt. The bodies themselves, well, they were fed to the huge furnaces which ran the boilers that were housed in the basement of this building. The fires were kept extremely hot, specifically for this purpose, and the corpses were usually so wasted by then, any smell of burning flesh simply blended with the other odors of puke, shit, unwashed bodies and strong disinfectant.

Rich took a minute to check his meter and to say, "Still no change, Shawn." Tony looked at his screen and uttered the same thing, primarily to hide his revulsion. Motioning with his light, Shawn indicated they needed to turn right down another junction. After they turned the corner, Rich continued.

"All this worked quite well for Doc McCane. He kept taking in patients when 'openings' came up, he kept collecting the money from families, and no one was the wiser. But then, in nineteen fourteen, it all came down around his ears. It seems that one of the employees became disgruntled with the doctor over a dispute about his pay. When he could not get his complaint resolved, he not only went to the sheriff in town, but proceeded to the local town 'watering hole' and started to talk about what was actually going on up at the Sanitarium. His stories so horrified the townspeople they spread the word to the surrounding community and, by that evening, a mob was headed out to the place to 'see for themselves.'

"The sheriff tried to intervene and keep some order, but the townspeople overwhelmed both he and his deputies. They stormed up here, forcing their way into the front lobby, shoving the staff aside and started going room by room."

"Everywhere they went, they were met with more horrifying situations – children locked in cages shaped like cribs, people wrapped and tied in wet strips of linen, shivering on the bare floors of their rooms. Other mental patients were locked two or three to a room, where they beat each other without mercy or interruption."

"What the townspeople saw so horrified them that they tracked down Dr. McCane in his office, dragged him as well as six other staff members out and hung them from the beams in the Common Room. They then started to unlock the doors to the rooms in an attempt to help the patients inside. Big mistake."

Tony held his hand up, "Ssshhhh, wait a minute!" Rich quit speaking. He had been looking down at the monitor when he thought he saw a flicker, a white image just fleetingly glide across the screen. Rich looked down at his meter. The needle was still at '0'. Shawn rewound his recorder and listened. Other than Rich's voice, nothing else was either interrupting or overriding his words. They waited for a couple more minutes, then Tony motioned Rich to continue on.

"Insane people can be hellishly strong. Even though there were quite a few patients who were weakened by their treatments, there were enough who were neither weak, nor docile. They were the violently insane and when they were inadvertently let loose by the well-meaning citizens they started a bloody rampage that only ended when the sheriff, the few deputies he had, and several men who did not go up to the Sanitarium with the crowd arrived with guns. By the time the mayhem was over, there were thirty five dead and at least sixty wounded."

Tony did another sweep with the Thermal Detector as they turned another corner. Getting no hits, he turned his attention back to Rich and the story.

"The State Governor came in and did a full investigation. The remaining patients were sent to other sanitariums or home with their family members who came to collect them. The rest of the staff were charged, tried and sentenced in court for torture, abuse and neglect. It was a devastating scandal that rocked this area of the county for years afterwards." The last comment was made in a low, almost inaudible whisper.

Tony looked at Rich. "Man, that was all kinds of messed up."

Shawn had moved a couple of steps ahead of them, head down. He'd helped Rich do the research but it never failed to affect him every time he heard it repeated. This is what made him determined to find out if this place was still haunted, the spirits of people involved in this tragedy still in agony and stuck here. His ultimate goal was to help release these tortured Souls, to give them some kind of peace.

The EMF Meter in Rich's hand let out a resounding screech. Shawn whirled around and in one stride made it back to his buddies.

The boys stood frozen to the spot, eyes bugged out, staring at the meter. The digital readout now pinged ferociously from 0.0 to 60.9 then back again.

The creaking of rusty wheels rolling erratically down the corridor in front of them filtered into their ears.

Tony slowly brought up the Thermal Detector to his eye level and looked at the screen. His free hand reached out and grabbed Shawn by the front of his shirt, tightening until the seams almost started to give. "Holy Shit" was all he could manage to stutter out.

All three heads turned to where they could look at the Thermal screen, none daring to actually look down the hall ahead of them. Looming ever larger in the frame, a metal gurney was being pushed towards the small group standing in the middle of the hall. They could discern a white sheeted figure on top. Rich blinked his eyes repeatedly, trying to deny what he was seeing, while Tony let go of Shawn's shirt so he could now hold the Thermal Detector in both hands to keep it from falling to the floor.

Shawn took a deep breath, slowly raised his eyes and looked in the direction of the noise. He brought his flashlight up and turned it on. The gurney was still making its way slowly towards them, but he could not see anything on it. He quickly glanced down at the screen again. In the screen, the white sheeted figure was struggling to sit up.

"Guys," Shawn breathed raggedly as he whispered to the other two, "Look up and tell me what you see."

Tony and Rich reluctantly raised their eyes and looked in the direction of Shawn's light. The gurney had just reached a junction about twenty feet ahead of them. Moving under its own power, it jerked its way around the corner that branched off to the right. The rattle and squeal of the metal wheels suddenly cut off as soon as it left their line of sight.

Shawn sprang forward, saying in a low voice, "We can't let it get away! C'mon!"

Tony and Rich looked at each other before hot footing it after Shawn, who had already reached the corner and rounded it. The two boys caught up with him about six feet into the new hallway. Shawn had stopped dead and was running his flashlight all over the area. There was absolutely no sign of the gurney they'd seen.

Rich flipped his flashlight up, slowly shining it forward, left then right. Tony focused on doorways, revealing other rooms branching off from the corridor. He stopped periodically and looked inside. After about five minutes, he leaned up against one of the musty smelling walls.

"Psssst! Psssst!" He hissed to get the other boys attention. They had moved further up the hallway, not realizing that Tony wasn't with them.

Both boys waited while Tony heaved himself upright and trotted towards them. When he got to where they were standing, he started playing his light in and out of the rooms that were around them. "Man, have either one of you noticed that these offices still have furniture in them? That they, like, except for the dust, look like someone could go right in and start working right away?" He now directed his light to the walls on either side of them. "And dude, have you noticed – there's no graffiti on any of the walls, man." He ran the light around the walls again for emphasis. "Not one damn bit."

Rich's eyebrows drew down in consternation. "Hold on," he whispered as he turned and loped back to the intersection. Shawn and Tony watched his light bob all around the walls, losing sight of it when he ventured further down one end, popping into view as he backtracked down the hallway they had come from. Finally the beam of his light hit them both as he made his way to where they were standing, waiting. He was breathing in short, quick gasps, but they didn't know if that was because of his running around, or because of the uneasiness which slowly seemed to be creeping up on them all. He nodded his head in the affirmative. No graffiti anywhere.

Shawn stared at the other boys. "Guys, do you want to go on?" His voice caught in his throat and he swallowed to clear it. "I mean, we've really caught on to something here and it would be a waste to leave now. Besides," he held his watch up to his face, squinting to read the glow-in-the-dark dial. "We've only got two more hours until sun rise. That means we've really got maybe an hour more to investigate."

A low moan rose out from the darkness at the end of the hall. It seemed to move towards them, and as it did, the moan went to a whine, blasting over their heads, the final crescendo a wailing shriek that sent them diving to either side of the hallway, covering their ears.

The shriek had barely died when they were enveloped by a slew of babbling voices, singing, wailing, and hysterical laugher. A verbal whirlwind swirled around the three boys, assaulting them from all sides. The incident lasted a couple of minutes, but to the three shaken kids it seemed like hours.

Suddenly, like a switch being turned off, nothing. Tony removed his hands from his ears. He slid down onto his haunches. Rich and Shawn made their way on unsteady legs to his side. They collapsed next to him, their backs against the wall in a defensive position, ready for any other type of assault. Tony was the first to speak.

"Well, Hells Bells, that answers that for me."

Rich looked at him in confusion. "Whattayamean?"

Tony stood up and brushed his pants off. "Hell man, we just got an invitation, don't ya know?"

Rich stood up, still not quite understanding, but Shawn caught on right away. "He means," Shawn said, "That we're gonna continue. This was like they threw the first punch. Get it?"

Rich grinned, the skin around his eyes and mouth shiny and tight. He readjusted the EMF Meter attached to his wrist, checked to make sure the batteries were still strong. "You guys check your equipment? Mine's good to go."

Tony leaned forward and grasped Rich by the shoulder. "My man! Let's go find out where these sons a' bitches actually are!"

Shawn nodded, suggesting Tony take point so he could let them know if anything was coming at them again. Shawn held the digital recorder up and next to him Rich moved the EMF meter up, down and sideways as they moved forward, ever deeper into the building.

Rich was the first to realize that he was catching glimpses of 'things' appearing just out of range of his vision. Angling his flashlight beam down to see if that helped, he let his eyes adjust to the darkness in front of him.

Sure enough, he was able to discern a pale face, peering out from one of the doorways on the left. He squinted, his eyelids all but shut in a concentrated effort to see more. Tony and Shawn noticed he had slowed his pace. They followed suit.

"Are you seeing what I'm seeing, man?" Rich's' voice was strained and lower than normal in a vain attempt to keep the nervousness from coming out.

Tony suddenly clicked his flashlight beam off and stopped dead in his tracks. "Tell me what you see, dude."

"Faces," "Figures," Shawn and Rich's simultaneous whispers sent the 'creeping chills' wiggling up and down Tony's spine. His voice took on an almost hypnotic quality as he spoke.

"I'm seein' hands, man. Hands reachin' in and out of the walls around us."

All three were now huddled together in the center of the hallway, watching as these images seemed to grow clearer and more distinct with each passing second.

For some reason, Shawn felt a sudden urge to look behind them. Try as he might, he couldn't resist, almost as if someone or something had taken hold of his head and was forcing him to turn around.

Fear and trepidation were fighting to take over his mind. He swallowed, the painful dry click in his throat adding to the panic attempting to encompass him. He had no choice. Closing his eyes, he felt himself turn.

His body was angled at a three quarter turn, his head moving in conjunction with the motion of his body. He took a deep breath and opened his eyes as wide as possible.

Moving with deliberate stealth, a thick, foggy mass was undulating up the hall, filling up the places where the boys had been, deliberately trying to catch them unawares. It seemed to encompass the hall completely, blacking out everything that had been there before.

Shawn caught glimpses of figures in the dark, forms that looked vaguely human, all shapes and sizes. They seemed to be trying to materialize, but kept getting swallowed up as the mass of darkness swirled and flowed ever closer to the three boys standing in the hall.

Rich and Tony were still facing forward, oblivious to what Shawn was witnessing. It was when the mass actually reached the office just fifteen feet behind them that Shawn was galvanized into action.

Shoving both his friends with all his might, he screamed "RUN!!"

Tony and Rich didn't wait for a second invitation. The two boys sprang forward, moving apart just enough for Shawn to shoot between them and take the lead. Instinctively Shawn took them straight down the middle of the hall, keeping as far away from the walls as possible.

Arms, hands, and fingers started sprouting from both sides, eagerly trying to grasp the fleeing boys. Dirty, grimy, fingernails broken and bleeding. Digits of all shapes and sizes pressed from the walls. Big, thick, skeletal, small, stubby fingered, long, feminine. They seemed to be coming at them from every space possible. Rich just couldn't believe the variety and number he was able to see in the dark.

"Now you've really gone around the bend, man." The thought flew through his mind as his feet flew on the ground, following Shawn's every move. His terrified brain was giving him mixed signals. He didn't know whether he should scream in fear or laugh hysterically. He found he could do neither. He was too terrified.

Tony's fear was tinged with anger. He too was seeing the hands as he ran right behind Rich, but his reaction was to strike back. He swung the flashlight, hitting the hands as he ran, smashing them with all his strength, and damned if he couldn't feel the impact every time he connected with one. He could feel a slight resistance, watched as the images would explode into sparkles of light. That gave him a feeling of grim satisfaction and helped ground him mentally. He redoubled his efforts, swatting and slamming as many as he could as he charged by.

Shawn spied an intersecting junction up ahead and aimed for the right hand side. Just as he was ready to turn, the wall of blackness appeared, filling up that space and blocking the way.

"Left! Go Left!" He screamed at his two friends behind him, praying they'd follow. All three skidded around the corner and continued to run.

For what seemed like forever, Rich and Tony followed Shawn's bellowed directions, dodging left, right, straight ahead – giving into blind faith that he knew where he was taking them.

Shawn sprinted along, memories of the layout of the place flashing in and out of his brain. Near exhaustion and just about ready to drop and give up, he caught a flash of light above and ahead of them. It suddenly dawned on him that he could see the outline of stairs. His terrified mind grabbed onto that fact – the stairs led up to the first floor! He forced his mind to shake off the ever encroaching fear and began to think. *Yeah, there are windows on the first floor level. Windows with broken and missing panes.*

He pointed. Energized by hope, he yelled, "C'mon guys! The stairs! We can get out!"

Needing no further encouragement, Tony and Rich picked up the pace, focusing on nothing but freedom from this insanity.

They took the stairs two at a time, nearly tripping over each other, desperate to get to the top. Once there, they scrambled to the side and paused, too spent to run any further.

Shawn slid to a stop, his whole body shaking. His eyes kept darting to the top step, waiting for the dark or for any figures to suddenly appear. He stood stock still, heart beating in his ears, staring for what seemed like eternity. Finally, unable to stand it any longer, he went and tentatively leaned over the railing. No darkness, no figures.

Tony and Rich were bent over their knees, trying to pull in great gulps of air as quietly as possible. Shawn gave them a few minutes to catch their breath and push some of the panic down to a manageable level. He looked around. A grimy, broken sign, hanging from the ceiling in front of them caught his eye.

He moved over to his friends and nudged Tony, the one closest to him. "Guys," he pointed. "There's our way out."

Tony stood up and the Thermal Detector hanging from his neck bounced against his chest. He winced, realizing there was going to be one hell of a bruise there later on.

Miraculously, the boys still had their equipment. They hadn't lost a thing, including the dead-weight batteries in Shawn's cargo pants. Tony looked at Shawn's bulging pockets and slammed both hands over his mouth, stifling the hysterical laughter that was trying to burst out.

Every single piece of equipment was dead silent.

Rich looked at his watch. "Guys, we've got five minutes to daylight. What say we get the hell outta here?"

The three turned as one and moved towards the sign which pointed the way to the 'Common Room'. In the photos that Shawn had seen during his research, the Common Room was set up like a huge ball room with couches, tables and chairs set in groupings of four to six, leaving an open central area for walking or standing. The East wall, though, was nothing but floor to ceiling windows, strengthened with mesh screening embedded in the glass. The patients had been brought in groups to that room, to "take in the sun and energize themselves," so the caption that went along with the picture read. Shawn was positive that a few of those panels at the floor level were more than likely broken out or loose. He stepped up the pace, eager to put this horrific place behind them.

Stumbling over the threshold into the room, the boys immediately began to look around, getting their bearings as to where the wall of windows would be. Rich noticed that the objects in the room seemed to be a little more visible. He switched off his flashlight to be sure. Yes, it was more a murky dusk rather than full dark. He nudged Shawn and held his flashlight up.

"Turn it off, man. It's ok. Let your eyes adjust, and you won't need it anymore."

Shawn turned his off, but for some reason, the hairs at the nape of his neck started to rise. He glanced back towards the double doors. *Strange, he thought, why's it seem like it's still dark over there?* Tony distracted him by grabbing his shoulder, spinning him around and pointing.

"There!" His finger shaking with excitement, Tony started moving towards the right hand side of the lower panes. A large portion of the window had been pushed out, the gap big enough that a person hunched over could pass through. Letting out a whoop of relief, Rich angled that way at a fast trot. Tony and Shawn started to follow when their equipment went haywire.

Darkness began to flow into the room. Starting at floor level, it worked its way smoothly around the walls, pouring over the furniture, blocking off the windows and the exit the boys were headed for, herding them back into the center of the room. The boys backed against each other, forming a triangle, faces pointing out towards the mass.

The cacophony of the machines cut off with a final, strangled screech.

The silence was thick, the boys' breathing muted, muffled. Somehow, the three felt that time was suddenly at a standstill. They watched in fascination and fear as figures started to materialize within the blackness.

They saw women in sackcloth, hair cut ragged, so thin only their breasts holding the cloth outwards could distinguish them from the men. They, with pants barely held up with pieces of string, straightjackets cinched over their upper torsos. Women holding babies, their eyes dead, features bereft of any kind of emotion. The babies' bodies were slack, the last tears they ever shed still glistening on their cheeks. Women and men were wearing the white and blood flecked uniforms of Sanitarium staff, faces still showing the shock of their own abrupt and violent ends.

Even more startling were the townspeople they all recognized.

Tony saw Mr. Ginty, his math teacher who had died of cancer four years ago. Shawn saw his grandmother, recognized her from the family pictures he'd seen, for she had died before he was even born. Rich recognized his cousin, Arlene, who had been killed in a car crash not three weeks earlier.

All three of the boys stood in the thick silence, letting what they were seeing flow through their minds, absorbing the reality that they were in the midst of not just a few ghosts, but from the looks of it, thousands.

Tony let out a tired, shuddery sigh. "Well, I guess we found what we were looking for."

Before either of the other two could respond, a little girl stepped out from the crowd and walked forward. When she had gotten to within five feet of them she stopped.

She was about five years old, dressed in a ragged pinafore of no discernible color, hair dirty and matted, feet bare. She clutched a worn out stuffed rabbit, fur all but rubbed off, stuffing leaking out from a ragged rip in the belly. Shawn noted dully that she had cute, dainty little features. Except for the fact that she had no eyes. She smiled at all three.

"Welcome back. Can you come play with me now?"

The suns' rays started coming in through the glass, slicing through the darkness. Dawn had arrived. As the room grew brighter and the night made way for the day, the boys watched, mute, as the men, women, children, all faded then disappeared at the touch of the light.

Only the little girl in front of them was left, smiling as the light inevitably released her. They turned to look at each other, and realization dawned on them as they too faded and disappeared when the light finally engulfed them.

The police cruiser pulled up to the chain link gate around 9 a.m. The Deputy turned off the ignition and waited for the Sheriff to make the first move. With a heavy sigh, the Sheriff popped the passenger door open and stepped out. The Deputy followed suit from the drivers' side.

Without a word, the Sheriff pulled out a huge metal key ring from his front pocket and proceeded to hunt through them, looking for the one to unlock the front padlock gate. He finally found it and with a muttered "Damn, I hate this," unlocked the hasp and pulled the chain through the links. Looping it and the padlock on the fence, he yanked one side open just enough for him and the deputy to squeeze through.

Glancing everywhere except at the building, he placed his hands on his hips. "Let's start going to the right and swing around the back. We can finish up on the side furthest from where we're at now. That should cover about everything."

The Deputy nodded, stepping forward to the crackle of dead leaves and crunch of dried grass. The Sheriff locked step with him and continued to talk. "Remember, we're not going in unless we absolutely have to. All we're lookin' for is any broken doors, footprints or scuff marks to show someone went in through a window."

Nodding, the Deputy zipped up his jacket. There suddenly seemed to be a chill in the air.

"I don't get it, sheriff. Why do we have to check this old place out? I mean, nobody ever comes out here, except to party at the dead end. From what I've heard in town, no one actually sets foot in this place. So, what's the deal?"

The Sheriff spat into the weeds and took a minute before he responded. "The fact is, someone called in and reported seeing lights out by the building last night. Most of the time, when they call about the kids at the dead end, we let it slide." He turned to look at the deputy walking beside him. "But, when someone says they see lights at this building, well, we have to come take a look."

The Deputy gave him a puzzled look and the Sheriff sighed, knowing he was going to have to tell. Seeing they had reached to within five feet of the buildings' brick walls, he started scrutinizing the doors and boarded up windows, looking for any sign of entry. He held his breath at each spot until he verified that the doors and windows had not been tampered with. The Deputy moved ahead of him, still within hearing distance, checking as they went along.

"Five years ago," the Sheriff started without preamble, "before you hired on, we received a call that someone had seen people around the building the night before. It was in the fall, about this time of year. So, I, my deputy who was partnered with me at the time and Don Gregson, the caretaker of this place, took a ride out here to see what was what."

The Sheriff stopped and peered at one of the windows where a board was broken. Assuring himself that it had not recently been tampered with, he motioned the Deputy to continue on checking ahead of him.

"The call that dispatch received was of some kids seen hanging around the actual building, which made us all a bit nervous. We got to the gate back there," he thrust his thumb back over his shoulder, towards the direction where they'd come in, "and sure enough, there was a little Ford Pinto parked on the side of the road. We checked it and saw that no one was there, so Don went up and unlocked the gate. Deputy Andy Grey and I went in first, followed up by Don, who closed the gate behind us."

"Didn't take us long to find the broken door where the kids had busted in. The tracks were easy for Andy to follow and soon enough, we found them, up on the first floor, in the big room."

Here the Sheriff paused until they'd swung around and had covered pretty much all of the back of the Sanitarium. They were level with the huge glass windows of the Common Room when the Sheriff stopped. Staring at the windows, he crossed his arms and continued to speak.

"They were layin' smack in the center of this room. It looked like they'd just collapsed where they was standin'. I motioned Don to stay at the entranceway, while Andy and I stepped towards the boys. All three of 'em were dead."

The Sheriff's eyes closed for a moment, recalling the sad and terrifying day. "Andy and I looked them over as best we could without disturbing the bodies, but we couldn't find a mark on any of 'em. But their faces," He couldn't repress an involuntary shudder, "well I almost had a heart attack just looking at them. All three looked like they'd died of extreme fright."

He made such an abrupt turn to leave the windows that he almost ran over the deputy. "Good Lord, man, keep on movin', ok?" The Deputy let the harshness in his boss's voice slide. He could see that this place was having a harsh effect on the old, experienced lawman.

Spitting in the grass again, the Sheriff cleared his throat and went on with his tale. "Now, while I was looking at the bodies, Andy was scouting the floor all around the base of the walls, and I noticed, about ten feet into the room. He kept to the outside of what he was looking at, but I could tell from knowing him almost all his life that something was beginning to really spook him. He finally stopped and in a shaky whisper called me over.

'Sheriff, I don't know what happened here. It makes no sense to me at all.' He started pointing to the faint tracks in the dust.

'"See here, where we came in, you can see our boot prints pretty clear.' He gestured with his hand. 'Now, look over here.' He squatted down and began pointing as he spoke. 'Here, you can see all kinds of prints. Boots, shoes, high heels, slippers, even bare feet.'

'Bare feet? What in the world are you talkin' about?' I looked at Andy as if he'd gone off his rocker. But Andy was one of the best trackers I'd ever met in my life, so in my heart I had no doubts as to what he was showing me.

"Andy's face had gone ashy grey. It was like he was like he was holding on to every bit of his self-control with only minor success.

'It's true, Sheriff. Just look.' He proceeded to walk me around the whole room. Everywhere from the back of the walls to about ten feet from the boys there were prints of all kinds. But none entered or exited the room. Only the boys and ours came from the doorway in.

"After he and I had been around the whole room, Andy stopped and stepped back towards the entranceway doors .'Sheriff, I don't know what happened here, but I can tell you that part of this is damn impossible. 'I was catchin' his jitters and it was getting to the point that we were both holdin' on by the thinnest bit to keep from bolting out of that room.

"I finally croaked out 'Explain.'

"Scanning the room and the footprints once more, Andy finally looked right at me. 'Sheriff, according to what I'm seeing, there were not hundreds, but thousands of people in here with these boys. And that, we both know, is impossible, no matter how big this room is.'

The Sheriff and Deputy finished their search at the back of the sanitarium. They turned the last corner, intensely scrutinizing the last twenty feet.

The Deputy saw the Sheriff glance at one door in particular at the end of their sweep then pick up his pace to get past it. He stopped and looked. The door at the bottom of these steps was less weathered than the others, the padlock on it barely rusted. Understanding hit him and he lengthened his stride, catching up with the Sheriff who was halfway to the patrol car. The Sheriff finished up his story in short, terse bursts.

"We called in the coroner and the bodies were picked up, autopsies done, the boys laid to rest. Andy and I never told anyone what we'd noticed in the room, and old Don was so deaf he hadn't heard a thing we said." The Sheriff reached the gate and waited for the deputy to walk through. He wrapped the chain back around the gate and snapped the padlock shut, returning the keys to his pocket. Waiting for the deputy to unlock the car, he went on.

"The day after we found the boys, Deputy Andy Grey walked into my office. Without a word he handed me his badge, gun and holster. He looked me straight in the eyes, said goodbye and left. That afternoon I'd heard he'd packed up all his belongings and left town as well. I never saw him again. About a week later Don Gregson came in and handed me the keys to this place. Said he was retiring and was too old to go out there anymore. I accepted the keys. Hell, it's my job, but for the first time in my career I didn't take any joy from it."

The Deputy unlocked the car. With his hand resting on the windowsill, he looked at the Sheriff. "So, the rumors are true. This place is haunted?"

The Sheriff pulled out of his reverie and looked across the hood at his man. "Haunted? Well, I couldn't swear to that, but," he glanced over his shoulder at the looming, rotting edifice, "even as far back as I can remember, my Granny would warn me to stay away from here, for in this town, this is the place where the dead have gone.

THE BLUE GIRL

Lindsey Beth Goddard

Frederick winced as he tightened the young girl's restraints. "Please don't do it," she begged. "I'm frightened!"

Her slender face, framed with a mess of tangled blonde curls, pressed tightly against the leather strap around her forehead. She arched her back. The flesh of her wrists and ankles turned white as she fought futilely against the restraints. A mere girl of nineteen years old, the sight of her struggling on the floor of the wooden box caused Frederick's heart to swell with remorse. Too much white showed in her panicked blue eyes. He wanted to soothe her, tell her it would be all right.

"Let me out! Let me out!" she screamed, eyes pleading.

Frederick felt the doctor's presence at his back. A large hand touched his shoulder. "Silence her."

The girl sobbed inconsolably as a rivulet of snot formed a thin, slimy trail down her cheek. *Even still, she is beautiful*, he thought. Frederick gulped. This part of his job brought him no joy. The task at hand was just that—a task. Something that had to be done.

She made no effort to bite his fingers as he popped the ball gag in her mouth. She merely whimpered, closing her eyes and trembling on the rough wooden plank. His sympathy only deepened as he eyed the scars on his hands where countless other patients had sunk their teeth in a last-ditch effort to escape the gag. This one was different: docile, full of woe. Perhaps water shock treatment was too extreme.

Frederick looked at Dr. Walters in his crisp, white physician's coat, always starched and ironed to perfection. Three decades his senior, the man bristled with energy. He paced the floor, eyes alight with anticipation, salt and pepper hair cropped close to his scalp.

"What did she do?" Fredrick's question caught the pacing doctor off guard. He stopped moving and blinked his eyes slowly, his train of thought derailed. He glared at his assistant, who gazed compassionately at the face of patient 5572 as she whimpered through the ball gag.

"Don't be fooled by her pretty face, my dear boy. She attacked two of our guards this last evening."

Frederick gulped. He ran a hand through his wild, red hair and double-checked the leather restraints. "It's okay," he said, attempting to calm her. "The gag will prevent too much water from entering your lungs. You'll be fine... good as new when this is over." His words had no effect on her rattled nerves. She continued to shiver, weeping with her eyelids shut against the horror.

His gaze lingered one last time on her plump lips and rosy cheeks, her long eyelashes slick with tears. Then he stood, shook off the effects of her beauty, and closed the lid of the coffin-like box. He flipped two copper latches, one at each side of the box, locking the lid into place. A myriad of holes had been drilled through the planks. He detected a flurry of movement from inside as she gyrated against the straps, to no avail.

Candlelight reflected on the glistening surface of the water as Frederick turned his attention to the pool. It was more of a tank, really, dug into the ground level of the asylum at Dr. Walter's request. *The water must be so cold. I am cold just standing here above the ground.*

He shook the thought from his head. Never mind such trivial things as the temperature of the water, the girl's fear. This would be over soon, and she would thank them. She'd be fixed.

Dr. Walter's methods had been successful in the past: bringing a patient to the brink of death and then reviving them before they passed away. This process, though frightening for the persons involved, provided a brand new start for the mentally ill. It was akin to wiping their slate clean, giving a second chance at life. As if the water itself washed their insanity away.

"We must lower it." The doctor's booming voice echoed through the room. The girl in the box screamed a guttural protest from deep within her chest, the sound muffled as it tried to leave her lips.

Thick ropes attached to the sides of the box began to tighten as a device overhead slowly moved. Nothing more than a heavy pole affixed to a Y-shaped base, the device resembled a well-sweep, the kind used for raising and lowering buckets of water from a well, only it was much larger, stronger, and capable of dragging a human trapped inside a coffin-like tomb.

The box plummeted into the tank with a resounding splash. Frederick cringed as water poured through the holes, filling the wooden box, sinking it.

"Don't look so glum, my faithful assistant. We need only stop her heart for a minute. Then we will bring her back." He watched air bubbles rising to the surface of the water, waiting for the young girl to drown. "Her mind will be reborn. Fresh and new. She'll feel better than ever. You will see."

Several Decades Later

The atmosphere inside the old asylum on Harper Hill could only be described with adjectives best suited for Poe: ghastly and somber, beguiling Mark into walking its decrepit halls and exploring its long-abandoned rooms. Sam didn't share Mark's enthusiasm. He'd been jumpy since they arrived, looking over his shoulder, arguing with Mark as they ventured further into the belly of Harper Hospital. He didn't like this. Any of it. As film projects go, he was certain they could have selected a topic of equal mystery and intrigue, and fewer—

Ghosts.

There. Sam finally admitted it to himself. He was terrified of encountering a ghost in these morbid rooms. Full of bad memories and the heartache of a thousand abused patients, this place permeated an aura of sadness.

The air was thick with it, pressing in on him, making it hard to breathe. Or maybe that was his fear.

None of it seemed to faze Mark. He strolled through the asylum in a state of awe, giddy at times because he knew this film was going to earn him some respect. He hadn't stopped moving since the moment they arrived. He would gesture for Sam to "come here" or "look at this", all the while narrating for the camera. This was his final year of college, and it was time to make things happen. Time to shit or get off the pot, as his father used to say. For years, Mark had dreamed of landing a position in the world of TV broadcasting. All he needed was for others to take notice. So many graduates let their dreams fall by the wayside, their majors all but useless in the real world. But Mark was going to make something of himself. With his best friend at his side, he couldn't fail.

Sam paused to catch his breath as they rounded a corner. The two-hundred-thousand square foot grounds of Harper Hospital was starting to take its toll on his body. A dull ache burned its way up his calf muscles. Reluctantly, he leaned against the moldy cement wall for support, resting as Mark poked his head into the nearest room.

Sam felt as if he had walked the college campus three times. This place was huge, and he was out of shape. His weight gain hadn't stopped at The Freshman Fifteen. Its successors, The Sophomore Twenty and the Junior Twenty-five had followed in its wake, leaving behind extra baggage. A steady diet of junk food and energy drinks was to blame. Parking his ass in a chair several hours a day didn't help. But he had to study. He was determined to graduate with honors.

"Right here," Mark said. "This is where we'll shoot the highlight piece."

Mark's eyes were alight with a new-found energy. He smiled, and Sam didn't like the look of that grin. It was too wide, too full of mischief. He said, "Come on, buddy. You've *got* to see this! Oh man, there is some creepy shit in here!"

As invitations go, this was a pretty lousy one. It didn't make Sam want to enter the room. This was their last project together at Griffin Film University, and it meant a lot to both of them. Sooner or later he would have to humor his friend, explore the "creepy shit" and capture it on film. But first he was resting his legs.

"Yeah, yeah, I'll be there in a minute." He waved a hand in the air to dismiss Mark, who shrugged and disappeared into the shadows of the room.

Sam fiddled with the hand-held camcorder. He was worried about the darkness of the old hospital building. Barred windows, set high into the walls, were the only source of light. He wished he had a better camera, but this one was lightweight and easy to tote around. He sighed and shrugged to himself, still resting against the wall. With enough editing, he would make the footage work.

Something stirred at the end of the hallway. Sam looked up. A portion of the hallway was illuminated by sunlight that filtered in through the bars of a narrow window. Everything else was cloaked in darkness. It was hard to make out anything in those shadows, especially from where he stood halfway down the long hall. He focused. His vision was drawn to the darkest patch of shadows, where the hallway turned down an adjacent corridor.

His heart froze. There in the inky blackness glowed a thin, pale face. A rush of both terror and sadness washed over him as he gazed upon her face, full of melancholy, framed by a mess of unruly blonde hair that looked as if it hadn't seen a brush in many years. She was half-hidden by the wall. One gleaming, silver-blue eye peered at him from where she stood at the bend in the hallway. He ran his eyes down the length of her body, noticing the rags she wore that resembled a tattered burlap sack. He gasped. She wasn't touching the floor, but hovering there in the darkness.

She floated sideways from her hiding place, coming into full view. Every hair on his body stood erect. "Mark!" he screamed.

Mark's reply from the other room seemed to come from miles away. "What?"

"Mark! Come here! Quick!"

The girl drifted toward him in a fluid motion, her feet still inches from the ground. Her skin was an eerie shade of pale blue, glowing faintly in the dimness of the hall. Her face was young and slender, and even though he was afraid, he recognized a natural beauty there. Yet the sickly blue color of her down-turned lips caused him to step backwards, away from the ghastly sight as it approached.

She was only a few yards away as she reached out to him. *"He's here,"* she whispered in his mind. She didn't speak the words aloud. Her lifeless blue lips never moved. Sam heard her voice like a gust of wind through his skull, a sense of urgency in the words. He shivered. The girl's unwelcome entry into his thoughts frightened him more than anything else.

"Who's here?" he stammered. The girl's foggy, white eyes flicked to the doorway.

Mark appeared in the opening, eying Sam with confusion. "What did you say?"

Sam gulped, eyes wide. "The girl," he said, pointing. But she was gone. Whipping around to check the other direction, he nearly lost his balance.

"Dude, what's wrong? You look like you saw a--" Mark paused. A shit-eating grin spread over his face. "Don't tell me you saw a ghost..." He teased his friend with a slight shake of his head, chuckling softy.

"I'm out of here," was Sam's only reply. He turned and headed in the direction from which they'd come.

"But you can't! We're not done!"

"Oh, I'm done!" Sam was fuming. He stormed down the corridor, camera in hand, determined to wait in the car. Yes, he would wait there until Mark agreed to call it quits. Why? Because there was no reasoning with Mark. Sam knew him well enough to know that if he explained what had happened, if he described what he saw, mockery and skepticism would be Mark's only reaction. He didn't have time for that. He trusted his own sanity; he knew what he'd seen was real, and he wasn't stupid enough to hang around a haunted asylum for the sake of a college film project.

"Sam! Sam, wait!" Mark's hand was on his shoulder. He eased around to block his path. "I'm sorry. I didn't mean to piss you off. You saw something?"

"Not just *something*. I saw a fucking dead girl, and she talked to me." There was silence then, tension so thick you could taste it in the air. Or maybe that was the dust and mold spores.

"Look, I'm not saying you didn't see something. This place is crawling with bad vibes. We'll get out of here, bro... No problem." Mark rubbed his chin as Sam waited for the catch. "But we're so close. The film is nearly done. I just need you to shoot one more clip. Then we'll leave... Together. We need to stick together."

Mark waited as Sam mulled this over. He sighed, gesturing to Mark with the camcorder in his hand. "One clip. No retakes. And you better talk fast. Because what I saw..." He trembled. "I'm not crazy. You know this."

"I do." Mark smiled, patting his friend on the back. "A few more minutes and we're out of here, I promise."

***

"We are now in the heart of Harper Mental Hospital. This place grows darker the further in you go, but its history is the darkest part of all. In this room on the second floor, I've discovered what I believe to be an electric shock treatment table. The electroconvulsive therapy--or ECT machines are no longer here, but these restraints," he pulled on one of the leather straps, displaying it for the

87

camera, "these were used to hold the patient down at several parts of the body: head, wrists, arms, torso, and ankles."

"Imagine being strapped to this table, forced to endure more than a hundred volts of electricity pumped straight into the brain. Under the care of the callous Dr. Walters, this was a harsh reality for many patients here."

Sam followed Mark with the camera, holding his hand as steady as possible despite his heightening anxiety. He couldn't wait to be finished. He felt more like an idiot with every passing second. Why hadn't he stood his ground and insisted that they leave?

Mark strolled away from the wooden table with the leather restraints, making his way to a straight jacket he'd found hanging on the wall. Thick cobwebs covered its surface, the fabric yellow with age. "When Harper Mental Hospital closed its doors in 1942, stories began to surface. Personal accounts of extreme cruelty within these walls. A few reports claim that patients disappeared, that they checked in but never checked out. None of these claims are supported by any solid evidence, and yet, standing here in this torture chamber, it's not so hard to believe." He paused to throw the camera his very best dramatic look. "Some patients were left in straitjackets for days on end, unable to perform even the most basic human functions."

As Mark delved into his narrative on the history of strait jackets, Sam noticed a cold breeze touch the back of his neck. Goosebumps formed there, causing the hair to stand on end. He rubbed his free hand over the chilled skin, warming it. Another draft whistled past his ear, cooling the side of his face. He clenched his jaw to keep from fidgeting and tried to hold the camera steady as an inexplicable breeze swirled around him.

An icy hand touched his forearm, and he jumped to the side, jerking the camcorder. It ruined the shot, and Mark stopped talking mid-sentence to furrow his brow. "What now?"

"Something touched me."

Mark spread his arms wide in front of him, gesturing around the room. "There's no one here but us, bro."

Sam breathed deeply, trying to calm his nerves, but the icy touch returned. Frigid fingers closed around his hand that gripped the camera. Sam looked down and realized Mark was partially right: There was nothing there. Nothing visible anyway. But he felt it, the cold grip of death. There was something foul in the sensation, an unnerving feeling that shocked Sam into a motionless stupor.

He looked at his hand, frozen in terror, unsure of how to react. One of the camera's buttons pressed down on its own. The footage began to rewind. Squiggly lines filled the viewfinder as the documentary rolled by in reverse.

"Okay, you're obviously spooked by this place. Let's shoot the straight jacket bit again, then we can call it a day."

"Mark..."

"Yeah?"

"Shut up."

The camera stopped rewinding in the middle of the footage. The rewind button was released with a soft clicking noise. The play button was pressed. Sam watched the video come to life, not knowing what else he could do.

In the viewfinder of the camcorder, Mark was walking the halls, narrating bits and pieces of information about the hospital's history. The footage had been taken only thirty minutes ago, but Sam's mind was so weary from his encounter with the ghost, it felt like much, much longer. Mark prattled on, practically walking backwards so that his face was the center of attention at all times.

Mark took a break, resting to catch his breath and wet his tongue as Sam poked the camera into random rooms, allowing a glimpse inside. He liked the way the dust motes swirled in the strips of light coming through each tiny window, the corners of each room lost in shadows.

Sam continued to watch as the view panned across one of the many rooms he'd filmed in that moment. The footage paused. "*He's here,*" her voice whispered in his mind.

Sam gasped, nearly dropping the camera when he realized where the film had stopped. On the paused screen of a camera operated by unseen hands, a man's face leered at him. A broad chin and bright, squinted eyes, pale against the blackness of the shadows that hid him.

"We've got to go... now."

"What? No. We need to finish this shot."

Sam flipped the camera around so that Mark could see the picture. "No, we don't. We've got company. And here's proof."

***

Sam put the camcorder inside the case he carried over his shoulder. A furtive glance through the door assured the hallway was clear. Their footsteps echoed through the corridor, hearts thudding in their ears as they quickened their pace with each stride. The overcast sky beyond the bars of the narrow, high-set windows cast eerie shadows on the mildewed walls. Sam felt as if those shadows were reaching for him, the memory of the cold hand still fresh in his mind.

Rounding a corner, Sam and Mark reached the stairwell and stopped. The girl was there. She waited for them at the foot of the stairs, an ethereal beauty marred by death and decay. Her knee-length dress resembled something a peasant would wear: torn and filthy, thick, stiff fabric that didn't flatter her curvy figure. But no attire could flatter her now. She was ghastly. Her skin glowed morbidly in the dim stairwell— pale blue, as if every particle of oxygen had been squeezed from her body. Purple splotches riddled the flesh around her lips, which were cracked, swollen, and perpetually sad. A mane of wild blonde hair flipped and curled at impossible angles, floating about her face. Her eyes were covered in a thick, white film, reminding Sam of a cadaver beginning to rot. The slightest hint of silver-blue shined in those eyes as she hovered there, gazing up at them.

"What do you want?" Sam screamed.

"*He's here*," she whispered, but her lips never moved. The haunting words echoed through their minds.

"Did you hear that?" Mark asked, his voice higher than usual. Sam nodded slightly, though his eyes never strayed from the dead girl at the foot the stairs. Her lips parted, mouth hanging open to reveal the darkness inside of her mouth. Soundlessly—without gagging or choking—her mouth began to leak. A trickle of water at first, and then a steady torrent gushing from her throat. She didn't clench her gut or double over in pain; she didn't heave. She simply stood there, mouth agape, water spilling from her like a spigot. It soaked her dress, slicked her skin as it pooled beneath her on the floor.

"Fuck this!" yelled Mark. He bolted down the staircase and dashed past the girl, nearly slipping. "Come on, Sam!" he screamed over his shoulder.

Though he was horrified, Sam couldn't look away. "Who's here?" he asked, descending the stairs. "What are you trying to tell me?" The sound of Sam's voice seemed to pull her from a daze. She closed her lips, turning, and pointed toward the main door of the hospital. She stayed that way, levitating with her toes inches from the floor, pointing the way for Sam, motionless aside from her wild hair which seemed to have a life of its own.

Sam's heart lurched as he slipped past her and made his way for the door. The air around her was so cold it made his muscles tense up, a chill jolting his spine. He maneuvered himself swiftly around the massive puddle. He hated the idea of putting his back to a ghost, but there was only one way out of this place. The girl's dead eyes burned into his back as he retreated. He looked to the stairwell as he swung open the door, but she had disappeared. The puddle was gone, too.

He stepped into the daylight, flooded with relief. Then he saw Mark standing near the car and knew their troubles weren't over. Mark cursed at the top of his lungs, balling his hands into fists. "God damn motherfucking shit!" he screamed. He delivered a swift kick to the Nissan's frame, planting his hands on the roof of the car and softly banging his head against the metal.

"What's the matter?"

"The tires," Mark mumbled without lifting his head. Sam looked down, turning his attention to the wheels of the car. His jaw dropped. The tires were completely flat, a jagged gash through each rubbery ring.

"Did we hit something?"

Mark raised his head, shaking it. "No. It's all four tires. Looks like the work of a knife." He rubbed his temples the way he always did when a headache was creeping up on him. "And I don't think it was your ghost friend in there."

"By the sound of it, I see you've met Anna." A stranger's voice caught the two friends off guard, and they turned to see an old man saunter out from behind a patch of sycamore trees. In his wrinkled, liver-spotted hands was a Smith & Wesson revolver, aimed directly at Mark.

"Woah, woah! What's with the gun? What did I do?" pleaded Mark.

"Who are you?" asked Sam, his voice shaky.

"Me? I'm just an old man who has grown tired of playing games with a ghost."

Mark and Sam glanced at each other through the corners of their eyes, quickly turning their attention back to the old man who approached them with a shambling, hunched over gait. "What games?" they asked in unison. This encounter was becoming a game of Twenty Questions.

"Her games. Always trying to tell her sad story and destroy my good name."

Sam rubbed a hand over the back of his neck. He scrunched his brow and bit down on his lip, thinking. "Are you... Dr. Walters?"

A series of chuckles exploded from the old man's withered throat. He looked to be around ninety years old, and his entire body shook with the maniacal laughter. He wiped a tear from his eye. "No, certainly not! Dr. Walters has been dead for many years. The man was thirty years my senior, and just take a look at *me*!" He smiled. "I'm the one nobody knows about. The nameless assistant... the underling." His lips curled into a look of disgust. "And that's how I'd like it to stay." He attempted to steady the revolver in his shaky hands, aiming it back and forth between the two younger men. "You shouldn't have come here."

"I'm sorry, really I am," Sam said, keeping his tone as calm as possible. "Here." He moved slowly, as to not upset the wild-eyed geriatric. He reached down to unzip the camera case.

"Stop moving!" the old man screamed.

"I'm just offering you my camera," Sam said in an act of desperation. He pulled it from the case, held it out to the stranger. "All the footage I've taken... it's yours. Just have it. My friend and I will drop the project. We'll never speak of Harper Hill again. Whatever bad memories lurk in this place, we'll leave them be. It's not our story to tell anyway."

"I'm afraid that's not possible. You've already seen my face. And you've already met dear Anna."

Sam gulped. He put every ounce of his strength behind it as he chucked the camcorder at the old man's hand. Mark and Sam were both shocked when the flying camera hit its mark. It slammed into the man's boney fist, sending the gun skidding over the gravel drive.

The old man's eyes widened as he dove for the gun. His knees buckled under the sudden movement, and he fell to the ground, jagged rocks digging into his skin. Mark got to the gun first. He plucked it from the stranger's grasp as he stretched his arms, reaching for it. Mark stood over their former assailant with a victorious smirk on his face.

"Why'd you do this?"

He didn't answer, but a swift kick to the ribs got him talking. "I heard you coming. I live in the house down the road. I've stayed there... many decades... protecting my secret."

Sam joined Mark. Their shadows fell over the man as he looked up at them with dark brown, malevolent eyes. "Look," Mark said, closing one eye to look down the barrel of the gun. "I'm tired of being forced to ask so many questions. So here's one more: Why don't you tell us this 'secret' of yours and I might consider letting you go."

"What's the point? If the truth gets out, I'll lose the respect of my family, of my friends. I'll be remembered as a monster, a murderer. Just kill me now." Silence fell over them. As if sensing the somber moment, the sun dipped behind a patch of clouds, throwing everything into grayness again. The man began to weep, tears trailing down his cheeks. "So many, many years I've lived with the guilt of what we did to beautiful Anna. She was the first to die at the hands of Dr. Walters and his brutal methods. He thought stopping the brain, then jump-starting it again was the best way to eliminate mental illness. I followed in his footsteps, but I never meant to hurt her."

He sighed and bowed his head in shame, still seated on the gravel driveway. "After Anna, we started using the crematorium for proper disposal of the bodies, but at the time of Anna's death, the crematorium was still being constructed." He paused to wet his throat with saliva, head hanging low on his neck to avoid eye contact with his captors. "Dr. Walters didn't want to risk being shut down or forced to discontinue his work over one accidental death. So we buried her, burned her files, made it so she never existed. The doctor insisted on perfecting his resuscitation skills, and with some patients the process seemed to work. But as the death toll rose higher and higher: two, three, four, five, six—I began to worry we were doing more harm than good." He wiped his nose, cleared his throat. "That's when I started to see her. She was everywhere I turned, mocking me with those blue lips and sad, lifeless eyes."

Sam glanced up at the hospital, picturing her in there, listening. Mark kept the revolver trained on his target. "So I got the place shut down by reporting the other abuse that went on here. It wasn't hard. And no one ever suspected me. I had Harper Hospital condemned before the authorities had a chance to discover the truth behind the missing patients. I only wanted to be rid of the past, to keep the name Frederick Stout from going down in history as a monster... a madman."

His frail shoulders shook as he began to sob harder. "You're not the first, you know. There was another young man who came here poking around. He saw Anna. He followed her, discovered my secret. He wasn't aware of me watching him, had no way of knowing I see everything that happens on Harper Hill. Up here... this is my world... just me, my house, and the asylum. I heard him coming, the same as I heard you. And I buried him down there with Anna."

Sam shivered as the grisly details were revealed. "And where is Anna?"

"Ask her yourself," growled Frederick. He lunged for Mark's legs, ramming his knees with all the force he could muster. Mark lost his footing as the blow knocked him sideways. He hit the ground, and Frederick was upon him, his speed shocking for a man nearly a century old.

They grappled on the ground, pebbles flying through the air. They were momentarily lost in a cloud of gravel dust. When Sam could see again, the old man was straddling Mark. In his hands was a pocket knife. He held it in the air, the blade shining in his shaky grip as he prepared to plunge it into Mark's chest.

Mark rolled sideways, crying out as the knife's blade grazed his arm. He reared back with both fists and delivered a double-punch to Frederick's sternum that sent him flying backwards. The old man hit the rocks with an audible thud. Sam approached, ready to dive for the Smith & Wesson that was just within Frederick's spindly reach.

But he had fallen unconscious when his skull hit the ground.

***

Sam watched as Anna's body was excavated. It was nothing more than a skeleton in a tattered, knee-length dress. The wild blonde hair had fallen away from her scalp. Even the word "scalp" didn't apply, he thought. No skin remained on the cold, hard skull. Her facial tissue had long ago turned into dust, a ghoulish grin where her lips had once been. Sam hoped it wasn't too late for the dead girl to find solace. He hoped she could finally rest in peace.

Officer McRyan strolled over, thumbs tucked into his belt. He stood next to Sam. "How did you know she was down here?"

"Easy. I asked her, and she showed me."

The cop wrinkled his brow, puzzled by the statement, then shrugged and made a beeline for the group of officers who formed a semi-circle around the corpse. The cellar was alive with conversation as they discussed the bizarre findings: a hidden room with a pool dug into the ground, a large well-sweep device looming over it.

The police had doubted Sam when they arrived on the scene where two young men held an older man hostage. Their self-defense allegations were hard to believe. Fredrick Stout, a frail geriatric of a man, didn't appear to have the vigor for an act of violence. But there was proof, irrefutable evidence. When Sam had thrown the camcorder to disarm the old man, miraculously the record button had been pressed. Frederick's entire confession was caught on video, and though Sam kept it to himself, deep down he knew a pair of unseen hands had caused this stroke of luck.

Frederick Stout had refused to cooperate with the police, not speaking a word to incriminate himself further. But someone else had provided all the information they needed. Someone who remembered every terrifying detail, who led Sam through the hospital as Mark waited for the police with the Smith & Wesson leveled at Frederick. She led him here, to Dr. Walter's hidden chamber of torture, where she had drowned, where she'd been buried and forgotten.

Photos were snapped and evidence was collected. The young girl's body would leave the asylum today. If only Sam could be certain this was enough to set her free.

Then he heard it. "*Thank you,*" her voice whispered in his mind.

"You're welcome," Sam whispered back.

He sighed and felt a gigantic weight lift from his shoulders—until he noticed the dead man in the corner. He looked around, but no one else seemed to notice. Mark stood outside the door, attempting to flirt with a disinterested female officer. The investigators went about their business. Sam turned his attention back to the apparition.

The dead man hovered there, above the dirt floor. A gunshot wound exposed a portion of his brain. Blood leaked from the hole in his cranium as his dark eyes bore into Sam. The ghostly figure reached out with a cadaverous hand, pointing to the soil with the other.

"Officer McRyan!" Sam called. The tall man jogged over. "Do you see that?" he asked.

"See what?"

Sam gulped. "The old man confessed to a second murder, and I'm pretty sure you'll find the body over there," he said, pointing.

The officer cocked his head. "How do you know? Did he tell you?" There was an awkward silence as Sam tried to determine if McRyan meant the killer or the dead man. He had a feeling the nerve-rattled cop phrased the question in such a way to avoid the haunting truth.

"Yes," Sam replied, leaving it at that.

The team set to work on digging up the second corpse, carefully removing the soil. Sam hoped this was the end, that there were no more souls trapped here. An eternity at Harper Hill was a punishment too severe for even the likes of Frederick Stout.

ROOM 309

Chad P. Brown

The creaking cables and the grinding gears came to a sudden, screeching halt.

Tony stepped off the elevator to make his rounds of the third floor, vowing to take the stairs from now on. Like everything else in Brookwood Asylum, the elevator needed to either be brought up to date or shut down completely.

But Tony figured it helped add to the haunting atmosphere that people shelled out good money to experience at Brookwood.

Brookwood Asylum was built in the mid-1800s and opened its doors to patients in 1864. It was originally designed to hold 250 mental patients but well over 2,000 patients resided within its over-crowded walls at its peak during the 1950s. Brookwood Asylum had housed mental defectives, epileptics, drug addicts, alcoholics, and even unwed mothers who were deemed morally deficient according to "mental health standards" at the time (Tony still found that last one shocking). Due to changes in the treatment of mental illness, it closed its doors in 1982. Abandoned and left empty for decades, rumors arose about how the old Brookwood Asylum was haunted by the patients who had died there, most of them by cruel or tragic means. In 2007, the building was put up for sale by the state and bought by an individual named Theodore Cox. A year later, Mr. Cox opened the doors again, giving guided daytime tours of the grounds and even offering overnight tours for the braver souls. The Brookwood Asylum Haunted Tour stayed open nine months out of the year, shutting down during the off-season from December to February. During that time, Mr. Cox hired nighttime security guards to watch over the building and prevent vandals and ghost seekers from breaking in.

Tony made sure all the former patients' rooms were locked up tight, noticing how the rundown appearance gave the building a spooky feel. The once white linoleum floor was now smeared with grime and God knew what other stains. Exposed, rusty ceiling pipes ran down the middle of the twelve-foot wide corridor. The walls were puke green, the paint chipped and cracked away in most areas.

As Tony made his rounds, a scream ripped through the air.

It wasn't an oh-you-startled-me type of yell or an I-just-saw-a-mouse type of squeal. But a blood curdling piss-your-pants scream.

Tony froze in the middle of the hallway. His frightened eyes danced up and down the empty corridor, on the lookout for any sign of movement.

When he heard the scream again, he considered jetting for the nearest exit. But it was his job to make sure the building was secure and no vandals or pranksters had broken in.

With a trembling hand, Tony reached to his side and pulled out his walkie-talkie from the pouch on his duty belt. He slowly raised it to his lips and pressed the talk button.

"Scott, you there?" he said in a low voice. "We've got a problem up on the third floor. Over."

The response of crackling static filled the air. He tried again, his voice tainted with a slight hint of aggravation.

"Answer me, Scott. I just heard screaming up here. Over."

There was still no response. If Scott had left the front desk to sneak outside and smoke a joint, Tony was going to kill him. They had been working together at Brookwood Asylum for the past two months as night security guards. Not a single shift had passed without Scott firing at least one up. He claimed it calmed his nerves since he worked in a supposedly haunted asylum. Tony figured he was just a stoner.

Tony considered trying to reach Scott again, but gave up and placed the walkie-talkie back in his duty belt. Letting out a deep sigh and steeling his resolve, he pulled out his flashlight from the other side and flicked it on, shining the beam around at the adjacent rooms. He noticed how the door to the room just ahead was slightly ajar.

Room 309.

The sound of running footsteps followed by receding laughter echoed behind him.

Tony jumped and spun around, the beam of the flashlight bouncing frantically from the walls to the ceiling to the floor. No one was there.

He shook his head, reassuring himself that he was just spooked and was imagining things. Turning back around, he shone his flashlight once again down the hall at Room 309.

The door creaked all the way open, the sound causing the hairs on his arms and neck to stand on end.

It was his job to go check it out and see what the hell was going on. But he was none too thrilled about going down to the room by himself. He would feel safer if he had backup.

Tony tried to reach Scott again on the walkie-talkie, but there was still no answer. He cursed his co-worker and replaced the walkie-talkie. Wishing he had a gun, he instead pulled out his issued Taser and walked down the hall towards Room 309.

When he got to the room, he flipped the light switch located outside the doorway. Nothing. The light should have come on because Mr. Cox left the electricity turned on during the off-season. Tony flipped it a few more times but the light still didn't come on.

The faint sound of giggling came from inside the room causing Tony to shudder. He lifted his Taser and held it in front of him.

"Who's in there?" he called out in a shaky voice. "Come on out where I can see you."

He stepped in front of the doorway and shone his flashlight into the room.

The walls were covered in splotches of faded, yellow wallpaper that had at one time covered the walls completely. Tony shone his flashlight around the edges of one exposed area of the plaster wall and swore he could see the imprint of fingernails. On the far side of the room, there was a huge window nearly five feet tall that would have allowed ample sunlight to filter into the room. Tony had heard how this was one of the steps forward in mental health care when Brookwood had first been built, replacing the housing of patients in dark, dank holes for open-spaced, sun-filled rooms.

Beads of sweat dropped down his forehead into his eyes blurring his vision. He wiped the sweat away with the sleeve of his shirt and blinked his eyes a few times trying to clear his vision.

Nothing seemed out of the ordinary and there was certainly nothing to indicate the source of the screams he thought he had heard.

Tony turned to leave but stopped when he caught something out of the corner of his eye sitting on the windowsill. He turned back around and squinted, shining his flashlight on the windowsill.

It was a child's music box.

It must be some prop for the haunted tours, he thought, although he couldn't remember having seen it or heard about it before.

The door swung shut with a thunderous slam that echoed down the empty corridor.

Tony dropped his flashlight onto the ground, busting the battery casing and smashing the lens.

"Damn it," he hissed, kicking the cheap, broken pieces across the floor.

Giggling from inside the room erupted again, louder this time, mocking him and his childish display.

Tony was fed up. He flung the door open, squinting into the darkness. "That's about enough! Come on out!"

A little girl cautiously stepped forward out of the darkness. Her long, light brown hair was pulled to the sides in pigtails. She wore a plain, red dress and white knee high socks. She was holding a teddy bear tightly to her chest. One of the button eyes was missing.

She slowly lifted up her head to Tony, a frightened look in her dark eyes.

Tony holstered his Taser and squatted down to the little girl's eye level. "What's your name?"

"Kayla," the little girl hesitantly responded.

"What are you doing in here?"

Kayla ignored his question. "Do you want to play hide-and-seek with me?"

Tony stared down at the little girl with a look of confusion on his face. "We don't have time to play any games. Besides, this isn't a safe place for little kids to be running around and–"

"Tony, you there?" a voice crackled from the walkie-talkie, cutting Tony off. "Check in, buddy. Over."

Tony yanked the walkie-talkie from his duty belt. "Scott, where the hell have you been? I heard screams up in Room 309 and there's some little girl up here who's lost. Over." He released the talk button, mumbling "son of a bitch" under his breath.

Kayla giggled beside him. "You said a bad word."

Tony smiled as his cheeks flushed red.

"Sorry, man," Scott responded. "I, um, stepped outside for a minute." There was a long pause. "Did you say screams... over?"

Tony could detect a mixture of disbelief and amusement in Scott's voice. He hoped Scott wasn't stoned; that was all he needed.

"You heard me. Now get your butt up here," Tony responded, careful to censor himself in front of the little girl.

He replaced the walkie-talkie without waiting for a response from Scott and turned to reassure Kayla everything was going to be alright.

But she was gone.

Concern swept across his face as he peered up and down the hallway, but there was no sign of her. He thought about waiting for Scott to get there first, but decided he had better go search for the little girl. They would have a major lawsuit on their hands if she ended up getting hurt or worse.

As Tony jogged down the hall to go and find Kayla, he could've sworn he heard the faint sound of music coming from the other end of the hall.

***

Scott opened the stairwell door and strolled out into the hallway. He hadn't worked at Brookwood long, but it was long enough to completely distrust the antiquated elevator. The stairs were a much safer means of getting from point A to point B without plummeting to your death.

"Tony? Are you up here?"

There was no response. Scott kept walking. His palms were sweaty and his breathing grew more rapid. He kept telling himself that he had misunderstood Tony; a combination of having just smoked one and the poor reception of the cheap Wal-Mart walkie-talkies, because there was no way Tony had heard screaming up here. The building was abandoned except for the two of them.

Either that or his co-worker was trying to pull a fast one.

Scott hunkered behind the corner that led to the hallway lined with the former patients' rooms, listening.

The click-clack of approaching footsteps echoed from down the hallway.

Figuring it was Tony, Scott peaked around the corner and nearly pissed his pants when he saw a woman walking down the hall.

She was wearing an ankle-length, dark gray dress with a white pinafore and a white, long cap that looked like a shortened version of a nun's habit. Scott had seen pictures hanging in the lobby of nurses from the early 1900s dressed in similar uniforms.

This had to be some prank Tony was playing on him and this woman dressed like a nurse from the turn of the century was in on the gag. Tony was probably getting back at him for the trick that Scott had pulled on him a couple of weeks ago. Of course, Scott had just made moaning sounds and yelled a few times while hiding in the former electro-shock therapy room. Tony's prank was way more elaborate. Scott decided to play along.

"Excuse me, nurse," he called out. "I need to ask you some questions."

The woman calmly strolled down the hallway, pausing at Room 309 to shut the door.

"How can I help you, young man?" she asked when she reached him.

Scott found the woman's polite, care-giver smile to be a nice touch, but also a little creepy.

He squinted and read the nametag on her uniform. "Phoebe Chaffin, huh? Well, Phoebe, have you heard any screaming up here?" Scott chuckled, really starting to enjoy it.

The nurse considered a moment before answering. "No, I haven't heard any screaming." She leaned in closer to Scott. "Not yet, anyway," she added with a laugh.

Scott didn't find her joke the least bit funny. "Seriously, though, where's Tony? Is he down in Room 309?"

"I don't believe we have a patient on this floor named Tony. This floor is reserved for that shameful lot of unwed mothers and their little screaming brats."

"Right," Scott replied sarcastically. He turned and walked down the hall towards Room 309. "Hey, Tony, are you in there?"

He flipped on the light switch and opened the door. The overhead fluorescents blinked a few times before illuminating the room in a cold, harsh glow.

Scott let out a gasp.

A young woman was hanging from the ceiling, a bed sheet tied around her neck. Her dingy, blonde hair fell in clumps around her face concealing her facial features. She was wearing a grimy hospital gown with dark stains. Her legs had multiple bruises. Some were a fresh, dark purple color while others were a fading, yellowish color.

"I told you there was no Tony up here," the nurse said from behind him in the hallway, "just the regular patients hanging around."

He looked down and saw that she was holding a scalpel in her hand, the sharp blade glistening. But he ignored it, thinking it was all part of the gag Tony was playing on him, his attention more focused on the woman hanging from the rafters.

Scott leapt forward and slammed the door shut.

"I don't have time for your games, you crazy bitch," he mumbled.

"Don't call me crazy," the nurse hissed from the other side of the doorway. He then heard the sound of receding footsteps as she walked away.

Once she was gone, Scott reached forward to open the door. He cursed himself when he realized he was trapped. The doors of the patients' rooms didn't have door knobs on the inside in order to prevent the chance of patients getting loose and wandering freely around Brookwood.

Scott banged and kicked on the door but it was useless.

He walked over to the woman hanging from the ceiling. Cautiously lifting up his hand, he brushed back her hair. Her skin was a bluish-purple color, her lifeless eyes were bugging out, and her swollen tongue protruded from her mouth. He stuck his hand out and touched her bruised leg. She was cold – real cold and real dead.

He quickly withdrew his hand and wiped it on his pants to get rid of the feeling of death clinging to his palm.

Scott glanced around Room 309 for a moment and then screamed in horror as the realization sunk in that the young woman was dead and that he was locked inside the room with a corpse.

***

"Kayla, where are you?"

Tony had walked over to the other side of the third floor, the East Wing, with no sign of the little girl. It was as if she had disappeared.

Despite his usual calm temper, Tony was starting to get aggravated. He didn't have time to run all over the asylum searching for a little girl that shouldn't even be in Brookwood in the first place.

"Come on, Kayla, stop playing games and come on out!"

"But I like playing games, especially hide-and-seek."

Tony jumped when he heard the little girl's voice. "Kayla? Where are you?"

"I'm over here, silly."

Tony's head turned in every direction but he couldn't tell where she was hiding. It sounded like her voice was coming from everywhere at once. He looked up and down the hallway, trying to pinpoint her location.

"Kayla, come on out," he yelled, the tone of his voice growing irater.

She giggled. "You have to find me first." Her answer was followed by more laughter.

Tony walked forward and stepped around the corner, spotting Kayla's teddy bear on the floor a few feet away. He bent over and picked it up.

"I've got your teddy bear. I bet he misses you."

"It's a she, not a he."

"Then *she* misses you," Tony corrected himself, trying to maintain his composure. "Please come out, Kayla."

"Fine," she answered after a moment.

Tony jumped and spun around when he felt a tug on the back of his shirt.

"Jesus! You almost gave me a heart attack."

"You're no fun at all," Kayla scolded, staring up at him. "Give me my teddy bear."

Tony tried to settle his nerves as he handed the teddy bear to Kayla with shaky hands. She took it from him and hugged it tightly to her chest.

"Where were you hiding?" Tony asked once he had calmed down and had the frame of mind to wonder how she had snuck up behind him so suddenly.

"I'll never tell," she answered, snickering secretively. "Can we go find my Mommy now?"

"Your Mommy?" Tony was taken aback. "Who's your Mommy?"

"She's a nurse here. She lets me play as long as I stay on this floor. I really like hide-and-seek. But you wouldn't play with me."

Tony stared down at the little girl in confusion, wondering if she wasn't perhaps a little crazy. "Kayla, there aren't any nurses here anymore. The asylum shut down years ago. Now, it's just a haunted attraction. People come here looking for ghosts."

Kayla gave him an inquisitive look. "Do you believe in ghosts, Tony?"

Tony thought for a second. "How do you know my name? I never told you my name."

"It says so right on your name tag, silly. T-O-N-Y."

Tony glanced down at his name tag and laughed. "I guess it does."

"But Mommy *is* here. Come on, I'll show you."

Kayla took off walking down the hall.

Tony stood for a moment trying to figure out what was going on. There was no way Kayla's mother was a nurse at Brookwood. The little girl had to be confused or maybe there was something wrong with her.

He shrugged his shoulders and followed after her.

***

Scott pounded hysterically on the door, yelling for help. But there was no answer.

With a sudden flash, he remembered the walkie-talkie at his side.

"Tony? Please come in. I need help," he whispered. "I'm in Room 309 and there's a dead woman up here and some crazy nurse with a scalpel. Over."

Scott waited for a response. When Tony finally answered, he let out a deep sigh of relief.

"I'm here, Scott. I can barely hear you though. What's going on? Over."

Scott pressed the talk button tightly with aggravation and fear. "I'm in Room 309," he said louder this time. "There's a dead woman up here and some crazy nurse with a scalpel in the hallway–"

"I told you not to call me crazy," a voice said behind him.

Scott spun around, dropping the walkie-talkie to the floor, and stared in disbelief at the nurse standing by the windowsill. She opened the music box and the tune of "Brahms's Lullaby" drifted across the room.

"How did you get in here?" Scott asked.

"Young man, I have access to all the rooms as a nurse on this floor." She closed her eyes and hummed along with the music box for a moment.

Scott pulled out his Taser and held it in front of him. "I don't know who you are or what you're doing in here, but you can tell your crazy story to the cops."

Phoebe's eyes flashed with anger as she slammed the lid of the music box down. "I am *not* crazy," she hissed. She stalked towards Scott, tightening her grip on the scalpel in her hand.

"Lady, stay back or else I'm going to send 1,200 volts of electricity right through you."

The nurse kept advancing, shoving the dead woman hanging from the ceiling out of her way. She stopped in front of Scott, the body behind her swaying back and forth. She raised the scalpel up so it was level with Scott's throat.

"I warned you," Scott said.

He fired the Taser but it didn't do anything. The nurse laughed. He banged on the side of it a few times and pulled the trigger again. But it still didn't fire. He helplessly dropped it to the ground and raised his hands in front of him.

"And I warned you," the nurse said as she swung the scalpel sideways, the blade slicing into his throat.

***

"You stay here, alright?" Tony told Kayla.

The little girl nodded her head and backed up against the puke green wall of the hallway. He gave her one more glance before walking over to Room 309.

"Scott, are you in there?"

When there was no response, Tony hesitantly reached for the door knob, a feeling of dread twisting his stomach into tight knots. He turned the knob and pushed the door open.

The lights in the room were on, which Tony found odd considering how they hadn't worked earlier. Inside, he saw a body lying on a gurney covered with a crimson-stained bed sheet. Beside it, there was a wheelchair, one of the old-fashioned, wooden ones that had leather restraints for the hands and feet of patients.

"What the hell is going on around here?" he mumbled to himself.

He walked over to the gurney and pulled down the sheet. He screamed when he saw Scott's open-eyed face staring blankly back at him, a gaping gash running across the middle of his throat. Tears filled Tony's eyes as he read the pain and torment twisted into Scott's face.

"I told him not to call me crazy."

Tony whirled around. A woman stood in the doorway wearing a nurse's uniform that made her look like she had worked at Brookwood since it had first opened its doors more than one hundred years ago.

"Who are you?" he asked her.

The nurse glanced down at Scott on the gurney. "A rude young man." She looked back up into Tony's eyes. "Extremely rude."

"What the hell did you do to him?" Tony shouted, shaking with rage.

"I told him not to call me crazy. But he persisted in using that impolite term in reference to me. So, I shut him up."

Tony balled his hands into tight fists until his knuckles turned bone white. "I'll kill you!"

The nurse laughed hysterically for a moment and then the door slammed shut.

Tony ran over to the door and began hammering on it with his fists, demanding to be let out.

The room went dark.

Tony felt something cold brush beside him followed by the sound of giggling. His heart thundered in his chest as his eyes darted frantically around the room cloaked in darkness.

He backed slowly away from the door. After taking a few steps, he felt something hit him hard in the chest, shoving him down onto the wheelchair. Tony tried to get up but he couldn't move. Something had him pinned in the chair, an enormous weight pushing down on him.

Something cold grabbed his right hand and fastened the leather restraint around it. Before he knew what was happening, the cold thing had his left hand and feet restrained as well.

Tony thrashed around in the chair, struggling to get free, but it was useless.

He heard the giggling again, turning his blood to ice.

The lights flipped back on.

Tony blinked his eyes and squinted, trying to adjust to the sudden harsh light.

The nurse stood in front of him with her arm around Kayla. Both of them were flashing malicious smiles, the sinister kind that Tony had only seen in the movies.

"Now, what are we going to do with him?" Phoebe asked Kayla.

Kayla thought for a moment before answering. "Something bad. He wouldn't play hide-and-seek with me." She stuck out her bottom lip, pouting.

Suddenly, it all made sense to Tony. "You little bitch," he said slowly. "You were helping her this whole time."

Phoebe lunged at him. "Watch your mouth!" she screamed. "Kayla may be a deceptive little monster, but she's no more of a bitch than I'm crazy."

"Yeah, show some respect for the dead." Kayla giggled.

The color in Tony's face drained as his mouth dropped open. His hands began to tremble with fear as he clutched the arms of the wheelchair tighter.

"Please, let me go," he pleaded, whimpering as he looked back and forth between the two of them. "Please!"

Kayla stepped forward.

The lights went out.

Tony screamed.

BROTHER KEEPERS

Lockett Hollis

When she first saw the stranger pulling his boat up on the beach, she thought, *He can get me out of here!*

It had been barely two months since Willa's last confinement to a seclusion room, and today was the first time she had been permitted to walk the campus unchaperoned, to wind at will down its roads and paths and past old, leaf-heavy trees and stark modern buildings all incongruently clustered on blocks of manicured lawn. She was nearly at the beach, her steps beginning to tend her southward down the longer aspect of the island, when she saw him.

Not a day over thirty, she thought, though that would still place him at ten years her senior. She found him handsome in a careless, roguish way. If she didn't spook him, if she could talk to him alone, who knew? She was not the insufferably cute pixie she had been two years ago, but she had seen herself in the mirror before leaving the pavilion for her walk. The many months of addiction, the torture of withdrawal, all the recent times she'd been sick, had aged her face a few extra years, but Willa could still pass for pretty at least— especially as she had freshened up a little before her jaunt. That was part of the treat. One of the nicer nurses had even dropped a complement.

The young man paused from his grunting efforts to haul up the boat. He lifted his head, swaying it to allow his hair to sweep aside from his eyes, and he smiled at her. Just a small smile—one of intrigued curiosity, perhaps?—but it brightened her whole day. She had meant to start out cool, casual, friendly. Normal. But that smile of his ignited in her all the desperation beneath the surface, all the craving to escape.

"Help me," she begged, approaching him. "I am being held here against my will."

His brow furrowed. "That's not good," he said. His wary eyes scanned the grounds and the water around them, then they widened, and with frantic resolve he lugged the little boat past her, puffing furiously, until both he and the boat were hidden behind the nearest manicured shrubs, where he remained crouching.

It was her turn to frown. What was his problem anyway? Big snob! And not bright either—if he wanted to hide the boat he should have left it on the *other* side of the bushes, or landed near the heavier growth at the southern tip of the island in the first place. If he was here to see a girlfriend on the island, this was a fast way to spoil their intended tryst.

"What are you doing back there?" she hissed.

His head protruded almost comically from his cover, gazing past her toward the water.

Willa began: "There isn't anything th—"

And stopped. No, there was something there.

A steam-powered passenger ship approached the island, passing from the dangerous bend in the East River which residents of Queens have long known as the Hell Gate. Smoke billowed from the prow as though from a dragon's nose, its plumes growing blacker and heavier every instant. As the steamboat maintained its mad windward course, the flames in the foremost portion of the vessel were fanned higher and higher, and they spread like eager demons throughout the double decking, where hundreds of people crowded, possibly more than a thousand, nearly all women and children.

The flames found them.

"Oh my God!"

The wailing was impossibly high, intolerably tortured, became ragged and bestial as the first of the people burned. Willa could see the crew scrambling forward with the fire hoses, but once the water was turned on the hoses quickly disintegrated in their hands, the water splashing impotently on their shoes as fire surrounded them. There was far too much crowding on the foredeck; some passengers had fallen, preventing the escape of others toward the temporarily safer stern of the ship. Desperate mothers cinched life preservers around their terror-stricken children, the canvas leaking puffs of some sawdust-like material, some of them even falling apart in the mothers' hands and spilling brown powder on the deck.

The children tossed overboard sank like stones in the useless 'life preservers', and when the mothers and others followed they were quickly swept down by their old-fashioned woolen clothing. Many of those who had jumped ship from the foredeck and had fought thus far to keep their heads above water were ploughed under and horribly mangled beneath the oncoming steamer's paddle wheel. Soon it was not just the screaming and the smell of smoke and charring bodies that reached the beach—the tide began to teasingly coax the dead onto the sandbanks, most of them face down, and very still. Willa noticed one child, probably not older than five, wash up on the beach, the little guy clad in a child's sailor suit complete with navy neckerchief, but the cap and one of his shiny white shoes were missing. An old nursery rhyme circled absurdly in Willa's mind as she raked her teeth over her knuckles.

Diddle diddle dumpling…

She bet dead boy's name was John, too.

The waterborne pageant of agony still slowly coursed by when Willa noticed the young man had stood up, and was staring out toward the water.

He sees it too! I'm not crazy! This is really happening!

But he seemed to be looking further upstream now, and not at the carnage but at the blank water, toward the unmoving buildings of the cityscape beyond.

"Don't you see it?!" she demanded. "Hey! Can't you see any of this?!" He shook his head slightly, and shrugged. Exasperated, Willa flung out her arm toward the suffering hundreds, turned her head to follow her arm.

The ship was gone.

The current churned by at a hurried clip, but there were no vessels on it now, and no bodies stacked along the sandbanks. The boxy arch of the gantry crane above the ferry slip stood in stoical iron idiocy, and on the mainland beyond, the city seemed to sleep in dust-colored indifference.

She turned.

The man was walking away from the beach, toward the building which acted as the island's morgue.

"Hey, wait!"

He halted but didn't turn around, looking over his shoulder. Was that pity on his face? A look that said, *'Sorry, I can't help you…sorry…'*? Willa debated over what to say next when he turned back, raised a small camera at the old brick morgue that once had been the structure of the island's chapel, and snapped a picture. Then he walked ahead.

Willa cursed and followed, worried she had already wrecked any chance he might consider helping her. He hadn't seen the burning ship because it wasn't there, though she knew that didn't mean it never had been. Since the start of her forced withdrawals, scenes of a similar sickening vividness would erupt into sudden being before her and then—usually after a hard pressing of her eyes or the needling of her teeth in her arm—those things would cease to be there.

God she needed a fix! And that man might be her only hope. There was no chance of getting more smack from the mainland brought here. After so many relapses the staff began guarding her more closely, and Hugo had stopped coming months ago. He had promised, *sworn,* that he would come back for her, help her get out of here or at least tide her over! But that had been before Valentine's, and tomorrow was May! He probably got another girl. That or they had caught him trying to bring the stuff and now maybe he was just upstream from her on the prison island—right down the block, after a fashion, just like the old times. But no Hugo, no junk, and without the junk there was no stopping the visions. It was the only cure that worked here, the only hero that really killed the pain—both physically and psychically.

The stranger snapped more pictures, then entered the morgue through a side door. Willa followed slowly, giving him space.

He glanced over at her, then continued taking pictures.

"It is an amazing place," he said, looking around.

She didn't expect that, didn't know what to say. It was a horrible place! Didn't he see that yet?

Luckily for them both, no living person lay on the other side of the door, though several sheeted shapes rested on gurneys in the cold-room. In this morgue, the dead were not sequestered to separate drawers or sections, but instead were kept collectively in one large and heavily insulated refrigerated room with a steel autopsy table in its center. Shuddering, Willa followed far behind the young man as he wandered onward beyond the morgue and up a nearby flight of stairs. She wondered as she climbed, *why was he so cautious and skittery before, but now clomps carelessly through the first building he came to? And why explore the morgue at all? Surely he hadn't come to visit a corpse!*

He passed the second floor, continuing to the roof. There he took pictures of the power plant and adjacent coal house, stepping gingerly so that his tread hardly sounded.

She smiled at him, feigning shyness. "I hope I'm not bugging you," she offered. He gave her a curious look, one not dissimilar to the strange smile he had offered at the beach, then he raised the camera and snapped a picture of her. She jumped in surprise.

"That's fine," he said, then turned away.

She followed him downstairs, but he was gone through the morgue and back out the door while she was only just emerging from the stairwell and into the interposing cold-room. Yelping in surprise she skidded to a stop.

Someone else was in the cold-room now—one of the doctors, or an undertaker. He stood at the autopsy table, his back to her, a steel instrument tray rolled up beside him. There was a body on the table: a young woman's,— Willa could see that, though little of her was visible past the man except her porcelain white left arm and her pale dead feet. The man lifted a knife from the tray, and after a few unseen movements of his hands in front of him, blood began to slowly run down the sluices on either side of the body.

Willa softly walked around him, trying to steal a glimpse of the body. She just barely saw one shoulder, and familiar tresses of strawberry-blonde hair, but before she could see the woman's face the man at the table turned a fierce scowl on her, and then the bloody knife. "Get away!" he snapped. Then they both were gone, as though they hadn't been at all.

Willa fled out of the empty cold-room and into the sunshine. She endured several moments of abject panic before the young man with the camera again emerged from the power plant, a building whose lofty brick smokestacks stretched high over the trees. Again he glanced her way, and before he began toward the rectangular coal house next door she thought his forehead creased uninvitingly, just a little, before he moved on.

She sighed, but there was no point in giving up. The bad sights were far more frequent, and far worse now than they ever were. She had to try to get off the island. She thought maybe they would stop once she got back to the mainland.

He was on the road leading toward the Nurses Residence and Doctors Cottage, still stopping and taking pictures. People smiled as they passed—other patients, the workers, a nurse. Many worked in other buildings in the complex and didn't know Willa either. She had been confined for the past two months to the TB Sanatorium, and though she remembered the campus well from periods of previous freedom, after her most recent recidivism there had been precious little of that.

A woman she'd never met passed opposite them, looking at Willa with a dark sardonic smirk on her hard, pallid face. The woman bore masses of black hair tempered with steely grey heavily piled upon her head and was dressed entirely in white, though if it was a nurse's uniform Willa didn't recognize it. The young man paid the woman no attention, but Willa thought she knew who she was.

"What?" Willa snapped threateningly, leering toward the spiteful apparition. The young man looked back over his shoulder for a moment but never stopped walking. Nor did the woman Willa was sure was Mary Mallon, who during her second period of confinement on the island had gradually graduated from restricted patient to laboratory technician. She had died on the island a long time before, sometime in the 1930s, but before that, during her life beyond the island, the woman had infected at least fifty people, and possibly hundreds more, with typhoid.

The glowering shade passed Willa by and then swiftly evaporated out of sight in a sunbeam falling through the tree-lined pathway.

Meanwhile the young man had passed the tennis courts and was on the path between the Nurses Residence and the Doctors Cottage, still taking pictures of nearly everything. Willa decided he must be a newspaper man, or maybe a policeman, or someone hired by concerned citizens to investigate the abuses on the island. Maybe he's working on a story that could blow the lid off this pressure cooker of abuse and neglect, where the some of the staff were as beyond gone as the patients were. Willa didn't want to follow him into these buildings and was perplexed by his brazen exploration of each and every one. The hesitation he'd demonstrated before was gone, and nothing seemed to be distracting him from his present task. In fact, he seemed to be thoroughly enjoying himself now.

While he explored the old hospital building Willa waited for him in the empty lobby, leaning in the doorway and gazing out across the lawn. She heard the sound of little feet across the lobby floor, and turned to see a little boy standing before her, dragging a stuffed rabbit behind him by one long fustian ear. The boy looked pale, his eyes red rimmed and his mouth pale and sad.

"Are you okay?" she asked.

His eyes flashed brightly then and he stuck out a tongue that was shockingly bright and pink, so that for a moment Willa thought he held a strawberry in his mouth.

A nurse ran over to the boy and shepherded him away from Willa while ignoring her completely. As they walked away, they seemed to fade to nothing in the light spilling in from a window on the far end of the lobby.

With all of her skin crawling coldly, Willa rushed back out into the afternoon sunlight, revolted even at the thought of the old hospital building and glad she hadn't followed the young man on his self-guided tour of it.

She trailed him distantly as he documented other buildings, such as the huge red-brick horseshoe-shaped 'School', which once had been the 'Service Building' during the hospital's first incarnation as a quarantine and leper colony.

While she waited outside for him, Willa plodded absently around the building, worrying. The man had barely spoken to her. She might as well go back to the pavilion and freshen up for dinner. But then again, it seemed that he would be heading to that very place soon anyway. If she accompanied him, and didn't harass him too much, then maybe there could be a chance...

She stared at her feet as she walked. Soon she heard the sound of people. Muffled voices were chatting around the corner of the building, and Willa heard the sound of large sheets fluttering in the wind. She expected to see bed sheets on clotheslines when she rounded the corner, but instead what she saw was a group of tents. People were lying inside, and as Willa got nearer, she heard one person moaning softly. His face looked pale and sick with a fever, and between moans his teeth ceaselessly chattered. White capped nurses popped in and out of the central tent which likely served for a nurse's station, carrying supplies and basins into patients. Two of them industriously assisted a doctor performing surgery inside one of the tents. Smoke ascended lazily from the wind-whipped shelters, and when one of the entry flaps was pulled aside to allow a nurse within Willa could see a wood-burning stove in with the patients.

From one of the tents the smoke began to rise more thickly, now accompanied by bright clusters of sparks, and the smell in the air had changed. Then suddenly the canvas sheet began to glow and pulse, and the shadows of those inside were thrown grotesquely against the fabric opposite the rising fire, their hands warding, mouths open. Then the shadows poured toward the entrance like black water and three people burst out of the tent. Yet there were still voices inside, one of them crying weakly for help, the other grunting in increasing panic. Seconds later the entire tent was ablaze, and the patients trapped inside began to wail. Men rushed with buckets of water, kettles, pans, anything on hand, but the flames were already dancing skyward, growling as though hungry enough to try licking the clouds. Within seconds the canvas was consumed, and the scorched remains of poles and cots and people smoldered in redder flames inside, slowly blackening, their flesh still sizzling. One of the nurses cried an 'Oh!' of surprise and, turning with her hand over her mouth, sprayed vomit on and through her fingers.

Willa heard the young stranger behind her. He had left by a different door and was heading toward the main north-south road that spanned the hospital's campus. She followed him, crossing the green newly-mown lawn that now bore no trace of tents or fire having ever been there. Her hands were quaking.

She began to grow more irritated with the young man, not just for being so pitiless and unfriendly, but because after he left the road to approach the enormous TB pavilion, he kept the most randomly meandering course imaginable, suddenly veering widely from a straight and perfectly unimpeded direction, as though avoiding something that wasn't in the way. Or he went about stepping sideways or suddenly lifting his foot in nearly a kick before landing and hoisting the other leg up. He also made movements beside his face with his hands, as though brushing away flying insects, or were those gestures directed at her? Was he, even with his back to her, trying to shoo her away like a pest?

She hurried and narrowed the distance, which wasn't hard since his progress was so slow and indirect. "You don't want to go in there," she told him. "That's the worst place here. Please don't."

He ignored her now, again making brushing motions with his hands and walking erratically in the vaguest direction toward the sanatorium and she thought, *Maybe he's committing himself for treatment. That guy's at least as bananas as I am!*

At last he came to the front of the Tuberculosis Pavilion. Above the stone porch, massive concrete blocks made up the posts and lintel of the front entrance, like the archway-shaded portal of some megalithic mausoleum. The central administrative tower rose oppressively above that archway. Its redbrick, fortress-like façade bore a patterned design of diamonds recessed in the brickwork, like dozens of sideways eyes. The wings, built with bricks of the same ruddy blood-cough color, stretched to the east and west like a cold-hearted enemy expectant of hugs. To the west, the children's ward and library were visible.

"You don't want to go in there," she said. "They won't help you. They—"

But he was climbing the porch steps. She swore under her breath and followed, nodding at a pair of chatting nurses approaching the porch from the sarcophagic doorway.

The color scheme was much cooler in the pavilion's reception area. Its walls were lined with chest-high baby blue tiles, and the lady at the reception desk offered a pleasant and unimpressed smile as the two wandered in. Willa was shocked when the young man audaciously photographed the receptionist at her desk without the least preamble. The woman's smile faltered slightly, but did not entirely dim. She seemed almost goaded into a kind of weird amusement by his action, then simply resumed perusing whatever lay on the desk before her, a novel maybe.

Willa trotted past the desk to catch up with him. He explored the building as though he were the absent owner, not even heeding the greetings of the staff or patients passing him. He took the central stairwell, whose walls were lined with yellow tile, and began methodically exploring hallways, patient rooms and staff offices. Some of the hospital workers asked Willa if everything was okay, and she just nodded and moved along. As she followed him down a corridor, a voice rose unexpectedly through the open doorway of an office and said her name. She froze by the door, which bore the name of Elliott Lily, md.

"I'm just getting some exercise, Dr. Mara," Willa explained, repressing a shudder as his eyes, so dark brown as to seem black as onyx, glistened over the unsettling smile.

Dr. Mara lowered his hands to the desk and appeared prepared to stand. "Have you been well lately, Willa? Have things been going better for you?"

Willa did not want to talk to him. Despite another doctor's name on the door, it was always Dr. Mara that greeted her from this office, from that chair; she therefore avoided this hallway as often as possible, taking the stair to one above or below, then back again if she ever needed to go somewhere on this floor.

"Yeah, sure, better I guess. But I really gotta go right now… sorry."

He chuckled dryly. "Maybe I'll be by to see you during rounds. We can talk then."

She nodded, fidgeting and nervous. Shifting back on her heels she turned and sprang down the hallway with a curt "'kay, bye" flipped back at him. She could hear his chair scrape and thought, *He's going to come and get me now.* Instead, when she glanced back over her shoulder she saw that he only stood calmly in his office doorway, watching her traverse the wide sunbeam-segmented corridor behind her quiet new companion, a tiny smile nearly hidden below his trim black moustache.

Willa lost the young man for a time. He had taken the stairs at the end of the corridor, but she was not sure whether up or down.

She tried downstairs first, thinking she had heard someone headed down there. When she entered the hallway on that floor she endeavored to walk quickly past each room, trying doorknobs whenever she chanced to be unobserved to be sure the doors were locked, and snatchingly surveying the rooms to which doors were open. Her strange potential savior was not on this floor.

A sudden snarling laugh caught her attention. She turned and saw Billy King sitting on the floor of his room. He was a recidivist like herself, but also simply one nasty son of a bitch. Willa was surprised they let this schizoid have his door open and unsecured.

Billy's spiky hair was so blond it was nearly white, but his eyebrows were black and so was the stubble all over his face. His closed mouth was smiling widely and his lips gleamed. He sat on the floor of his room rocking back and forth, coloring on the wall with pencils and crayons. He had drawn some sort of crucified plant-like creature in reds and yellows, and all around it he had detailed disembodied eyes, some crying, others just staring. He was extending the pattern along the wall when he saw her and starting chortling.

"I'm not a bullshit artist," Billy giggled, grinning. "No, no, this is serious, bitch! I'm on to something here! This is gonna be the safest Christing room in the whole bughouse!"

As Willa turned away to move on, Billy hurled a handful of crayons at her. She caught one in the folds of her shirt above her hip, and kept it there unconsciously for a moment with her hand as she bolted away from him. The rest clattered all over the hall. As she hurried away his voice bellowed into the hallway:

"Go on then you uppity little whore! Skinny-ass high-horsey bitch! I DON'T NEED ANY OF YOU BITCHES!!"

Already pavilion nurses were hurrying up the hall, into his room, berating him. One of the male staff grunted, "How many times I gotta tell you don't do that shit on the wall!" The struggle and cussing ensued, and Willa was backtracking to the stairs during the confusion when she nearly collided with Robin, one of the nurses from the floor where Willa's own room was.

"Willa, you okay?" Robin asked.

"Yeah, just Billy got to yelling at me. He's getting bad again I guess." Willa realized the crayon she'd caught was still in her hand, and she stowed it away in her pocket.

Robin sneered contemptuously at the thought of Billy King. "That asshole," she muttered. "Okay, well, be in your room in time for dinner. Don't make me have to come find you, understand?"

"Yes ma'am."

"Good girl," Robin said, already walking past Willa, her huge bottom jigging like pillowy pistons as she approached the commotion, unable to resist high drama.

Willa climbed up the stairs, past the floor where Dr. Mara had accosted her, and on the next level she conducted a search of the rooms along that corridor, torn now about the exploit, wanting to find the young man but loathing the very sight of this corridor.

Along both sides of the hall ran the doors to the seclusion rooms. Rectangular peepholes peered through doors reinforced by sheets of heavy galvanized metal and secured by both a long iron bolt and a latchkey. Inside, addicts so incarcerated endured the unimaginable agony of cold-turkey withdrawal with no further amenities than a lumpy mattress and a mess bucket. Wide windows looked out from the far side of the rooms, granting a view across the water and toward the city beyond, but their panes were protected from the patient by screens of heavy wire mesh that were kept closed with padlocked chains whose links were as thick as Willa's little finger. Perpendicular from the outward-facing window, another smaller window—similarly armored—permitted supervision of the patient from the Nurses' Station, but of course not all of the seclusion rooms had this feature. Typically the rooms adjacent to the Nurses' Station were reserved for the very sickest of the withdrawing patients. Willa had spent the first few days of her first week-long confinement in seclusion in this very room. She remembered how when the nurses had lowered their heads to look inside at her, their faces had been minced into inhuman hatchwork by the mesh, almost like the view of them from a fly's eye.

After those first black and unremembered days of rolling and heaving through gut-clutching torture, she had been moved, and it was in that even more secluded seclusion room that she first had been visited by Dr. Mara, and the never-before-mentioned injections began, and their associated nightmares.

The nightmares that had never since ended for her.

Where was the young stranger now? Willa decided if she wasn't prevented she would follow him back to the boat, and beg him, weep, offer her body, promise him anything, and then maybe, just maybe, she might convince him to take her off this wretched island. If not, she would be absent at dinner. Then her new and minute freedom would be lost, and she would be punished. She didn't want that, *God!* she didn't want that! But escape was still worth a try.

She heard a noise from the hallway and leaned into it to see without being seen.

It was the young man!

"Hey! Sir!" she tried, but without acknowledging her he stepped into the next room down the hall.

"No, oh no, don't please," she whimpered, hurrying that way.

She stepped in behind him as he surveyed the room. It was identical to the other Seclusion rooms, except it was missing the supervisory window in the side wall. From this room, aside from the birds in the treetops at eye level outside the window, no one could view the room's sole occupant except through the narrow rectangular slot in the door.

Willa knew this room very well.

"Please," she begged. It was now or never. She couldn't help the sniveling, the curling of her lips, the tugging twitches of muscles in her cheeks and eyes. Her face was breaking down; soon she would be sobbing uncontrollably. *Why did he have to come in here?!*

"Please take me out of here," she whispered wetly. He gave her an incredulous, furrowed look. Then he once more raised the camera and took a picture of her. The flash hurt her already sore and anguished eyes.

Fury seized her.

"YOU BASTARD! What, are you just playing games with me?! Just get out! GET OUT!!!" She began to thrash around the room (old habits die so hard), shaking the screens in the window, punching and kicking at the walls and door and the old mattress on the floor, spitting obscenities. The young man fled the room and still she fumed, her hands throbbing and bleeding, one knuckle swelling, probably broken. She crumbled to her knees for a moment, out of breath, then arose in a panic and desperately flung herself toward the door while calling him.

"Wait! Wait, please! Don't go!"

She turned out of the room to hurry down the hallway, more pleas ready in her mouth, when she slammed full tilt into the white-jacketed chest of a man. Stunned, she backed away even as his hands lowered to her shoulders, and looked up into the face she already dreadfully knew would be there. The old dark eyes, the thin moustache, the lips curled into the same sadistic smile.

"Hello, Weeping Willa," he cooed, using his pet name for her that she hated. "Have you decided you need a little time alone again?" He chuckled. "Such a proactive girl. I'm glad you're so... *committed* to your own health."

Willa tried to move away, but the only unimpeded direction was back into the room, and his grip had already grown into iron, his fingers pushing deep into the muscles in her back, his thumbs on the nerves beneath her collarbones, digging, sending singeing signals of pain down her arms even as she raised them to ward him off. He moved with her into the room as though they were dancing, as if she were no more than a large doll.

"No! No, let—" but he clamped her mouth shut with one large hand and with his foot shut the door behind him. He did it softly, gracefully. The door didn't slam, it snipped shut. Behind his hand Willa's terrified negation could not be more than muffled sonorants: "NNNNNNN!! mmph, NNNNNHH! mmmmph phNNNNNNNNNHHHHHN!!!!"

But even these sounds ceased soon after Dr. Mara brought the syringe out of his pocket.

***

Home at last, Brian uploaded his photos and began a slideshow review of them while hungrily munching on takeout lo mein. It had been one hell of a big day, and all he had brought to eat on the island had been a couple prepackaged cookies and a stick of beef jerky. He must have walked a few miles total, not counting the calories it had cost to paddle out there on those currents and pull his kayak up onto the island and hide it. There had been a damn close call—if he hadn't heard the patrol boat's soft putter ahead of time he might not have gotten himself and the kayak hidden soon enough. Thankfully the overgrowth of vegetation reached so close to the beach that he'd had little trouble ducking out of sight behind the massive tangles of kudzu and honeysuckle.

The light from the computer was the only illumination in the room. He avidly watched the pictures scroll by and smiled. This was going to be a brilliant article, as soon as he got around to writing it to accompany his photography. North Brother Island was a fascinating place. Abandoned since 1963, it had been converted into a bird sanctuary, and all the remaining buildings of the Riverside hospital were left to decay 'naturally' for half a century. Ever since its establishment as a quarantine in the late nineteenth century, for many of the patients kept on the island, Riverside had been a place of perpetual suffering and desperation. Overcrowding had led to the use of tents for some of the patient population, exposing them to the elements and to the fate of burning to death when the stoves used to heat the tents set them on fire. The hospital had often rationed both heat and food in the winter when the inadequate facilities equipment could not provide for all the buildings, and when storms or the freezing of the East River hindered delivery of desperately needed supplies. The remoteness of the hospital, with its objectionable conditions and the long and unrewarding shifts, led to a recurrent absence of physicians and inappropriate and inadequate medical practice. Sometimes in the absence of doctors the nurses improvised beyond what knowledge they had. All these things, with the abuses and corruption of staff extending from the earliest years to the final ones when the island had been employed to sequester drug addicts for treatment, all contributed to making North Brother Island—as once described by a convalescing patient—as bad as the "Black Hole of Calcutta". Riverside had also been the scene of the holocaust aboard the Passenger Steamboat General Slocum, one of deadliest disasters in US history, and had also housed the infamous Typhoid Mary for more than a quarter of a century, during those times when she hadn't been free to infect the general populace.

In a place with such a history that had then been left in complete isolation for nearly all of the past fifty years, Brian couldn't blame himself for feeling a thrilling shiver of fear and dread while there, especially since he was trespassing on Park Services property and could very well have been arrested by the Coast Guard if caught. But he had also suffered from the paranoid idea he was being watched out there, like someone was constantly near him, constantly approaching. It had made him nervous and jumpy; he had spun around several times, expecting someone else to be standing there, and kept glancing over his shoulder. He had taken to talking to himself in instinctive resistance to the oppressive solitude. All this had exhausted him even more, but at the end of such a day, it made watching the pictures he'd taken all the more gratifying.

The first shots were of the western beaches, with the gantry crane and the coal dock. The concrete slabs of the latter were drastically sunken and cracked, their timber supports disintegrating. Nearly all of the uppermost planks had long ago rotted apart and washed away, leaving the upper eight inches of the long iron bolts to rust. Brian thought there was something quietly exclamatory about all those vertical bolts standing on the dock like hair on end, and he smirked as he chewed.

Several shots of the morgue scrolled past: the hole in the ceiling, made by bricks presumably fallen from one of the shattered chimneys of the power plant's smokestacks. Inside the plant, surrounded by walls of red brick that had faded to pale gray, Brian had taken shots of the huge coal boilers once used to heat Riverside's buildings. The boilers rose to about three times Brian's own height, the rusty cylinders toward the top resembling the eyes of some huge robotic monstrosity. Trellises of riveted metal beams and rusting pipes of various sizes were engulfed by vicious masses of kudzu and Asian bittersweet. The coal building next door had been even more dilapidated, the wooden roof shattered and its boards spread all around the decaying walls as though it had been bombed.

Beneath layers of dead leaves, he had found chunks of disintegrated asphalt, manhole covers, curbs, sections of the paved roads and walks between the various buildings. He had nabbed a picture of a rusty but intact fire hydrant, having exposed a bit of the curb beside it with his foot. The chain-link fence surrounding the tennis court was also rusted through, and large trees grew right through the court's surface, so that it merely seemed to be a fence in a forest boxing in an otherwise unremarkable section of the same forest.

Brian was fond of his photos of the iron spiral staircase which corkscrewed through the southern end of the Nurses Residence. The staircase stopped at a sheer drop to the next floor down, and black dusty debris from the constantly crumbling ceiling covered the steps. Plaster dust blanketed the floors also, as plentiful as beach sand. One photo in the same building displayed a window lodged lopsidedly, near completely fallen out of the frame, the sash poised like a desperate yet hesitant jumper. Down one residential hallway many of the doors, complete with knockers and room numbers, still bore the nurses' names beneath. The doors' blue-green paint was cracking squamously, resembling reptile skin. On the fourth floor the ceiling was utterly gutted, exposing skeletal rafters and slivers of sky. Dead leaves littered the floor and fallen boards in the hallway.

Now he watched the photos of the decaying Service Building. In one room, hundreds of brass keys, oxidized to a minty blue, lay spread across the floor. Brian had been unable to discern if some of the stains on the wall were the colors of mildew and dry rot, or the last remaining splotches of ancient paint. More pics displayed the high grimy ceilings in hallways so poorly built that the walls were bulging away from the metal support structure, causing the frames of several doors to shift one part away from the other, so that the doorways themselves appeared to be striding widely toward the center of the hall, like cowboys stepping into a street for a pistol match. One door proclaimed the slanted room beyond it, angled as though modeled from a Cubist painting, to be the PRINCIPAL'S OFFICE. The door itself seemed to be the only thing keeping the sorry room from rolling itself headlong into the hall.

From there he had walked north, through ever thicker baskets of cable-tough vines. He had nearly tripped several times, had to widely skirt trees fallen from the parasitic overpowering of kudzu and porcelain berry, or climb through dense ropey thickets with hardly room to plant his feet on the ground. He had paused to take pictures of some of this tendril-wrapped jungle.

At last there began the sequence of what Brian thought the creepiest of all the photos: those of the Tuberculosis Sanatorium. Built in the early 1940s, it was a monster of early modern architecture. The tall central portion, formidably keep-like, was encrusted with autumn red patches of dying ivy, causing the building in the first of the pictures to appear to be caked in blood.

The inside had been robustly built, but fifty years had still contributed much to the rotting of the wallboard, and plaster crumbled in layers from white to yellow to brown and then granted a peek at the bricks beneath. Almost every window was open, and invasive vines of porcelain berry groped inside through the windows, forming abstracted shapes in the air over the floor like wire sculptures.

Brian was surprised to find that so much brick made up the inner walls of the TB pavilion. It gave him a sense of how quiet that huge building must have been, room to room, and how utterly cut off an inhabitant would have been there, especially those locked inside the seclusion rooms.

Even in the warmth of his apartment Brian shivered. Those had been the worst places. The nightmarishness of the very idea of being kept in one of them gave him goose pimples, and then there had been those moments when, in the last of the seclusion rooms he had visited, the eerie silence had been shattered by a pandemonium of pounding and the battering of the screens and chains and walls inside. Brian would have dropped his camera and kept on running, possibly unable to work up the courage to go back for it, had it not been strapped to his wrist. Those were some of the last of the photographs, and they were almost here.

Then they were, and were not what he expected. Something had lanced like light across the lens, some kind of artifact in the photo he couldn't clearly make out, but in parts gave him the sense of a shoulder shaded by soft strawberry-blonde hair and a lean and plaintive woman's blurry face, her features lost in a strange effect of misplaced and twisted light. He reached up and punched a key which paused the slideshow, before it could return to the beginning.

The walls in that room hadn't been covered with eyes like that, had they? Were the pictures shuffled and out of order, so he was looking at one of the amateurish frescoes from the floor below? No, for the heavy mesh over the windows was clearly visible in the left of the shot, but the walls were inexplicably covered with crude drawings of eyes and crosses, sketched in crayon. Some were turned sideways, some upright, some with lashes, some with tears beneath, and some closed. And some just vacant, staring.

He began to feel something unexpected in the pit of his gut.

He felt suddenly, deeply sad.

"I'm sorry," he said.

The girlish shape in the photo, and the eyes all around her on the wall, all the things that hadn't been there, stared, and Brian stared back.

What else could he do?

***

She was awake, and he was gone. For now. But Dr. Mara would come back. He always came back. "I like you," he had said after sticking the needle in, before she had lost consciousness. "In all my time here, and it has been a very, *very* long time my sweet, you have been one of my favorite patients."

It was dark. The distant city lights blinked bleakly across the shining black water. Dr. Mara had left the scrap of rag where he had shoved it in the peep hole. She staggered to the door and pulled it out, allowing knifelike fluorescent light to slice inside through the narrow glass. Then she crouched, still dizzy, and crawled across the floor. She found the crayon in her pants pocket, took it out, dropped the pants again where they lay and, still naked, struggled back to the wall. There, she began to draw the talismans against the Evil Eye, and the crosses. Those were the only symbols of protection she could think of, and Willa had no other sources of safety or sanity, and no one else to watch over her. She thought it had been bad before, but Dr. Mara had only just begun with her. When he had first started experimenting on her, she tried to tell her nurses what he was doing. "Willa, stop imagining things please," Robin said to her. "You've wasted enough of my time. I told you, I checked the directory, and then I even checked the hospital records. There hasn't been a doctor by that name on the island for more than twenty years."

As she drew over and over again on the wall, Willa thought about the body she had seen being dissected in the morgue, and wondered at the kind of sick and twisted universe she existed in, to allow her to see her own ghost there upon the autopsy table.

ETERNAL ASYLUM

Sarah Cass

"Why did I agree to this again?" Maddie let her flashlight arc across the floor to the corners of the room. Dust, drywall, bricks and wood, years of neglect piled on the floor. The walls were left pockmarked by time.

The smell of death and fear crept into her nose and took residence. Out of obligation to her boyfriend, Charlie, Maddie snapped a few pictures.

Pops of blue and yellow light blinded her in the moments after the camera flash. The realization she'd be blind again after every shot made her stomach twist.

Ghost hunting.

Charlie's bright idea.

Definitely not hers. She didn't believe in ghosts – but she did believe in vagrants, rabid animals, and her friends that lived to play practical jokes. Any one of those things could work to terrorize her in this building.

Poeke County Lunatic, Idiot, and Epileptic Asylum.

Asylum. What a joke. The tour guide told them about the kind of 'asylum' the patients here had received as recently as sixty years ago. Nothing short of torture to 'get the devil' out of them. The 'devil' of disability.

A person like her brother would have rotted here. Died here.

A shuffle in the hall whispered into the room, followed by the world's most recognizable giggle. Nan couldn't hide to save her life. She'd always been the most fun to play hide and seek with because the seeker always found her.

"Boo!" Nan giggled and stumbled into the room, "I got you, didn't I?"

"Sure did," Maddie tried to keep the sarcasm out of her tone. Then again, sarcasm *was* her tone. Always. "I hate this place."

"Scary as hell, isn't it?"

"No. It's creepy and stupid and full of hateful reminders of what monsters humans are." Maddie lifted the camera and snapped a shot of Nan to blind her. "And if it wasn't because Charlie already paid for the tour to 'surprise' me I wouldn't be here."

Nan rubbed at her eyes, squinting when Maddie shone the flashlight in her face, "Well Charlie loves the ghost hunting shows. It's sweet of you to humor him. Don't worry, we only have the three hour tour anyway."

"Goody. We're on the SS Minnow of ghost hunts." Their laughter echoed through the small room. The flashlight flickered and she wacked it before picking up the camera to search through the pictures she'd taken.

The first one to appear was the last she'd taken of Nan. Nan's already pale features washed out in the flash, and an orb of light hovered above her shoulder. Maddie gasped with mock elation, "Oh. Mah. Gah! It's an *orb*."

"What? Really? That's so cool. Let me see," Nan darted over and squinted at the LCD screen. "Whoa."

"Please. It's a piece of dust. You're so gullible, goober." She pushed Nan away and flipped through the rest of the photos. Just before she turned the camera off the last picture appeared on the display – the first picture she'd taken.

The decrepit room she now stood in didn't show in the picture. Instead two beds nested under the fully glass paned window, sunlight streamed in across the floor. A young woman sat hunched on the bed, long blonde hair curtained her face.

"Maddie, did you hear me?" Nan shook her shoulder. "I said we should find out what the others are doing. You coming? What are you looking at? You look like you've seen a ghost."

Maddie tried to smile at Nan's joke but couldn't manage. She didn't know any way to explain the picture on the camera. Before Nan could try to figure out what had her spooked she shut off the LCD and shrugged. "No ghost, just more dust. Dust dust dust. We should have worn masks."

"You're such a complainer."

Hard as she tried, Maddie couldn't stop her mind from wandering back to the photo. A few feet outside the room the realization dawned on her and she stopped. Charlie had used her camera at the start of the tour. He must have snapped a shot of one of the photos hanging in the tour center.

But the photos in the tour center were all black and white. The picture on the LCD screen had been color. Nope, Charlie tried to scare her that's all. Anything else would be pure lunacy.

"Maddie?" Nan's voice echoed back down the hall toward her. "Where are you? I thought you were with me. Man, my flashlight went out. Could you help?"

"I'm right here," Maddie called back with a sigh. "We're supposed to be hunting ghosts, why use a light?"

"Uh, there's a bunch of crap on the floor and I don't want to trip." Nan's laugh twittered with nervous energy. "Just turn on your light."

Maddie dropped her camera strap over her neck and lifted her flashlight.

Madeline. A whisper of air brushed along the back of her neck. Charlie's voice, but he never called her by her full name.

"Charlie?" She spun around and hit the button on her flashlight. No sign of him, and she hadn't heard him dart into a room. "Really, Charlie? Come on, I'm not up for practical jokes."

"Mads, who are you talking to?" A few clicks and a bang sent a fresh beam of light down the hall from behind her. Apparently Nan got her flashlight working.

"Charlie's around here somewhere trying to scare me."

"Uh, Charlie went to the morgue with Steve. By now they've probably locked each other in the freezer in the name of getting evidence." Nan stopped next to her and searched the rooms on the left with her light. "No one's here but you and me. I think Carrie and Sharon went up to the nurse's quarters – that's two floors above us."

The hair on the back of her neck stood up but Maddie forced a smile, "Got ya."

"Jerk," Nan shoved her with a chuckle. "You're going to make me think you believe in this stuff. Come on, let's go scare Car and Shar."

Mrs. Durant. You must stop. A voice shouted, the echo lingering until it died into the breeze.

Durant was Charlie's last name, not hers. The part that freaked her out though, is that Nan didn't react at all. Not even a hint of a gasp at the loud bellow. Maddie stopped in her tracks again and swept her flashlight back down the hall.

In the flash of the beam she swore a man appeared, but in the second it took her to stop her sweep and go back he was gone. "Shit. Did you see that, Nan?"

"What? Oh, don't you start Maddie. I'm not falling for it again." Nan's beam met Maddie's at the end of the hall. "Hey, what's that room?"

"I don't know. Let's go find out." So she really wanted to find the man, but the room provided a great excuse. Rather than go slow like she had been for the first part of the night she tore down the hall as fast as she dared. She hopped over debris and stopped just in front of the door.

Nan started coughing as she stopped, "Dang girl. You kicked up enough dust running. What was that about?"

"Just curious I guess." The end of the hall afforded no escape but the room in front of them. Nowhere for the man to go except behind the door.

I'm sorry Madeline. You're talking nonsense. You're hysterical. Charlie's voice held a coldness she'd never heard, enough to wrench her heart.

Her breath caught in her throat, and she struggled for air. Crushing pressure in her lungs shoved the last bit of oxygen from her body.

Bang! The flashlight rolled away, the beam stopping on a pair of military boots.

They stepped forward and disappeared into the shimmering dust.

"Maddie? *Mads.*" A sharp sting dug into her bicep, Nan's nails piercing her skin.

Air. She needed air. A deep gasp didn't bring any air into her shrunken lungs. Her knees buckled, the floor moving closer with a thud to her knees.

"Charlie," Nan sounded panicked.

Charlie's voice filtered in through the growing haze of her oxygen-deprived brain. *I don't know what to do, doc. Since I told her I was going to fight she's been like this.*

Don't worry, young man. The strange voice pierced her heart. *We'll take care of her. You go ahead, your wife will be here when you get back.*

The air rushed back into her lungs moments before pain knifed through her temple into her skull. All the air she'd just taken in left in a scream that hurt her own ears. She gripped at her head to try to push out the pain.

And then, everything was gone.

Air entered and left normally, the sensation of claustrophobic drowning faded into a lingering shake in her hands. The stabbing agony in her head tapered down to a whimper of a migraine. After a lifetime dealing with migraines several times a week, she could tolerate this small headache.

"I don't know, she just freaked out." Nan's whisper cut through Maddie's self-assesment. "No, I don't think she was teasing me. I don't think she heard me. I'm serious Charlie. It's weird."

Maddie reached out, gripping onto the denim of Nan's jeans. She took a breath and winced as the air itself stabbed along every inch of her lungs until she had enough to talk. "I'm fine," she rasped. Was that her voice? So hoarse, too hoarse. Her lungs ached like she'd been drowning.

"What? Then what the hell was that? What? No, Charlie. I don't know she says she's fine now. I swear,

Mads, if this was some kind of sick joke it's not funny." Nan yanked her jeans out of Maddie's grasp. "And I'm not playing. I don't know Charlie, if you want to see her, she's on the third floor. I'm going."

"Just the dust, and a migraine." Maddie tried to get to her feet, but her knees didn't want to work. So she reached for the flashlight and tried to ignore how much her hand shook as she did. "I'm sorry. The dust must have… I don't know."

"Whatever Mads. I'm heading to the nurse's quarters. You're the one that doesn't believe in this crap anyway, so you'll be fine by yourself." Nan stormed off in a huff. Her footsteps carried down the hallway until the door to the stairwell slammed shut, the bang echoing through the empty rooms.

Maddie sank back on her rump with her hand pressed to her chest, trying to catch her breath. Nan was right. She didn't believe in this stuff. What the hell was her problem? Seeing things, hearing things – like she believed in ghosts or something. The power of suggestion had her thinking ghosts called her name. Ghosts that looked like…

"Charlie." Maddie jumped when he knelt in front of her. "Where did you come from? I didn't hear you coming. I swear I hear everything in this place, even mice scurrying across the floor make a racket."

Madeline. Why do you insist on calling me Charlie? His brows pursed together in that familiar edge of frustration.

"It's your name." She blinked a few times, letting her eyes readjust to the dark. Her heart started to pick up the pace again moments after finally slowing. This wasn't Charlie. Not really. Charlie didn't have a mustache. Or wear glasses. He wore contacts only, glasses made him too geeky. As if ghost hunting wasn't enough for that. "Charlie?"

Doctor. I thought you said she was better. Charlie turned his head toward a man that formed behind him out of thin air.

A hallucination. She had to be hallucinating. Moments ago she'd been unable to breathe, she'd almost collapsed. Yes. A hallucination. A disturbingly real, intimidating hallucination sitting right in front of her face.

I'm sorry, Mr. Durant. She was this morning. I told you her lucid moments come in bits and pieces. She seems to lose more of herself each time. That voice again, filling her head and sending shivers down her spine. Fear she'd never felt drove into every muscle fiber until she wanted to run.

"I have to go. I must get out of here. Air. I need so much air." Her body wouldn't listen. No matter how much she tried to get to her feet weight shoved down on her shoulders. "I must."

It's time for drastic measures. We've tried so many therapies, we need to go a step further. The voice was so cold, her mind immediately imagined it belonged to the ugliest of faces. She had to, because all she could see was shadow. *It could be all that brings your wife back to you.*

Then do it. If she doesn't come back, Charlie had never been this cold. So detached, and the love that softened him disappeared into harsh lines. He pulled back when she reached for him, *then she isn't my wife any longer. Her treatment will be up to you, Doctor Miller.*

"Charlie?" Maddie pressed her fingers to her forehead trying to eliminate the hallucination. She had to get the hell out of there. Far, so far away. She'd been a fool to agree to this.

She braced her hands against the wall and tried to push herself to her feet.

Screams echoed down from above. Nan had managed to get Carrie and Sharon. Maddie shivered and almost fell again. The doorknob felt sturdy under her grip so she used it to brace herself further.

Almost there. Just another few inches and she'd be supporting her own body all by herself. All of this would stop.

Snap. The world dropped out from under her only to smack her right in the face when she landed.

A groan rumbled through her still sore lungs as she tried to assess the different levels of pain. The worst still seemed to be the rattling ache in her lungs, so she must not have hit her face too bad. Although the mild throbbing in her cheek made her think there'd be an ugly bruise tomorrow.

"Damn it. How do I always end up in – what the hell?" Just a foot from her stood a row of tubs. Half-rusted out, long and tall, with no spouts, no drains – just tubs. She pushed off the surprisingly clean floor to a plank before hopping to her feet.

The room shifted, her vision blurring until she stumbled and gripped the edge of the tub. Screams filled her ears, begging and pleading to be released. *So cold* her own voice rang through her head. *Please, please. I'll be good. I'll be Madeline.*

Her stomach twisted, tears burning at her eyes until she had to blink to clear her vision again. Planks of wood stretched across the top of each of the tubs. Shackles hanging under them, bolted to the floor.

Aching prickles like a sunburn itched at her wrists. She rubbed at the pain on her right wrist before she pulled the camera off her neck. The desire to take a picture won over logic. She had to see if she'd see something like in the room down the hall.

The flash burst through the room, and everything fell silent. The sounds of the night disappeared, bugs and animals stopped all noise. The distant echoes of the highway faded, and the breeze died down into suffocating stillness.

Her fingers went lax the moment she lowered the camera. *Bang!* The sound jolted through her, but she couldn't back away. In front of her stood the faceless man, so close she could smell cigars on his breath, the breath that came from a mouth she couldn't see.

"Hallucinations," she whispered. Her heart hammered in her chest. None of this was real. She should grab the camera and leave. Leave now.

Come now, Mrs. Durant. This won't take long. He didn't wait for her response, just turned and headed across the room to another door. Nothing good could be behind that door. Nothing.

She pressed her hand to her chest. Her heart had to stop pounding so hard.

Air grew thin, her lungs once again starting to rasp and wheeze. Asthma. An asthma attack. Inhaler, she had to find her inhaler.

Pressure shoved into her back and forced her forward. She tried to back up, but the force of energy wouldn't let her go. It didn't make sense. Ghosts weren't real, they just weren't.

She tried to turn around to face whatever pushed on her, but found nothing there and only ended up on her ass at the door the faceless man had disappeared through. The door gave way under her back and the floor again met her with a vengeance.

Pain arced through her head from the point of impact, blinding white light filling her vision as the pressure in her lungs grew worse. A gulp of air couldn't give her enough to scream, nothing would. She groped for the inhaler in her pocket, but her hand seized when the white pain disappeared into clear visions rushing through her head.

All around her men forced her backward. Somehow her short blonde hair now flew out long and tangled. Her thin fingers grasped for purchase on anything as the men dragged her to a tub deeper than the others in the first room.

Until the bubbles stop rising, the voice of the faceless man stilled her fight, bringing back the urge to throw up.

Her fingers closed over her inhaler in her pocket even as she watched herself being forced into the deep tub and pushed under the water. Just as water trickled down her throat she took a hit off the inhaler, and the images flickered away.

With the shaky fingers of a fresh hit she tried to put the cap back on but another spike drove into her temple. The white heat didn't disappear. It pierced through each of her eyes until she felt her own sob rather than heard it.

Through the blinding light she heard the voice. Pressure wrapped around her wrists, tight enough to numb her fingers.

I'm sorry Mrs. Durant. You must accept that he's dead. Died in the war.

"No," she screamed at the voice. The fear crawled up her throat and clawed at her vocal chords, "He's not."

Strap her down tight. I need to give her a stronger jolt this time.

Jolt? Jolt of what? A fresh hot poker of pain drove through her forehead and the scream forced its way out despite all efforts to keep silent. A thunderbolt passed through her, electric heat raced along her spine until she arched with another scream.

Wave after wave hit until the world went black.

***

The sweet scent of pure oxygen distracted her from the haze in her head. A steady high pitched blip to her right.

Beep. Beep. Beep.

Her heartbeat. A hospital. Now she could only be grateful for the oxygen, the sterile smell of hospitals always turned her stomach. Had since her first asthma attack.

"Is that really necessary?" Charlie's voice was so quiet she could barely hear it over the machines.

Maddie forced her eyes open a sliver to find him. He hovered near the door speaking to a man in a white coat.

"The proprietors said when they found her she was completely incoherent and out of control. If she becomes like that again she could hurt herself. As it is, once she wakes we'll probably have to sedate her." That voice, the voice of her nightmares.

She had to get the mask off. Find out why Charlie was talking to her hallucination. The moment she tried to pull off the mask she realized her predicament. Cushioned pressure wrapped all the way around her wrists, soft but firm as handcuffs.

The heart monitor's steady beep jumped, increasing in pace. The oxygen became bitter and unfulfilling, her lungs refusing to let any more into her chest. She rasped in short breaths, trying to speak but her throat felt raw. Like she'd been screaming for hours.

Charlie's face hovered in front of hers, the warm smile she knew so well melting into concern. "Baby, you've got to calm down. Relax. Please."

Her Charlie. Once again. Not a stranger with the same face. She tried to grab his hand, but her arm wouldn't move more than a few inches. The tickle of a tear slipped along her temple.

"That's it baby. Just relax. Dr. Miller is going to take care of you."

Miller. Her eyes widened, and she twisted against his hold. The doctor of her nightmares had the name Miller. It couldn't be, that would make everything real.

"Baby, please. Calm down." Charlie's gentle grasp grew tight, squeezing hard enough to send pain through her shoulders. "Stop. I need to know what happened, and you can't tell me like this. Please calm down."

"I need to sedate her," The voice again. Cold shivers twisted through her spine when the doctor moved and lifted a syringe to the IV. At the angle he stood she couldn't see his face. Why couldn't she see his face?

She fought against Charlie, against the restraints. Pain coursed through her body from the tight bands around her wrists and ankles to her lungs and back into her head.

The moment the syringe attached to the IV she froze. The syringe moved so slow she thought she could measure in microns. Whatever a micron might be.

Despite the mask covering her face, her breath came in painful rasps. Short quick seconds that ticked away each tiny bit of the drug that entered the IV. Down the tube into her arm until she felt the cool tingles slip along her arm toward her head.

The quick rasps slowed into almost non-existent whispers of air. Just before the doctor turned all the way around everything went white.

Pure white peace.

***

She opened her eyes and the sounds returned. Horrible screams echoed through the building, the coughing of a tuberculosis patient across the hall. The crowd of patients in the yard enjoying a rare day outside.

One she hadn't been able to be a part of because of her treatment. Days upon days in that tub of cold water left her swollen with moisture even though her wrists remained tiny and frail.

The tips of her fingers wrinkled into rough ridges, yet the skin felt so delicate it might just slough off if she rubbed too hard. Days in the water. She'd sworn to be good. To be Madeline again. Why did she need to swear such a thing?

She sat on her bed, hunched over and watching the dust motes. Glad that for now her husband's money kept her in the quiet of this room. One of the few not overcrowded with patients – just one roommate that didn't speak or move much.

A flash flickered across her vision, out of place with the dust and sunlight. She lifted her head and stood, crossing the few feet to the window. What could have caused the flash?

Boo! A voice she hadn't heard in years broke under the usual sounds of the hospital. A whisper so soft her imagination might have been the source.

Madeline spun, gasping at the sight before her. Nan. No, not Nan – she'd died, hadn't she? "Nan."

Another person was there. They spoke, another flash came just as Madeline tried to set her hand on Nan's shoulder. Then Nan moved and Madeline saw – herself. Shorter hair and wearing pants of all things – but it was her.

What was happening? Had she crossed the last threshold into full insanity? Up until today she'd never wondered over her mental stability like so many others had.

You're such a complainer, Nan whispered in her ear.

"I'm not," she tried to contradict but Nan disappeared. A shadow of her friend, not really there. If she had been, where could she have gone? "Nan?"

Madeline crept to the door on her bare feet, peeking out with just one eye. No need to draw the attention of the nurses. Last time she did, she'd landed in the water treatment for three days.

No nurses lingered in the hall thankfully, but there was also no sign of Nan anywhere. She couldn't have gone far. "Nan?"

She slipped into the hall, walking slow and steady. If she ran someone might get upset. This time she'd sworn to be good. If she broke that, goodness only knew what might happen to her.

Nan flickered into view again down the hall. She looked so panicked, so upset. *Maddie? What's wrong?*

"Everything. Nan, why can't I see you very well? Nan?" Her pace picked up a little. Nan wouldn't look at her, she needed Nan to see her. To prove this was real and the doctor was wrong. "Nan!"

"Mrs. Durant. You must stop," Dr. Miller voice bellowed down the hall, drawing nurses out of the water treatment room.

Madeline's race to reach Nan came to an abrupt halt, and her friend disappeared before her eyes. "Nan, don't go. Please come back."

"Madeline," Charles oozed disappointment into every syllable. She wasn't surprised, the disenchantment happened so long ago she couldn't remember how he'd sounded when they'd courted. There'd been kindness there once, hadn't there? "Nan is dead. She died of influenza five years ago. You know this."

"Charlie," she gasped. Every bit of her soul told her she was right, that everything wasn't some sign of insanity. No one ever believed her. Her heart started to race, tears slipping down her cheeks. "Nan was just here. She was right here, I swear it. I saw her. In my room and right here."

"I'm sorry Madeline. You're talking nonsense." Strong hands gripped her shoulder before he spun her to face him. Disgust twisted his lips into a grimace, "You're hysterical. Enough is enough."

"Charlie, please."

"Madeline. Why do you insist on calling me Charlie?" His grip on her shoulders disappeared, and he went the extra step to wipe his hands on his pants. Like she might transfer her insanity to him through touch.

"It's your name," Madeline whispered. Charlie was his name, wasn't it? Yes, Charles – Charlie. Charles. She used to call him Charles until the first time he'd brought her here. "Charles. Please believe me. Nan was standing right there."

A nurse that looked nothing like Nan stood where she pointed now. Short and dumpy, the nurse's eternal scowl deepened. This didn't bode well. She'd end up back in the tub.

Panic overrode her logic and she grabbed Charles by the lapels, "You have to believe me. I swear she stood right there. I saw her. I'm not insane."

His nose wrinkled and Charles peeled her fingers off his jacket. He turned his head toward the doctor. The man stayed half hidden behind Charles. Only the jacket of his white coat could be seen. Charles sighed, "Doctor. I thought you said she was better."

"I'm sorry Mr. Durant," the voice that chilled her to the bone shattered her grasp on calm. As she began to whimper, she could swear he chuckled low and deep. "She was this morning. I told you her lucid moments come in bits and pieces. She seems to lose more of herself every time."

Charles couldn't listen to him again. He had to listen to her.

"Charles, you loved me once. Believed me once. Please try again. Look at me. Don't let him do this. Charlie," she tried to grab his hand but he shoved her back so hard she hit the floor hard. Pain shot through her weary bones and a strange keening wail erupted from her throat. "Please."

"I think it's time for drastic measures," Dr. Miller's back now faced her, Charlie leering over the man's shoulder at her. The doctor touched Charles' arm for a brief moment before his voice dropped. Even made quiet, the basso tone carried right to her ears. "We've tried so many therapies, we need to go a step further. It could be all that brings your wife back to you."

"Then do it. If she doesn't come back," Charles' eyes narrowed. "Then she isn't my wife any longer. Her treatment will be up to you, Doctor Miller."

"No," barely a whisper of her pain escaped. She couldn't move. Every inch of her body went numb until Charlie turned away. The simple movement sent years of fear and anger rushing through her body.

She flew to her feet and raced toward Charles with a banshee-like shriek. Platitudes and begging fell into desperate screams as hands grabbed at her and dragged her away.

The humans that might be behind the energy tearing her from Charlie no longer mattered, they didn't even exist. All that mattered was making him see, but the more she tore at them and tried to get to Charlie, the further he walked away.

Until a solid door slammed, and another, and all that remained was her and the fight to survive. Screams echoed through the room and she struggled against the brutal force pushing her toward the tub.

"Until the bubbles stop rising," the doctor's chilling words stilled her.

The second her fight stopped, somehow her body kept moving. She realized two men lifted her by her arms and legs. Nothing touched the ground. Everything else stilled, her heart pounding in her ears as she floated through the air, the ceiling above her, God knew what beneath her.

Water soaked through her dress, tickled her back. "No," she arched her back out of the water. Another scream shot out until water filled her mouth and nose.

Every struggle she made met with brute force. Pain wrenched her joints, pierced her shins and shoulders where the men held her down. She reached out, nails cutting through flesh as water forced its way down her throat.

Her lungs ached for air and she stilled, wanting nothing more than to take a deep breath. Above her the water churned, shielding the doctor's peering face.

Every muscle twitched in protest, trying to help her escape again. Black seeped around the edges of her vision.

You must accept that he's dead. Died in the war. She shouldn't be able to hear the doctor, but she did.

"No." The uselessness of crying out into the water wasn't lost on her. Charlie wasn't dead. He didn't fight in the war, he'd been a child.

Strap her down tight. I need to give her a strong jolt this time.

Jolt? What did that mean?

Blinding pain blasted through her skull. Her back arched, and she opened her mouth to get air for the scream.

Water flooded in through her mouth and nose, rushing into her lungs. Another convulsion shook her body and she went lax.

White light filled her vision, peaceful quiet filling her soul.

***

"Mrs. Durant?" Doctor Miller touched her shoulder, a not-gentle shake rattling through her aching body. "Did you hear me?"

Maddie didn't want to leave the quiet of her own mind. She didn't want to hear this doctor spout any more lies. She took a ragged breath and ventured a peek. The man remained behind her, just out of sight.

Instead she saw his desk, the stacks of papers piled up, leafs poking out randomly throughout the stack. The typewriter off to the side, the ash tray next to it.

Above the desk hung a picture of planes, war planes. Obsessed with the damn war, everyone was so obsessed with the war. The damn Nazi's. So obsessed that Charlie now lie – dead? "No. No, he can't be dead," her voice didn't sound like her own. Hoarse, cold, flat. She'd once felt joy, hadn't she? She couldn't remember. So many memories were hazy now thanks to Miller's 'treatments'.

"He was shot down by German forces over Poland. Allied forces recovered the plane – and his remains." Miller sat down behind his desk, the stack of papers obscuring him from her view. Smoke from the doctor's cigarette billowed into the air, whirling around in an endless run of Rorschach tests.

"He can't be," she dug her nails into the arm of the chair. Charlie had to come back, he'd promised. If he came back she could finally leave. He'd save her. He had to save her before it was too late. "No. He's not dead. He can't be dead. He can't be."

"I'm sorry Mrs. Durant. You must accept that he's dead. Died in the war." Each word was punctuated with the click of a typewriter key. *Ding*, the bar moved to the next line as the callous man kept typing.

She wrapped her fingers around the arm of the chair, twisting until her palms smarted in pain. None of it could be true. This horrid man couldn't be telling her this, someone she loved should be telling her. "No. He's not. Where's Nan? Nan should tell me. I have to see Nan!"

"Nan is dead too. You remember. She died while working as a nurse at Pearl Harbor. That was over a year ago, it's why your husband went to fight. Did you forget all

171

of this again?" The typing stopped and silence fell over the office.

Maddie swallowed against the lump in her throat, searching her memories for the truth. Hot tears burned her eyes and ran cold trails down her cheeks, "No. No they aren't dead. They can't be dead. They aren't dead."

"You must calm down, I won't tolerate this. I have other patients to give news to today. Return to your room."

"No." She flew to her feet and shoved the stack off his desk. The waterfall of reports splashed to the floor and spread out in a pool of lies. A laugh she knew to be inappropriate welled and she didn't stop its escape.

Maddie jumped forward to kick at the pile of papers. Another laugh escaped as she grabbed an armful and threw them all in the air, turning her face to the rain of paper and file folders.

Shouts tried to break through her laughter, laughter over the absurdity at the thought of Charlie being dead. Nan dead. All dead. She had no one. "No one," she shrieked at the ceiling before the bruising grasp of two large orderlies suffocated her arms attempts to fight.

She dug her heels into the floor to slow their efforts to drag her, and twisted against their crushing grip. "He's not dead, he can't be dead, he's going to save me, save me from this hell."

The orderlies ignored her, glimpses of the patients ducking into their rooms were all she saw before she was pushed into the familiar room with a harsh shove to her back. She stilled the moment the door closed leaving her with the orderlies, Doctor Miller, and the equipment that would soon send incomprehensible levels of pain through her.

Pain that couldn't touch the ache in her heart.

Charlie – dead. Nan – dead.

"Come now Mrs. Durant. This won't take long," Miller's quiet glee made her nauseous. The elation in his voice every time they entered this room, "Strap her down tight. I need to give her a stronger jolt this time."

This time. Just yesterday she'd been in here. Yesterday Charlie hadn't been dead.

A shove to her back took her to the table, but she wouldn't make it that easy on them. She stood ramrod straight until they were forced to lift her and set her on the table. This time she wouldn't fight, but she wouldn't help them either.

The biting sting of raw skin shocked her wrists as the leather was pulled tight. She closed her eyes before Miller began to attach the wires. Her body jolted with each strap, words passed through her periphery as mumbles of sound.

Charlie – dead. Her Charlie.

"Please hurry," she whispered. "I want to forget."

For once she wasn't disappointed. The moment the leather strap was shoved in her mouth the blast of energy sent sparks of light across her eyes.

"Set the level higher," Miller's dark laughter ran through her ears.

A smile formed around the leather and she closed her eyes, welcoming the thunderbolt of pain through her skull. Her body jerked against the straps, pain coursing through her until the next flash of power raced along her scalp and into her brain.

White light poured over her and erased the pain.

Peace.

Quiet.

***

"Don't fall asleep Mads," Charlie nudged an elbow into her ribs. "Pay attention."

Maddie grinned and opened her eyes, she gave him a wink. She leaned in to whisper, "Why? I don't need to know the history, do I?"

"It helps to bring the ghosts out, to know what they went through." Charlie squeezed her hand, "You said you'd be good."

"I am. I will, for you." She leaned in and gave him a quick peck on the cheek before turning her attention back to their tour guide.

"For the past seventy years it's simply been known as Poeke County Mental Hospital – but when first built the full name was the Poeke County Lunatic, Idiot, and Epileptic Asylum. It's been the largest mental hospital in Ohio since it was first built in 1856." The red head handed a picture to Charlie. "That's a picture from 1887, when the hospital was run by Dr. Miller – at the forefront of his field at the time."

A passing sense of déjà vu threatened her attempts to poke fun at this whole event. Like she'd heard this whole speech before, done this whole ghost hunt thing already. But why on earth would she have gone on a ghost hunt before? Only Charlie had the ability to charm her into something this ridiculous.

"Take a look at least, please?" Charlie's lip quirked up into that adorably crooked smile – the same one that had convinced her to come today. He grinned when she took the picture, "That's my girl."

"Just remember that when it's my turn for a favor." Maddie searched the picture for the doctor, finally locating the man that stood off from the others. His face was blurred with motion, but still he sent a chill down her spine. "Forefront of what? Back then they almost tortured the disabled, didn't they?"

"Mads," Nan groaned. "Your brother didn't live then, he lives now. Chill out and let us hear the rest."

"So-orry," She handed off the picture. With a huff she sat back in her chair and folded her arms across her chest, ignoring the tour guides answer to the question as best she could. Tales of the horrors they called treatments weren't helping her mood.

Mrs. Durant, a cold voice echoed in her ear. Cool air brushed along the nape of her neck. *You won't ever forget.*

SCREAMS

Alex Chase

Some nights, when the moon is high and the wind carries the first, frigid gusts of winter, I can swear I'm back at that damned asylum. Those few short hours have been branded into my memory will remain there until my dying day.

It was a bitter night in late October. The leafy boughs of the trees had just begun the metamorphosis from lush, green puffs, leaving them with an array of brilliant reds and yellows. Phillip Ottenhiem, my best friend, was doing a report on local lore for a graduate anthropology class. He claimed that he 'really needed an A worthy paper' because 'the jerk is failing me' (I didn't point out that Phil rarely went to class).

I'd had been out of college for nearly a year at that point and was working on establishing a career as an author. Tragically, it wasn't going well, since every publisher I turned to seemed to be on the lookout for the next Robert Heinlein or Isaac Asimov. Who was I, with no publishing credits whatsoever, to assume that I was worthy of being published at all? I did have an open door to teach fictional rhetoric at my alma mater, but didn't want to accept that for a wide variety of reasons, the least of which being that I wasn't comfortable speaking in front of others. Besides, in the foolishness of youth, I felt that teaching would have meant failing to make my mark as a successful writer.

Kelsey, Phillip's sister, had accompanied us. As children, they'd been inseparable, only rarely succumbing to the bitter conflicts of sibling rivalry and only over small matters such as who would get the last cookie or whether or not Pluto should still be a planet. When it came to anything of significance, such as who liked who, Kelsey having failed American Government (again) or whether or not James Borte deserved a second chance after being caught with half a grand in meth, they were like two magnets that had been glued together.

She also loved ghost stories, so when she heard where her brother was going off to, no amount of insistence on her brother's part could make her stay behind. Either way, she had been twenty (Phil was twenty-two, barely, and I exactly one year older); if she'd wanted, she could simply follow us or go alone some other day. Phil reasoned that it was better to take her along because she was just as obstinate as he was and at least he could watch over her and keep her safe. I suggested that I too could watch over her, but he insisted otherwise, insisting that his 'baby' sister would need her brother, not someone else.

Phillip and Kelsey met me at a bus station a few blocks away from our destination- the allegedly haunted halls of the Eastburn Psychiatric Rehabilitation Facility. The actual town of Eastburn had faded to oblivion long before and had been the subject of rampant whispering for decades, vicious rumors defacing any remaining memory of the two like mental graffiti.

Setting off down a narrow path that wound through the nearby forest, I listened to the quiet crunch of our feet on the crisp, leaf-strewn ground. I was pleased to note the utter lack of signs of civilization; there were no crumpled McDonald's wrappers, no crushed beer cans or half-smoked cigarettes, no amorous couples defiling the serene nightscape with their sexual exhibitionism... though the sensation of being alone in the wilderness soon became unnerving. Thankfully, Kelsey breached that void with conversation.

"So, Phil, what are we in for? Resident ghosts? Intelligent spirits? Poltergeists? Shadow people?" Kelsey grinned, her eyes seeming impossibly large behind her wire-rimmed glasses.

"Sorry, I haven't heard of anything more extravagant than one intelligent ghost. Some reports suggest up to thirty or forty residential ghosts though." Phil looked up at the sky. His shaggy brown hair, which had fallen across his eyes, was tucked back behind his ears. He made a point to hide them whenever strangers were around because he thought they were freakishly large.

I followed his gaze, briefly admiring the specks twinkling amidst the darkness, wondering if anyone would notice should one or two suddenly go out.

"Thirty or forty, huh? How'd one building get so many ghosts?" I wondered aloud.

"Well, legend says that the doctor who ran this place

wasn't too nice about the way he treated his patients. Sure, at the surface, he was caring and supportive, but he really just wanted to use his patients as guinea pigs. I guess he figured that once he made some breakthrough, he'd become rich. One day, a patient caught on and went on a rampage. Locked the entire staff inside with the rest of the patients then just walked away. Left the whole lot of 'em to die." Phil had always been a skeptic and this was one of the only areas in which his sister and his opinions were notably different; his flat voice betrayed how little regard he held for such lore.

"Oh man," Kelsey shuddered. I wanted to reach out and steady her, let her know that I'd protect her, but stopped myself. "Talk about negative energy. No wonder they're trapped."

"If they're really still here," Phil pointed out, arching the fuzzy caterpillars that he referred to as his eyebrows.

"What about the intelligent one?" I glanced over, half interested, half speculating as to whether or not my own face resembled a member of the animal kingdom.

"That'd be the doctor, or so they say. Some feel he's looking to make amends for what he's done, others say he wants more test subjects. Personally, I think that if he was really that smart, he'd move on." He tucked his thick hands into his coat pockets, contenting himself to block out any portion of the world he disagreed with. Along with ghosts, he felt that aliens, narwhals and honest politicians also did not exist.

"Maybe his intelligence is what's keeping him here. Sometimes, really smart people have trouble keeping faith and believing in the afterlife, which would mean that after this life lies oblivion; he might be here because he's scared that he'll cease to exist." I rubbed my chin, allowing my eyes to drift out of focus, trying to wrap my head around what might happen at the end of my life. It scared the hell out of me, and death was far off, right? I had no reason to be afraid.

"Ya' know, I think this is the most I've ever heard you speak at one time," Kelsey laughed. I'd known the Ottenhiem's since my mom and I moved to Densen's Forge, a small town in southern Pennsylvania, twelve years earlier, after a messy divorce sent us running from central New Jersey and my dad running to the plastic woman he'd met at a sleazy, so-called gentleman's club.

"Yeah, I'm usually pretty quiet," I chuckled sheepishly, feeling the blood rush to my cheeks.

"You are," she nodded. "But I like what you have to say. You should talk more."

I looked over at her, but she'd snapped her gaze forward so we couldn't make eye contact, my own eyes focusing on the pointed slope of her nose. My mind whirled, trying to figure out if she was being friendly or hinting at something else, trying to be subtle enough that her brother didn't notice but also being so subtle that I too had missed the significance. It wasn't clear if her possible affections were simply the workings of my imagination, so I opted to leave the matter alone.

Besides, Phil had once spoken with me about his sister's love life. All he needed to say was that, no matter how much he trusted a guy, he wouldn't trust them enough to date Kelsey. Though I hadn't revealed my feelings directly, his knowing stare informed me that he, at least, was aware of my regard for her. I respected them both too much to ignore his directive.

It didn't take us long to reach the hospital. Passing through a hole in the surrounding chain link fence, we crossed to the front door of the building, skirting the overgrown plant life that attempted to stop us from proceeding by ensnaring us in thorn-covered tendrils. The cracked face of the building glowered down upon us, bearing all the scars and latent hostility of a nightclub bouncer.

As if protesting our approach, the harsh weather kicked into overdrive. The wind began to scream as it whipped past us nearly twice as fast as before. It tore at my jacket, causing it to billow out behind me. Shivering, I pulled the sides together and drew the zipper up, nestling my chin down against my chest. It wasn't a cold night, but the wind had a piercing bite to it. I was seized by the sudden notion that the hounds of death were already nipping at us, ready to sink their teeth into fresh meat.

"Come on, it's freezing out here! Let's go inside," Kelsey whispered hurriedly. She seemed to glow, the moonlight glinting off the crests of her dirty blonde hair. I kept wondering why we allowed her to come; haunted or not, abandoned buildings can be very dangerous, and we could've been arrested whether we wound up injured or not. Part of me insisted that we should turn back just to make sure she was safe, but I rarely got to spend time with Kelsey. Though it wouldn't be long, and we would be in the company of her brother, I wanted to spend the time with her.

I should never have been so selfish.

Phil banged his fist against the glass doors, then slammed his shoulder into them, but gave up. "The building is shut tight," he called. His failure to open the building did not surprise me. Despite his strength, he was a very direct person who would hesitate to proceed if the most straightforward attempt failed. That's certainly not saying he was flawed for behaving this way, since that would be to insinuate that a majority of people are flawed, but I like to think I'm slightly more creative in my approach to problem solving.

"May I?" Phil jumped; I was, in my younger days, able to walk silently. Most complained of my tendency to sneak up on them, but it was one of the few pranks I tended to pull. I was proud of very few things, but my agility always made me smile.

Phil laughed, "Do you have some sort of magic spell to allow us to gain entry, oh great wordsmith?"

Smirking, I tapped at the glass, examining it for weaknesses. Tugging my sleeve down over my hand to protect it, I threw a right jab and shattered the entire pane, the tinkling of shards on the ground comprising the door's final, pleading attempt to protest our entry. "Open Sesame."

Stepping over the shattered glass, I found myself in the foyer of the sizable facility. It was dusty and papers had been strewn about, but it could probably be fully operational with a few days of dedicated cleaning.

The whirr-click of my camera seemed to echo through the empty room. I took shots with and without the flash just to be sure I canvassed everything. Besides, the moonlight made for some really haunting lighting, and the sudden mechanical illumination ruined that effect.

"Hey," Phil muttered, coming up beside me and coughing as the dust in the air coated his lungs. "Nice job, slugger."

"That's probably the only time I'll ever hear those words directed at me," I snickered. While I was fast and agile, I was nearly famous for how awful I was at sports; some said I had the grace of a cat, and the hand-eye coordination of one too.

"You aren't that bad at sports," he lied, though we both knew he didn't believe it.

"Sorry Phil, but the only way he could get any worse at sports is if he were crippled," Kelsey droned from behind us.

I turned back, grinned, and snapped a picture of her, forgetting that my flash was on. I'd feel uncomfortable repeating the string of expletives that followed.

"Sorry!" I winced. "I didn't mean to blind you."

"Just keep in mind that you owe me one now," she growled.

"But I'm always nice to you! Can't you look the other way this one time?"

"We'll see, buddy," she smirked menacingly, yet I would've sworn her words were somehow flirtatious. I again blamed my imagination because she couldn't possibly have been flirting with me, not there, in a ghost-filled asylum, in front of her brother. Or so I thought.

Turning away as I tried to swallow the lump in my throat, I glanced down at the picture of Kelsey. There was a shadow across the screen, like someone had been standing over her, except it wasn't just a shadow; it was a thin wall of impenetrable darkness. The academic in me tried to assuage my fears and assure me it was nothing but a trick - maybe some dust had blocked off part of the lens. The photographer in me knew that wasn't what happened. It was a black streak with discernible human characteristics. Dust doesn't look like that.

I shrugged it off and took another few shots as we wandered past fallen security gates and into a dark hallway where we found that my occasional flashes were our only source of illumination. Phil flicked a switch and, predictably, found the power didn't work. With every snap of the shutter, we got a glimpse of the cold walls and discarded medical equipment that was strewn about the cracked linoleum. It sent a chill up my spine, but at the same time, the raw, near-apocalyptic nature of the building drove me onward. I felt like I was being called deeper into the building.

Maybe, just maybe, I never really had a choice in the matter.

"Did you bring a flashlight?" Phil turned, bumping into me. A burst of light exploded down the hall as I accidentally took another shot.

"Are you talking to me? I thought I was the camera man," I prodded. I did, in fact, have a flashlight on me, just in case.

"No," Kelsey mumbled, sounding nervous. "I brought my iPhone, but that's not the same... Didn't you bring one?"

That was the tragedy of thinking so alike; they often shared the same opinions on who should do what. When Phil thought Kelsey had something covered, she often thought he'd done it, leaving the task incomplete. I'd learned to anticipate this and wordlessly drew two pen lights from my back pocket. I handed one to each of them.

My thumb slid over the memory button on my camera. The screen displayed the picture I'd taken when Phil bumped into me. There, looming just to the side of the doorway at the end of the hall was a translucent silhouette. The hospital gown was in clear detail, though the face was mangled. I couldn't tell if this was from the bad angle or from some mutilation experienced just before death.

The shock must have registered on my face because I heard Phil say, "What's wrong?"

I shook my head. "Nothing, that picture was just really good." I've always been a good liar. This was no exception.

"Huh, you're welcome, then!" He beamed. I saw Kelsey crack a weary smile, but something seemed to be weighing on her mind.

Continuing down the hall, we came to what appeared to be a dayroom. There seemed to have been some sort of physical confrontation. Though the bodies had since been cleared away, the furniture nearby was badly splintered and the tiles had the sickly brown-red hue of a stain that no cleaner could remove.

The rest of the room was otherwise untouched. The windows were dirty, but intact. A pharmaceutical station stood at the edge of the room, its shatter-resistant confines still guarding the likely-expired medicine within. There were two sets of double doors, one to our left and one to our right, though one was shut with a heavy padlock. The cracked ceiling shook loose a pocket of dust as the wind outside caused the building itself to tremble.

"Maybe we should go," Kelsey whispered. My gaze fell on a set of elevator doors; they were wide open, revealing the collapsed carriage, which had undoubtedly fallen through the shaft and become unusable many years earlier.

"Are you ok, Kelsey?" I turned back.

"Yes, I just... I don't know, I feel like we aren't welcome here." She shuffled about like a foal that was too scared to stay and face danger, but unable to live without its herd. Something shifted in me. Now, more than ever, I wanted to stand by her side, though this time, all I wanted to do was protect her.

"Then let's go," I nodded. She smiled and I smiled back.

"Hey, we just got here! And what about my grade? I

can't write ten pages on my trip through the lobby, I need the full tour."

"I bet he could," his sister jutted her thumb towards me. I looked at the two, not knowing if he was too proud to admit fear or to stubborn to accept the possibility that the building really was haunted, making me debate showing him the photos I'd taken. Though I wanted to convince him, I didn't want to scare Kelsey and opted not to draw attention to them.

"My vote's on leaving. I can help you with your essay if you like, but there's no sense in forcing ourselves through this." While waiting for Phil's response, I glanced down and began scrolling through the pictures I'd taken of the dayroom, opting to peruse my optical evidence in hopes of finding the perfect shot to get us the hell out of there.

My camera showed a security guard lying prone, the leg of a table having been thrust into his chest. His head had lolled towards the camera and fixed empty, white eyes upon me. A patient with his head bashed in sat in a nearby armchair. The petite nurse from the drug station was surrounded by empty bottles of Lithium and Prozac, desperately trying to avoid experiencing the prolonged agony she'd been left to suffer.

I put my eye to the viewfinder and spanned the room, eventually focusing on Phil and Kelsey. The pale beams of light from outside were falling across them, but something caught my interest. It was like a source of light forming behind them, but it wasn't quite light, it was like pure energy that formed into the shape of a man.

Looking at the camera, I saw a hideous, slack-jawed man standing behind them. The ethereal figure held some sort of rod - maybe the leg of a chair or a guard's baton - and seemed to be glaring down at us. I snapped a picture, wondering if the thing was real, wondering if I'd lost my mind, wondering if ghosts could hurt people, and hoping like hell that the answers were no, no and no.

Dropping my hands, I looked at my friends. There he was, standing behind them. I could see the figure and instantly realized the answers were yes, no and yes, respectively. This wasn't just some resident spirit - this was a hungering ghost, a thing I'd only heard about in anime. It wanted blood as compensation for its pain.

The figure lifted its weapon.

"Move!" I yelled, pointing only because I was too far to physically intervene. It was stupid of me. I should've been closer. Phil spun, saw it, and yanked Kelsey out of the way. The being was fairly slow, but I didn't want to see what might happen if we let it get too close. I heard an odd whistle-growl sound coming from it. Looking closer, I saw a gaping hole in its neck, the edges rimmed with teeth marks.

"Let's go!" Phil dashed for the doors across the room. They'd only lead us deeper into the abandoned institution, but we couldn't double back. It wasn't likely that we could bypass our attacker.

The hall we'd found ourselves in was pitch black and smelled of rotting flesh. Though the lights I'd given them were still shining brightly, the beams waved about erratically, making it difficult to see. I had enough physical awareness to catch sight of a pile of debris directly in front of me. I leapt over and slid in the dust beyond it, keeping my momentum going.

A bang resounded from behind us as the doors slammed open. Then I heard a second bang. A third. Fourth, fifth, and by the sixth I was beginning to wonder where these noises were coming from. I noticed other doors on the sides of the hallway. Though I couldn't read the plates by each, it didn't take a genius to know that these were patient cells.

Which meant that there were at least six of them coming after us.

Something caught my eye - a plate different from the others. "This way!" I yelled, pointing. Phil had to stop and turn, but Kelsey and I darted off towards where I pointed, down a side passage.

Kelsey was ahead of me. I couldn't see much. My world faded into the crushing blackness of the hall around me. Focusing only on the door now illuminated by her thin beam, our feet slammed across the dirt-caked floor. A crash came from in front of me as she slammed open the metal doorway to a stairwell.

We raced inside. Holding it open for Phil, I slammed it shut as soon as he made it in. We didn't know if a door could stop the spirits from following us, but we knew we had to try.

A quick sprint up the stairs led us to the second floor. Phil led the way, holding the light as steady as he could while a small chorus of ghouls howled behind us, calling us to join their ranks. He stood in the center of a four way intersection and shone the light around, making visible the charts and files that had been flung to the ground as dozens of panicked individuals went from being selfless medical professionals to frantic captives. Kelsey joined him, pointing the opposite way, as I scrutinized our options. Ahead of us seemed to lay a seclusion wing. The two side halls were too long to see in their entirety, but they appeared to lead to more cells.

There was a bang, quickly followed by another as the door behind us shot open. The light couldn't reveal much, but we were able to make out a series of semi-formless humanoid figures storming towards us. A fetid wind blew through the hall, carrying their screams and sending us running in the other direction.

We had no choice but to dash to the seclusion ward and pray the tide of enraged spirits wouldn't be able to crash down on us.

I found myself at the back of our minuscule group. Phil took the lead, shoving the door open. Though the doorway was but a few feet away, I was almost certain that I'd never make it. I could feel my heart stop as icy fingertips grazed my back, tearing at my shirt. I felt the fabric give way, though I didn't hear a sound over the collective roar of my attackers.

Flinging myself through the open door, I tucked my shoulder, rolling through dirt as Phil slammed the door shut. Making the most of the meager visibility offered by the two lights, we spotted a shelving unit. I leapt forward and helped him shove it against the frame, keeping the ghouls at bay.

"What the fuck was that?" I panted, stepping back as the door pulsed inward, but didn't open.

"Don't worry... we're safe... I think..." Phil's chest was heaving. We felt the stiff, dead air of a room that hadn't held a live human in decades.

"Hey," Kelsey whispered. She was looking at me. "You don't owe me anymore."

"What do you mean?"

"If you hadn't said something... who knows what would've happened." Her voice shook like dead leaves in the wind.

"Don't worry about it." Is it considered selfish to save a friend if half your motivation is not wanting to be alone? I cleared my throat and shook my head. "Phil, are we really safe here?"

"We should be. Most of what I read on the internet said that some ghosts, like poltergeists, can't move through walls like the others. They can only possess objects that use energy, like televisions and appliances."

"So what do I do with this?" Kelsey waved her phone.

"As long as they're not in here, we're fine." He rubbed his eyes. "We should be able to leave at dawn, when they're at their weakest."

"You know, I pulled enough all-nighters for one lifetime. I didn't intend on doing it again, especially not in a haunted asylum," I grunted. "Maybe we can think up an escape plan?"

"Sure. You start, I'll add on once you can find a way out of this room that doesn't involve walking back through a horde of bloodthirsty spirits."

Grunting, I began to pace angrily. Phil gave me space, knowing that I hated being in closed spaces since the time I'd been locked in a janitor's closet overnight by Isaac Clem when I was in tenth grade. That night was certainly no exception. The stale air of the seclusion wing was rife with the stench of desolation; it was the bitter, lonely smell of bones that had decayed to dust.

"When a spirit is trapped in our realm, it's because they die with too much emotion pent up inside them. That emotion binds their soul to our world until they can resolve it and find peace. Some die full of pain or anger, others just can't let go... and it looks like these want to use us as their way out," Kelsey whimpered.

Glancing over, I could see her eyes shimmering. I knew I was scared. I couldn't begin to imagine how she was feeling, knowing that her beloved ghosts may very well kill her

"I'm going to check these cells and see if there's a way for us to leave," I approached the locked seclusion cells, fear twisting my stomach like wet rag.

"How are they going to help us escape?" Phil shined his light on me.

"Did you notice how old this place is?" We spoke softly, despite the fact that our pursuers already knew where we were. I suppose some primal portion of our genome had kicked on, triggering survival instincts that our ancestors had so kindly honed for us. "Some portions were falling apart. A piece of the lobby was practically caved in. If I'm right, we should be just over the day room. If part of the ceiling caved in, maybe we can use the hole to scamper out of here."

"Good thinking." Kelsey tried to smile, but her quivering lips failed to disguise her helplessness.

Foregoing my feelings on doing so - and Phil's - I stepped forward and hugged Kelsey. "It's okay. We'll get out of here."

She leaned briefly on my chest. I held her in the quietude of the cell and, for a moment, things seemed peaceful. Phil watched us, not seeming to object. Regrettably, I had to pull myself away and examine the cells, but we both seemed a little stronger, a little less shaken. We shared one reassuring smile - a real smile - before I turned away.

"So, Phil," I cautiously approached the first door. "Remind me about that one smart ghost?" Kelsey coughed; I turned and she handed me her light. I urged her to stay close to her brother, where it would be safer, but she seemed reluctant.

"Right, his name was... uh... Doctor Harris. They say that he thought he was doing the world a favor, using those sick patients for 'the good of mankind', but at the end of the day, he was nothing but a sadist and a murderer. Those he didn't kill got to turn the table and rip him apart."

"What might that mean for us now?" I looked back, nodded, and threw the lock on the first cell. Pushing the door open, I saw nothing within the cell. It was filled with padding and dust.

"I have no idea. Like I said, the only things I really know at this point are the rumors. Maybe he's still as whacked as his patients; maybe he's trying to make amends. He hasn't helped us so far, though, so I doubt he's going to get involved... Kelsey?" His light flitted around the room. He sighed, "Oh, good, don't scare me like that."

The trembling girl was huddled in an arm chair across the room. Her arms hugged her knees to her chest. It sounded like she was trying not to cry. Phil's light fell across her like a show light on a porcelain doll and she looked all the more frail for it. Though he would normally be by her side, I couldn't help but notice that Phil wasn't moving.

I sidled over to Phil and nudged him with my elbow. "Go to her. Your sister needs you, man."

He shook his head. "No... she needs *you*. Brothers are for making sure that women are safe... people like you are for making sure that women *feel* safe. I've taken care of her so far, but... now it's your turn. I think you both deserve that chance." I felt a hand on my back that guided me forward. His light turned away, but I caught him smiling begrudgingly at me.

A lump caught in my throat. What was I going to say? I realized that, during my years of dreaming of confessing my feelings to Kelsey, I never thought about the actual words I'd use to do so. I especially had no way of knowing what would be right for our clusterfuck of a situation. Who *would* know the right words?

Then I realized that there probably weren't 'right' words for this and decided to wing it. Kneeling beside her, I laid my hand on her shoulder. "It'll be ok, Kelsey. We'll get through this." She shuddered and tried to nod, but ultimately just shook harder. "Listen, the doors keep them out... for some reason... if you want, we can stay here till dawn, not opening anything, not touching anything, just focusing on waiting them out. They don't come out during the day, right? So if you'd like, we don't have to do anything."

Disembodied blue eyes stared at me from the darkness, faintly glowing from my beam of light. They pleaded with me, begged for me to help them escape their fate, but I knew the best I could offer was my embrace. Though I wanted to leave as quickly as possible, we were both aware that, should she ask, I'd stay by her forever, without hesitation.

"We... no... I..." Her voice was distant and disconnected. "I'll be ok. I can handle myself, it's only that... I don't know, I guess I wanted to find ghosts for so long that I... I didn't know what it would be like when it actually happened."

"I think I know what that's like," I chuckled weakly. When we'd met, I was barely twelve, and even though my mom laughed, I swore I'd marry Kelsey some day. My feelings hadn't changed. "Listen, though. Whatever you need, let me know. I'm here for you, ok?"

Those lost eyes seemed to shine a little brighter. "Got

it." That voice - that soft, beautiful voice - sounded more stable now.

"Would you like me to continue looking through these cells, or would you like me to stay here?"

I heard her breath catch. Something in the air between us seemed to whisper, 'Stay,' but she lifted my hand from her shoulder. "I'll be alright. You... you keep looking."

Nodding, my body stood and walked away, though my mind screamed that I was making the wrong decision. She was there; she wanted me by her side. Yet, as much as I wanted to go back, I knew that men must, at times, suffer to ensure that the women in their lives are safe.

Understanding this, I steeled myself. I'd bear that night a thousand times if that would ensure a single one with her.

As I approached the bank of cells, Phil gave me a slow, approving smile. I returned it in kind and flipped open the lock on door number three. The rusted deadbolt shrieked in response, but eventually gave way.

Pressing the door open, we were immediately assaulted by the stench of foul water. My light illuminated a small hole in the floor. The room below held a pool, no doubt for some sort of hydrotherapeutic purpose. I breathed out heavily, angry at the fact that the aperture wasn't large enough for us to slip through.

I gingerly stepped across a pile of rubble, among which I noticed ceiling panels. Phil and I both aimed our lights up, but we let out a collective sigh of disappointment, noticing the roof was too high for escape.

Containment room four was much harder to open than its previous counterparts. The bolt released easily enough, but the door itself seemed stuck in place. Ramming my shoulder into it sent the aged metal crashing to the ground. I stumbled and nearly fell, hearing a sharp intake of breath behind me.

Kelsey had her hand over her mouth, her eyes wide. Her other clutched her iPhone, its brilliant LED display blinding my dark-adapted eyes. "Don't worry, everyone. I'm fine. It was just loud."

Looking over my shoulder, I noticed a patch of the wall was flickering. In the sudden illumination, I saw a charred outline surrounded by melted padding. The flickering was becoming a flame. That flame became a hand, which was soon followed by an arm, groping madly for some material foothold in its ethereal eternity. I edged backwards as an entire figure pressed itself out of the wall and angled for me.

"Guys? The door is broken, what do we do?" I yelled, stumbling backwards. My foot caught on some debris and I crashed to the ground. The burning ghost moaned and reached out towards me.

"What do... holy shit!" Phil yelled.

Scrambling onto my front, I attempted to get to my feet and sprint away, but the ghoul fell towards me. I felt those hands, those appendages of unending immolation, coil around my calf. They dragged me back, igniting my jeans as the heat seared my flesh. The pain moved higher as burning digits clenched around my thigh.

The furious jolt of my muscles drove my knee into the floor. I heard a gut-wrenching crack as my kneecap split, though I was distracted by the sudden, acrid stench of burning flesh. The pain in my throat told me that I must've been screaming, but I couldn't hear. I couldn't see. I couldn't think. As that burning pain arced through my hips, up my chest and began to throttle my heart, my instincts kicked into overdrive. All I knew was one thing: I wasn't about to let myself be killed.

With adrenaline coursing through my veins, I tore myself away, propelling myself across the room with my good leg. Its fingernails ripped into me, tearing away ribbons of smoldering skin.

My back slammed against the far wall. I used my good leg like a kick stand, forcing myself to remain standing so I could face my attacker. My chest heaved and my eyes blurred, but a brutal, animalistic rage filled me. I'd accepted that I would die, but I vowed to die fighting.

Phil grunted and I watched the shelving unit we'd placed against the door topple forward onto the walking pyre. It did nothing; the spirit floated through it, scorching the metal in the process.

The door to the room crashed in as a wave of poltergeists flooded toward us. Kelsey's phone exploded as the entire score attempted to possess it at once. The thin lights of our flashlights were snuffed out in an instant, plunging us into darkness. The only thing we could see was the area around the flaming ghoul.

The spirits shrieked and wailed as the lights above us snapped on, filling the room with a blinding whiteness. We shielded our eyes as it drove them back, out of the room. I watched the burning one disintegrate to ash once more.

Spying a chair to my left, I immediately collapsed into it. My heart was racing, but my nerves were too wired for action to feel pain. Sitting on the edge with my right leg extended, I glanced around at Phil and Kelsey, who were staring at me with abject horror.

"Who might you be, and what are you doing in my hospital?" An austere and rotund figure glided forward, dressed in a pristine lab coat with 'Harris' etched into it. His figure was more solid, more real, than that of the other ghosts; he appeared in such detail that I could make out fine grey hairs along his chin.

Taking a moment to glance around, I noticed that the debris had been cleared away. The walls were white, the ceiling was intact, the doors were back on their hinges and, if I hadn't known better, I would've sworn we were in a functional asylum. The building had been restored to its pre-abandonment state

My friends were silent; their jaws hung open, their widened eyes locked on me. I was more concerned with the new ghost, though.

"Does it really matter?" I growled. "After all, aren't you just going to kill us?"

He looked over at me, his translucent figure spinning effortlessly in the air. His face contorted, as if angry, but suddenly fell. "Oh my," he said softly. He cleared his throat, "No, I don't intend on hurting you. It appears I may be needed for quite the opposite."

"So, you must be Doctor Harris."

He straightened up and nodded. "Yes, I am Doctor Neil Harris, that's correct..." He cleared his throat. "Did one of my patients give you that horrible injury?" His hand waved at my leg.

"What are you talking about?" I sputtered. Despite having transcended death, the doctor looked unnerved.

"Your leg, son," he gestured more pointedly.

"What?" I looked down.

I'm not sure if it was actually seeing the damage to my leg, or if it was knowing that we weren't in immediate danger, but one of those set me off. All I know is that moment is when the pain hit me.

Clamping a hand over my mouth, the agony I felt when in the flaming clutches of my attacker came back tenfold. I stared down into an open wound that tore from the middle of my thigh to the base of my calf. Exposed sinews and useless muscle seemed to throb as I looked at it, the pain intensifying as my musculature begged for the privacy screen we call skin. Ribbons of flesh dangled, some dragging across the shining floor, leaving black streaks in their wake. The skin was so burnt that the injury couldn't bleed; the veins had been cauterized. Knowing I might not lose the leg was hardly a blessing, considering that it barely looked like a leg.

Trembling, I extended a finger and, despite the voice

in my head that begged me not to, prodded the depths of the injury.

I was right. My finger hit bone. I had been burned so badly that only bone was left in some places - a fourth degree burn. I drew my hand away, my finger coated in the ashes of my ruined leg. My pulse surged and my injury responded, sending spasms through what remained of the muscle.

I nodded and swallowed hard, suppressing my pain. "I might need medical attention," I whispered, my voice shaking. Looking at it made me dizzy, so I forced my eyes shut as an arctic chill swept through me. My dizziness only amplified as I began to feel giddy as well, so I looked up at them, since I couldn't suppress my symptoms.

"We've got to get him out of here," Phil said. The ghost seemed to seethe as my eyes drifted in and out of focus; Doctor Harris was a water bed in a vacuum, floating and distending in odd directions. It made me laugh, which in turn made Phil look at me in concern.

"Perhaps. You may not trust me, but I can still aid him, if that's what you desire. Otherwise, he may succumb to shock and perish before you manage to get him to a hospital. I'll require a small sacrifice on your part, of course. Nothing is free." The ethereal man grinned.

"Hold up, you're a ghost. You're not even human anymore, and besides, weren't you some sort of mad scientist when you were alive? I'm not letting you experiment on my friend." Phil stepped between us.

"Not human?" He seemed taken aback. "May I ask

your name?"

Phil seemed wary. "Phillip... why?"

"Phillip, you're young, so I don't blame you for not knowing this, but there is yet a great deal for you to learn. There is much more to being human than one's biology - or lack thereof, in my case. Humanity is about your actions, inactions, goals, and fears, not physical form. And as for your second point, no. I was a psychologist and a researcher. I sought to end human suffering. That is all I ever wanted, and I continue to do that now." His voice had a comforting gentility that reminded me of my grandfather. I was surprised to find myself smiling. No thought was more comforting than curling up against his chest and taking a nap, like I did when I was a child.

"Didn't a patient kill you because of your abuse?" Phil prodded.

Doctor Harris sighed. "I died because I was careless and did not see the extent of a man's delusions. I admit that my professional expertise was greatly tested by that patient; I failed that test. My inability to cure him of his torment is my only regret," his voice wavered. The apparition slumped, still shouldering the burdens he bore before his untimely end.

"And if we want to leave... can we?" My leg hurt too much to care about his undead state. All I could think of was the warm cocoon of blankets I'd forsaken to go to Eastburn.

"Yes, you can. As I said, you may not make it far. Or you might arrive at a hospital, get treated, and live happily for many years, though that chance is slim. I can help, if you'd like to work out some form of arrangement, or you can take that chance." His words were loaded; I knew there was something strange going on, but my head was swimming. I was weightless, hurtling through the dark. Nothing but a hunk of planetary rock cast from a supernova.

Phil looked at me. "Do you think you can make it?"

I shrugged, then used my shaking arms to push myself to my feet, bearing my weight on my working leg. My one fumbling attempt to move caused the injured limb to drag, which, in response, sent lightning through my veins. Collapsing to the ground in tears, I quietly wretched, heaving the contents of my stomach onto the pale tiles beneath me. Kelsey dropped down, cradling my head, and pressed a hand to my forehead. She was so cold. I tried to push her away. I remember being scared that my heat would melt her.

"Phil, he's burning up." Her voice echoed inside my pounding skull.

"I'm afraid the boy is going into shock. He isn't going to make it." Doctor Harris sounded genuinely concerned.

"Please, help him. We'll do anything," Kelsey interjected, holding me tighter.

The doctor stared down at her, his head cocked at an odd angle. His eyes seemed to widen as some unheard message passed between them. "So be it," he held up his hand.

A wheelchair rolled into the room. My heart slammed about erratically as I was lifted into it by unseen hands. Looking around uneasily, I had enough presence to pull out my camera and begin taking pictures, though they were, in retrospect, awful shots. When figures actually showed up on film, they weren't the rabid, deranged ghouls from before; these spirits were donned in scrubs. They almost seemed peaceful.

"I know you don't trust me, but even in death, I try to follow the Hippocratic Oath. I will do everything in my power to ensure you do not die of this injury." The doctor waved for Phil and Kelsey to follow as he took hold of the handlebars on my chair. I found myself being wheeled through bright, clean halls. Clipboards, mops and other items floated around as their ghostly owners continued the tasks they'd been assigned in life.

"So... what do you do now? You know... now that you're dead," Phil fumbled awkwardly. I heard a smack as Kelsey swatted him and couldn't help but give a delirious smile, sure that things would be returning to normal. We'd arrived at a set of metal doors. Doctor Harris pressed a button.

"Why do you ask?"

"I'm curious. I mean, I'm writing a report. On local lore, you know, for a class."

"Ah, college students! To be young again," he sighed wistfully. "Of course, I'd settle for simply being alive." A ding resounded as the elevator arrived and the doctor moved to push me through the opening doors.

"Wait," Phil stopped him. "This elevator was broken. How...?"

"Hush. We don't have time for parapsychological philosophy right now." We moved into the waiting carriage and it escorted us smoothly to the ground floor. As the elevator opened, we found ourselves in the 'refurbished' day room. I continued to take pictures, wondering how they'd turn out. It was all I could do at this point - my ears had begun to ring and echo strangely, distorting their words like a children's game of telephone. What few words I heard were unintelligible.

Doctor Harris brought us through the doors that had been padlocked before. They now stood open. He'd led us to the hydrotherapy chamber. Like I predicted, there was a pool, though it was now clear and inviting. I was given a pill and took it without question; my hearing slowly returned, though I was still euphoric and disconnected.

"Oh, dear me, I believe I forgot to answer your question," Doctor Harris turned to Phil as I was lifted onto a gurney. "You see, in life, I did what I absolutely loved. I continue to do that now. I help people. I also continue to run experiments, when people are kind enough to donate themselves to my cause." A tray with salve and gauze floated over. He took a small amount of the ointment and began to dress the wound. Whatever he was using managed to take some of the pain away - but not much.

"Help people how, though? People don't come up here, so how can you help anyone? ...and what do you mean, donate?" Phil looked on inquisitively. Kelsey watched the process too intensely, biting her lip all the while.

"You came up here, didn't you?" the doctor smirked, skirting the last question. Through the haze that surrounded me, I was dully aware of a light pinprick in my arm.

"Well, yeah… but not to meet with you." The fog in my head receded. Whatever he'd given me was pushing the delirium away.

"Everyone needs me, one way or another. You get hurt, then I get what I want," he let go of my leg. "This will prevent you from going into shock. Now… my payment, please." He was looking at Kelsey.

"What are you trying to say? You can't have her," I looked up, confused, though the searing fog in my head was thinning.

"Oh, poor boy, I already do. Why do you think I agreed to help you?"

My jaw dropped and my stomach heaved again. I didn't want to understand what he was saying. I was reminded once again of how fragile and precious she was as a tear rolled down Kelsey's pale cheek.

"I'm sorry. I just… I couldn't. You got hurt because I encouraged you to keep looking through those cells. If I had stopped you, you… you…" she broke into sobs.

"No! Damn it, don't you touch her!" Phil ran forward, directly through the doctor, and collapsed to the ground.

"Foolish child. I'm a ghost. I don't have corporeal

form unless I want to, so how could you possibly hurt me? Besides, you don't have a say in this matter. She and I have an arrangement. His life in exchange for hers."

"So, you sick your ghosts on people, wait for innocent visitors to get hurt, and then force them into some crooked deal?" My gaze bore into him. "Then let's switch it up - take me instead. Free her."

"No!" Kelsey sputtered through her tears. "You don't deserve to die for me."

"My patience is wearing thin. I'd like to collect on this debt. Now. Besides, I just *saved* your life when you would've died anyway. You mean nothing to me." The doctor stood taller, somehow, and loomed over us.

"I..." Kelsey jerked backwards, pulled by some unseen force towards the pool, the waters of which seemed to seethe with anticipation.

"What happened to the Hippocratic Oath, huh?" I snarled.

"I'm not hurting her, child," he smiled mockingly. "Death is liberation. I'm freeing her from the pains and trappings of life. Look at her; she is so scared, so weak and so breakable. She's nothing but a stained glass window - great to look at, but she could be destroyed in an instant. She'll be much safer now, and happier too. Happier than you could ever know."

"Kelsey..." I stared at her.

"I'm sorry... Since the first day we met I... I liked you, you know? I wish..." She smiled weakly at me.

Stumbling backwards to the edge of the pool, we locked eyes for one last instant. Her voice was barely audible as she said, "I wish we could've had more time together." Then she jolted backwards and disappeared beneath the surface of the water.

"KELSEY!" Phil roared, diving forward. He slammed into the surface. It was unyielding, as if he'd struck a thick pane of glass. "Damn it!"

Throwing myself from my prone position on the stretcher proved useless. I wanted to try to help; no, I had to try. However, my leg still couldn't support my weight.

Phil continued punching at the surface of the water, trying in vain to save his sister. He screamed, tearing at his hair.

"Doctor! Let her go... please!" I began to sob now. The only thing worse than the aching in my chest was how utterly helpless I was. The girl I loved had sacrificed herself for me but all I could do was crawl to the edge of the pool and watch her die.

The stagnant waters below gave us a perfect view of her frail and fading beauty. The perfect blue of her eyes shimmered, dulled, and disappeared as her eyes closed.

Sheer anguish overwhelmed me. I had no choice but to scream. I can't recall what I was yelling, but my voice reverberated off the walls and into the halls around us, my quiet nature unable to suppress the pain of losing her. Phil was silent. He'd exhausted himself in trying to save her. He mourned his sister in silence.

Minutes ticked by that way. My screams and swears

were at odds with Phil's soundless weeping. Eventually I turned to threatening Doctor Harris, though I know those comments were in vain. It didn't take long for my voice to give out.

The wheelchair creaked as it rolled into my peripheral vision. I dragged myself over to it and hoisted myself into the seat.

I'm not sure how long I sat there for, but I didn't look up until the chair began to move. "We're gonna get out of here, come back with a fucking army of priests, and send that dickhead straight down to the fiery pits," Phil growled from behind me.

"Agreed," I said, my hoarse voice creaking.

The halls were still immaculate. The shining linoleum floors and pale plaster walls did little to ease my spirits. I didn't need to ask how Phil was holding up; rage and anguish emanated from him. Part of me believed that, had I turned around, I would've been able to see the air around him shimmering like the air over a road on a hot summer's day.

With the front doors in sight, I couldn't help but notice that the sun was just barely peaking over the horizon. Knowing that Kelsey would never see it rise caused my heart to seize up. I prayed it would stop beating; I didn't deserve a life she'd died for.

"Going so soon?" A voice called from behind us.

I heard Phil whisper, "Kelsey?" His hands relinquished my wheelchair. Grabbing the wheels, I spun myself to face the translucent apparition of the woman I loved.

"I guess I don't blame you. There's nothing left for you here, is there? You got your report, Phil, and you..." she looked at me. "You got to know how I feel about you."

My mouth hung open. I could feel myself fumbling for breath. My lungs felt filled with water; I was sure I was slowly dying, just as she had.

"Besides, I didn't say you could leave yet," a darker voice hissed. Phil raced to the doors. Sure enough, they wouldn't budge. The window I'd shattered had been replaced.

"What do you want?" I moaned. My leg was starting to throb again.

"It's not what he wants... it's what I want." We looked at Kelsey. "He was right. Death is... *spectacular*." She lingered on the word, savored it. "It's such a rush. You can't imagine the power you have when you don't have a body weighing you down."

Phil's breath was ragged too. "What... what do you want...?" I said hesitantly.

"Company." She smiled sweetly. There was something in that expression that I didn't recognize, but I ignored it.

I looked at Phil. He stared back.

"Boys... I want someone to spend eternity with... but the doctor says I can only have one of you stay. So I want you to choose."

"Kelsey... no," I said.

She looked disappointed. "I'm very sorry, then, but if that's how you'd like to play it, you'll both die." The way she said such a thing so casually made me sick. It couldn't really have been her... but I couldn't believe otherwise.

"Wait," I held up a hand and then turned to Phil. "I'll stay. With my leg the way it is, you've got the best chance at getting back to town anyway."

"No," he snapped. "You've suffered enough. You're going."

"Phil, she died for me! The least I can do is return the favor." I felt like my seated position weakened my argument.

"Damn it, don't you understand?" He sighed, "Brothers are for keeping women safe... which means that I failed. I failed the both of you. I let you get hurt... and let her get killed. I'm doing this, and I'm not giving you a say in the matter." Phil stepped in front of me and shoved the chair against the door. "You're a great guy. I'm sorry I got between you two before... but I'm not sorry now. Take care of yourself."

Before I could protest, something clicked behind me. A powerful wind swept through the lobby and blew me backwards, wheelchair and all. I careened through the open doors and out into the open air.

The wheels shuddered and struck a rock, flipping me over. My head hit the ground and everything faded to black.

***

Waking with a start, I found myself in a hospital bed. There was a thick bandage around my leg. I could see my toes poking out from beneath my sheet and breathed a sigh of relief. My head felt fuzzy and the pain was barely noticeable. I'd watched enough television shows about hospitals to know that I was on a high dose of morphine.

A quick press of the 'call nurse' button on my bed frame brought a concerned woman to my side.

"We didn't expect you to be awake so soon," she placed her hand high on her chest, her face contorted by worry.

"Well, I'm up," I slurred. "What... what happened?"

"You... you were found by the Lippincott Street bus stop with severe burns on your leg... Do you remember what happened?"

Of course I did, but I could hardly tell her. I shook my head. She bit her lip and rushed off to find a doctor, certain that I had a concussion. Ironically, I did, but that's beside the point.

I'll spare you the details about the numerous skin grafts and months of physical therapy designed simply to teach me how to walk again. Here's all you need to know: it cost a fortune, it hurt like a bitch, and I need a cane to walk. My days of running and agility are over.

Reviewing my photographs of that night, I realized that they showed far more than I'd thought. Upon printing, I was able to see the blurred outlines of men who'd lost all sense of reason.

Some were simply the images of one man attacking another. Others showed blatant cannibalism.

The girl who'd died in the pharmaceutical station was there, in my photos, her form bloated and purple with bloody foam oozing from her lips.

A guard, still in uniform, stared at us from his post in the station near the lobby. A baton was lodged firmly in his eye socket.

The pictures from our flight through the hallway were worse still.

But, sadly, none of those matter. I have never shown them to anybody, nor will I ever. They are the last memories I have of my best friend and one true love. For better or worse, these images die with me.

My friends deserve to rest in peace, though I know they never will because, on nights when the moon is high and the wind carries the first, frigid gusts of winter, I can hear them screaming.

SLEEPOVER AT OLD ST. MARY'S HOSPITAL

Kimberly Lay

I was sixteen in 1988 and had lived in Nevada for almost a year when I drove up to Virginia City on Six Mile Canyon road for the first time. That was the most uninspired name for a road I had ever heard. Literally six miles up a gravel, washboard-and-pothole-covered, windy, dusty, canyon road that led up the mountain into the back side of Virginia City. When the canyon ended, the mountain flattened out near the top, and opened to an expanse of sagebrush and the occasional outcroppings of trees. The houses scattered randomly about along several streets just before the last steep incline up onto Main Street of the once booming gold mining town of Virginia City. The tall false front old-west-style buildings, built in the 1800's on Main Street, were lined up tight, side by side, and only opened for an occasional side street that either led steeply down to the residential area below, or on the other side of Main Street, led steeply up to the courthouse, opera house, and other varieties of important buildings on the street above.

The first place of interest that could be seen on the left of Six Mile Canyon Road, once the canyon opens and flattens out, was a large, well-maintained building, several stories tall. It stood by itself along the less-populated back loop road that skirted the busier parts of the old western tourist town. The closest neighbor to the lonely building was the cemetery. The building, much bigger than any house, was built in the style of a red brick old colonial mansion. White framed windows with crisscross grilles covered the glass. Columns held up the second story porch surrounded by a white railing. A broad staircase descended from the porch on the main floor to a path in between two small patches of lawn in front. The front of the third floor had only three windows set inside white wood on the triangular roof front. A long narrow drive led to the basement door on the side of the building. The long narrow drive was separate from the main arched drive to the grand steps in the front. The few trees in front of the property did not block the view of the house from the road. Sagebrush grew everywhere else in the desert sand.

The place appeared benign, regal and well-maintained, but the ambiance it exuded was haunting. I didn't know anything about the place, but I felt as if something was watching me from the top floor windows when I passed by in the car. How could anything be watching me from up there? Yet every time I drove down the back loop road, I would speed up a little faster so I could hurry and pass by the place. Fear filled my throat and tightened my chest with painful, escalating anxiety until I couldn't see the building any more. Any talking or even thinking about ghosts made me feel that way. I was wildly afraid of something I had never seen or experienced. Now I was afraid of a place I knew nothing about.

The place looked important, but with no signs in front, I could never figure out why the large lonely building sat by itself on the far end of town with only the cemetery as its neighbor.

Several months passed before I could finally ask someone.

I was in a car with friends when we rode up Six Mile Canyon Road and passed by the building that tormented me with its quiet presence. Overcome by the same tight, fear ridden feeling, I could finally ask someone and hoped they would finally put my over-active mind to rest.

"What is that place?" I asked my friend Jenny. She lived at the base of the canyon and for years she had ridden the bus to school up the canyon road to Virginia City.

"Now it's an artist's residency center, but years ago it was St. Mary's Hospital. On the top floor is where they locked up all the insane people. They say it's the most haunted place in Virginia City because a fire broke out and the smoke killed them all when they couldn't get out, you know, because they were crazy and needed to be locked up."

"That's probably a rumor meant to scare tourists. How do you know it's haunted?"

"Susie says it is. She lives there. Her father is the caretaker. Are you scared, Kay?"

I lied when I shook my head.

***

After observing Susie over the next few weeks, I couldn't believe that she could live in a haunted house and be normal as if she lived in just any other normal house.

When I learned that I would be going over to Susie's for a cooking demonstration with my church youth group, I quickly became a basket case. I had nightmares about ghosts on the top floor for several nights before we attended the class.

I was completely unnerved when the day of the cooking class arrived.

The hairs on the back of my neck stood on end and my heart raced when we pulled into the long narrow drive just as the sun sank down, about to disappear behind the mountain.

I played it cool, but I was hyper aware of everything around me. We walked through the door into the basement floor, headed down a narrow hall towards the kitchen. Right away the topic of discussion was about whether or not Susie's home was haunted.

"Is it just a bunch of talk?" one of the younger girls asked.

"No, it's not talk. It really is haunted," Susie said, nonchalant.

"So what happens? How do you know it's haunted?" I couldn't help but ask since everyone was interested. But they probably weren't freaked out the way I was.

"Well, most of the time the fan turns on by itself. Sometimes it's not even plugged in. Occasionally the lights flicker on and off. The cabinet doors will slam open and shut on their own. But that hasn't happened very often. Only like once or twice."

On the way in, we passed a fan on the cluttered ledge in the hall that led to the kitchen. Sitting at the table, I had a clear view of the fan. I couldn't take my eyes off it after that.

"Sometimes things will fly across the room."

"Aren't you scared?" I asked, almost expecting something to hit me upside the head.

"No. I'm used to it. It's just their way of telling us they're here."

There had to be more to it than that. I was sure of it. The place had kept insane people locked up and they all died a terrible, fiery death. Fire was my other worst fear, right up there with ghosts.

The hauntings dominated the conversation, even though nothing out of the ordinary happened that night.

When it was time to go, I had to hide my fear even more. The darkness outside made every sight and sound more ominous. Night seemed like a better time than any other to see a ghost. I stared at the ground when I headed for the car and diverted my gaze from the windows as we rode up the narrow drive to the road. When we passed the arched front drive on the back loop road headed for home, I couldn't help it, I had to look.

Susie said no one lived on any other floors in the old hospital. With no artists in residence that night, the top floor should have been dark. But there was an odd, faint light in one of the windows. I decided then and there I would never come back.

At school the next day I still felt the hairs on my arms rise when I remembered the eerie light in the window. I had always been scared of everything and I couldn't believe I had actually spent a few hours in a haunted house.

"Susie said we could stay the night next weekend." Jenny said, eagerly. "She wants to give us a tour."

"Wonderful," I replied flatly, full of dread. Because I was such a weak little pushover, she talked me into tagging along. But I wasn't tagging along. She would have to drag me.

I had hoped that the days would pass slowly, or some big disaster would happen, but I had no such luck. Everything went smoothly.

Friday night arrived, which was unfortunate for me, because I couldn't find a way to back out. I really wished I wasn't such a pushover.

Jenny picked me up and I didn't have much to say in the car as we drove up the crazy, windy, miserably rough road to Virginia City.

Jenny, oblivious to my anxiety, carried on about how excited she was and she hoped we would see a ghost or even two. She told me other people, actual ghost hunters had stayed and left with proof that the old hospital was haunted.

I sighed in misery. Jenny wasn't helping me at all as she babbled on. We turned onto the long drive to the basement entrance. I longed to return to my peaceful, unhaunted home. I didn't have the courage to insist on bringing my car, so I couldn't escape before the ghost party started.

As soon as we stepped out of the car, Susie burst out the door to greet Jenny and me with a hug.

It was already dark when we carried our backpacks, pillows and sleeping bags into Susie's home.

"There is no one staying here this weekend so dad said we can stay in whichever room we want. That is if you aren't too scared to stay in a room alone." Susie glanced at Jenny and gave her a wink.

I barely caught it and I was glad I didn't miss it. Something was up with those two and I was skeptical. But I waited to voice my suspicions as we headed up a narrow staircase to the main floor. Susie led us down a barely lit hall in the back of the old hospital. Doctors and nurses must have kept supplies in the row of white cupboards that lined the hall.

The hall opened into the main entry. The room was much larger than I thought it would be. Susie turned on another lamp. But the light still didn't fill the room and it bothered me. Small, ornate Victorian lamps on antique side tables, barely put off enough light to navigate the main room, furnished with a couple of Victorian sofas and stuffed arm chairs. Everything looked new, or at least well-maintained, but a musty odor filled the stuffy, warm room.

"Dad doesn't want to waste electricity up here when there are no paying guests. We can only use the lamp light." Susie looked at Jenny just a little too long and I saw the slight turn of her lip when she said it. Something was definitely up.

Susie showed us around the rest of the old hospital. The place had been extensively renovated. There were bedrooms furnished with antique metal framed beds covered in handmade quilts. The lamps in most rooms looked like old oil lamps but they were electric. As she took us upstairs to the third floor there was another large room with another Victorian sofa near the stairs and some older worn armchairs. She showed us several more bedrooms.

Then Susie stood in the main room on the second floor after we finished the tour on that floor.

"Do you want to see the upstairs? It's used mainly in the day time as the artist's studio. We can't sleep in there but I like it up there. You can see the most of the old houses out the front windows and you can see the cemetery out the one on the side. Not much to see over there at night since there are no lights over the cemetery." Susie waited for my answer. So did Jenny.

This must be what they were planning. To scare me after all the nonsense they told me.

"Wasn't this place a hospital?" I knew it was, but I was stalling. I didn't want to play their game.

"Yes. Can't you tell?"

"Well, is it really haunted, or have you two just been trying to scare me all this time?"

Susie's eyebrows raised in disbelief, as did Jenny's, but Jenny started to smirk, and then she burst out laughing.

"I'm sorry, I couldn't help it. I knew you were scared of ghosts and we thought it would funny to play a joke on you. Come see." Jenny grabbed my hand.

My cheeks burned, I pressed my lips together tight and glared at Jenny.

I would obviously have to work harder on my face of fury, because Jenny ignored it and pulled me up the stairs. I reluctantly let her drag me up to the top floor. When we reached the top, a blurry figure was illuminated on the wall while eerie ghost sounds and clanging chains filled the room coming from a projector and boombox hidden under a table.

"I really don't think this is funny." I crossed my arms at the top of the stairs and squinted at them. "Why would you think it is funny at all to try and scare someone like this?" I turned and with my cheeks flaming, I stomped down the stairs.

"Shh." Susie ran down the stairs after me and pulled my arm.

"Why? No one's here."

"My dad doesn't want to have to come up and tell us to be quiet," Susie said, as her mouth turned to the side and she looked back upstairs.

"Why are you looking up there like that? Your pathetic attempt to scare me failed and your dad's not up there." I turned my arm out of her hand and shoved my own into my pockets.

"No, he's not, but Jenny is and she shouldn't be left alone up there." Susie was about to head back up when we heard something rolling across hardwood above our heads.

"Is she bowling?" I asked.

Alarmed, Susie took my arm and pulled me up the stairs after her.

"What was that?" Susie asked.

"I didn't hear anything." Jenny was on her knees, crawling under a table to unplug the boombox.

I crossed the room to see if Jenny had pool table balls or a bowling ball near her, but I froze when I noticed the padding under my feet. The whole room was carpeted with plastic mats under easels along the walls of the large open room. Clenching my fists and my jaw, and dread rising in my chest, I turned to Susie.

She chewed on her lip with her shoulders stiff near her ears.

"Are you playing games with me?" I had to ask, knowing she wasn't. I headed for the stairs. I shivered as the air suddenly chilled. I took a few more steps and the air turned stuffy and warm again. My eyes widened and I gripped the rail.

"Let's go." Jenny shivered, bounding down the stairs past me, leaving me behind on the top stair.

I didn't care if they were joking or not as I rushed down after Jenny. The hairs on my neck and arms stood on end and the painful tightening in my chest wouldn't let go.

Susie was right behind us, and then she was in front of us, as we headed down the next flight. We stopped on the main floor near the front double doors to catch our breath.

Jenny and Susie both bent over and laughed hysterically.

"You guys are toying with me." I was fed up with their antics.

"No, that was real," Susie said.

"Why are you laughing?"

"It was funny!" Jenny answered.

"No it's not."

"Maybe not for someone who is scared of a few ghost stories. It's just a bunch of noise," Susie replied.

"And cold air," I said.

"You felt a cold spot?" Susie asked.

"Yes!"

Susie didn't say another word as she headed for the pile of sleeping bags. "Do we want to sleep in here on the floor or do you guys want your own room?"

"Umm, I don't want to stay anymore. You guys have had your fun," I said, picked up my stuff, ready to go anyplace else other than where I was.

"Seriously, it's not a big deal." Susie unrolled her bag across the floor.

"Susie lives here. Nothing bad has happened to her. She's fine. It isn't a big deal. I think this is fun." Jenny had her bag and unrolled it next to Susie's. Jenny pulled my bag out of my hands and rolled it out next to hers. She sat down then patted the floor.

I had no choice. I couldn't call my mom to come get me. It was late and at least thirty minutes up the hill. Besides, she had never been to St. Mary's before. I resigned to stay, sinking down to my knees onto my sleeping bag.

Jenny opened a bag of chips. Susie handed me a soda. They told stories for hours. I tuned them out. I was the first to lie down and attempt to fall asleep. They giggled and talked about boys they thought were cute at school.

I always had insomnia in new places. Which became a huge issue for me as the room fell silent except for nasally breathing from Jenny and a bit more of a snore from Susie.

Moonlight spilled across the floor from the big front windows.

I don't know how long I had laid there but I was regretting the soda I had hours earlier. I sat up slowly. The floors upstairs creaked with old house noises as I crept my way to the bathroom on the other side of the stairs. At least I wanted to believe they were old house noises. My heart was racing as I turned on the light and closed the door. The bright light in the tiny space brought me some relief, but being completely alone didn't. I hurried to finish washing my hands. I paused with my hand resting on the door handle. I took a deep breath as I turned off the light, just before opening the door, so I wouldn't wake Jenny or Susie.

Right outside the door, the faint light of a transparent figure of a woman was in front of me. I stumbled backwards almost falling on my butt. I gripped the door frame with my eyes locked on the woman. She was faint at first, and then the all the details came into focus. She wore a long dress that would have touched the floor, but she hovered above it. I had never seen a nun before but I could tell she was one. Her head was covered in a habit.

She gazed up the stairs, in concern, and then searched around the room. I thought for sure she looked at me but she didn't acknowledge my presence as her hand pressed against her chest as if she was frightened and the other hand lifted her skirt as she hovered up the stairway.

I hesitantly took a few steps into the room to see where the nun had gone. My heart thundering in my ears made my head feel like it might explode. She hovered in the middle of the stairway and I saw the transparent figure of a boy wobbling at the top. She hurried the rest of the way up. The nun bent over the boy with protective arms to pull him closer as she looked around for help.

My eyes were transfixed on the nun as she led the little boy, whose legs were stiff with the ghostly braces he wore, away from the stairs. Something compelled me to follow her up to the second floor to see where she had taken him.

I scanned the room but she was gone. Soft humming of a lullaby and the creaks of a rocking chair on hardwood came from one of the rooms. When we had gone through all the rooms earlier, there had been no rocking chairs and all the floors were carpeted. I gripped the handrail tight.

The sound of little children giggling came from the far side of the room and rapidly swirled around, moving to the other side. Then the haunting giggles were right beside me as frosty air washed over me. The laughter filled my ears and it died down, moving away, until the giggles dissipated. I wanted to run down the stairs. I wanted to be anyplace else. I couldn't move because I was frozen with fear. The lullaby started again along with the rocking.

The tables in the room rattled. A man's wicked, cackling laughter whooshed up the stairs behind me. I ran from the sound over to the other flight of stairs leading to the top floor. I only made it up three steps when I froze again. The room was quiet once more and I didn't dare go to the top floor with everything that had already happened on the first and second. The pain in my chest was unbearable and I started to hyperventilate.

The main room on the second floor glowed red. The walls danced with a reflection of flames. On the ceiling, smoke swirled about in the room. A flash of light crossed in front of me. I tracked it over to the wall. Huddled in the corner was a panic stricken man, fearfully looking all around. Red and orange light flickered all over the room and grew brighter. I wiped my sweaty brow and coughed from the smell of smoke noticing that the temperature continued to climb. I jumped when a chill passed through me just as the back of the nun's head appeared in front of my face. I gasped. She walked through me on her way to the ghostly man on the floor. But there was no fire. The nun attempted to coax the man to leave with her but she was unsuccessful and struggled to pull him away from the wall. He slumped over instead as she continued to tug on him. She suddenly looked up at the ceiling and shrieked, covering her face with her arms. Then she and the man both evaporated at the same moment with the red and orange fiery light. The room plunged into darkness again as moonlight spilled in the windows across the floor. The temperature in the room was stuffy warm again and the smoke vanished.

I sighed with relief.

Something rolled across the floor above me. The same sound I had heard earlier that night. I couldn't help the tears that filled my eyes as I trembled. I made myself take a step down when a blast of air shoved me forcefully backwards. I landed hard on the stairs with the wind knocked out of me. There was no one there. I pulled myself up to sit, reaching for the edge of the stair with my heel to ease myself down to the next step. An air blast knocked me back again. Something took hold of my hands. It yanked my hands over my head and some unknown force dragged me up the flight of stairs.

"Help!" I yelled. My calls were muffled. Groans and moans echoed in the room above me. My arms were unable to pull away from whatever had me. But I could move my feet and I stuck one in between the rails. My foot stopped whatever pulled me up to the top story of what had been the insane asylum. I only stopped myself for a moment before my entire body was yanked away from the stairway, pulled all the way up until I was just above the landing. Once I was let go, I fell into a heap on the floor. It took me a moment to take in what had happened. I scrunched up in a ball to hide my head. I didn't want to see anything. The room echoed with the most wretched and anguished human sounds. But they weren't human at all because I was the only human there. I covered my ears. My hair swirled up in the air around my head and then it was yanked hard. I had no choice but to move my head where my hair had been pulled.

"Please, stop!" I pleaded, as I was shoved once more by air against the wall. All the easels in the room shook violently and crashed to the floor at once. Transparent figures roamed around the room. Then they all headed towards me, reaching for me. I pushed myself away with my heels as I slid along the wall crying. Men in straitjackets staggered towards me. Women with floating hair and no eyes reached for me. A couple of very thin children used only their arms to crawl across the floor in my direction. They didn't just moan and groan. They were saying words.

"They put me away, let me out."

"Set me free."

"Where's my mother? She left me here."

"They won't let me out to my find my gold!"

"They said I was crazy, I'm not crazy."

"Help us leave!"

The ghosts' pleas filled the room as they surrounded me. I held tight to my hair and clutched my head in silent terror. They pulled at my legs. I couldn't kick them off. They dragged me across the floor.

"Stop! Please stop," I cried. I reached for the table leg and took hold. Whatever had me pulled harder. I had to let go of the table when it turned over and crashed to the floor. They let me go in the center of the room, far from the stairs. My clothes were yanked in all directions. I screamed.

They were unrelenting.

"Set me free."

"Where's my mother?"

"They are going to steal my gold!"

"I want to go home."

The voices, next to my ears, cried out louder and louder.

"Please, oh please, in the name of Jesus Christ, I plead for you to stop! Please save me." I trembled all over, on my back, protected my head with my arms and pressed my eyes shut.

The room fell silent. The tugging stopped. Light permeated my eyelids even though I still had them tightly closed. Cautiously I started to open my eyes. Maybe Susie was there because she heard my screams and turned on the light.

I gasped. The light hadn't been turned on by Susie or Jenny.

Directly in front of me, the figure of the nun brightly illuminated the room. She stood between me and the all the other faint ghostly figures. She pointed for them to move away. They backed up slowly. The nun's ghostly face turned to look at me and smiled. Her eyes were not hollow like some of the others. She could see me and reached out to reassuringly touch my shoulder. I felt freezing cold where I should have felt her hand. She hovered over to the window to look outside. The light from her ghostly shape still filled the room. Every ghost in the room silently approached the windows.

Rattling chains and wooden wheels on gravel could be heard outside.

The nun floated over to the stairs and gestured for them all to depart. Each ghost either went down the stairs or disappeared through the floor.

"Thank you," I said.

The nun nodded then she followed the last ghost.

I could still hear rattling chains and what sounded like horses stomping, and protesting, outside. My heart still pounded as I pushed myself up off the floor and tentatively walked toward the window.

My jaw dropped as I watched a ghostly apparition of a horse drawn carriage pull up to the side of the building. No horses pulled it but I could still hear them and no one guided the carriage on top. It was longer than a normal carriage should be. Two doors opened in the back. I realized the carriage was meant for carrying off the dead as ghostly men carried the bodies of the ghosts that had surrounded me earlier, out the door, placing them one by one in the back of the carriage. Ghost after ghost was carried out. The last two figures to be placed in the carriage were that of the little boy in leg braces, and then the man in the fire. The last one out the door was the nun. She climbed into the back of the carriage, and paused to look up at me before she shut the doors.

The chains rattled with the sound of crunching gravel and horse hooves as the carriage floated away from the basement door disappearing into the night.

The house was absolutely quiet. Not even old house sounds. I shivered. I didn't shiver from cold because the room was stifling. Slowly at first, I headed for the stairs. I was afraid the ghosts or blasts of air would return to throw me against the wall again if I tried to leave, but they didn't. Once I knew they weren't going to stop me, I ran down every flight without pausing.

Jenny and Susie were snoring right where I left them. They never heard my screams for help. I would have run out the front door, but the carriage with all the ghosts had to be out there somewhere, so I buried myself under the sleeping bag. I didn't care if it was too hot. I moved as close as I could to Jenny on the floor and curled up in a ball facing her, pressing my eyes shut, desperate for sleep. I didn't want to see or hear anything in the house for the rest of the night.

While I lay there, my body throbbed with the pounding of my heart. Sweat dripped off my face.

At some point I must have fallen asleep because a sudden bright light startled me awake. I instantly sat up, covering my eyes with my forearm. Blinded, I struggled to focus my eyes on the dark figure with illuminating light as bright as sunlight around its head, hovered over me. I slid backwards in a panic. My back crashed into the ornate sofa. I pushed my long hair out of my eyes.

It was Jenny, holding my sleeping bag in her hand and laughing hysterically.

I was obviously very entertaining to her.

"Did you think I was a ghost?" Jenny let go of my sleeping bag.

"Umm, yes," I said, sitting up the rest of the way, attempting to tame my crazy, static covered hair.

"What happened to you? Why were you buried under the sleeping bag?" Susie asked.

"I saw ghosts last night. Far more than I ever wanted to see in my life," I said, taking a donut out of the box Susie held out in front of me.

They both laughed at me.

"I did. I'm sorry Susie, but I don't want to come back and stay the night here ever again." I stuck the donut in between my teeth and folded my sleeping bag in half to roll it up.

"I am sure you were dreaming." Jenny smiled at me as if she knew better.

I took a bite of donut and said, "Nope. It wasn't a dream. I saw a nun, and a little boy. There was horrible laughter and a man on the second floor with the nun in what seemed to be fire and smoke. I was pulled up the stairs to the top floor and was attacked by all the crazy people up there." I ran my hand over my head and pulled out a handful of loose hair. "See, they pulled my hair out. I screamed plenty but you guys were no help at all. You slept through it. But the nun saved me. She sent them all away. I watched as the ghosts were loaded up into a death carriage and left."

"You are just making this up to get back at us," Susie said. But her face showed me she wasn't all together sure I was making it all up.

"Go upstairs and see for yourself. They knocked all the easels over and the table too." I stuck the donut back in my mouth so I could finish cleaning up my things.

I knew they still doubted me as they ran up the stairs, chatting away.

Even though it was daylight, I still didn't want to go back up there, but Susie and Jenny had been gone too long. I took another donut and waited until I finished it before I found the courage to see what was taking them so long.

When I found them, they were setting up the easels in silence. I stood at the top of the stairs with my arms folded.

"I'm sorry I laughed at you, Kay. I believe you." Susie heaved the table back up on its legs. "At least once a week my dad says he has to come up here and fix all the easels. I guess we know why now."

There was something on the floor near her feet when she stepped away from the table.

I leaned over to pick up a beaded necklace with a cross that dangled at the bottom. I held it up to examine it.

"That's a rosary. My dad finds one in here every time the room is a mess like this," Susie said.

"It has to be from the nun. She probably left it when she sent all the ghosts away. I think we should leave it here for her. She is probably why your family is always safe," I said.

"Probably." Susie shivered just before she hung the rosary over the post to the handrail near the stairs. "I will tell my dad to leave it here."

When it was time to go, we said goodbye to Susie and headed for the car. I stood by the car door for a moment before I got in. Something reflected in the sunlight as it swung in the top floor window. I wasn't all together sure, but it looked like the rosary. If I could pick a ghost to see before I left, I would have chosen the nun. I decided I was never going to return to the very haunted St. Mary's Hospital.

***

I couldn't believe fifteen years had passed since that night at St. Mary's as I headed to Virginia City with my children and husband to take in the tourist sites for a family reunion. We drove up Six Mile Canyon Road so my husband could remember the good old days of when he rode up the mountain on a school bus. The road had been paved but was still as winding as ever. The canyon opened up and flattened out. To the left, the old St. Mary's Hospital was still there. Just like it looked fifteen years ago, with a fresh coat of white paint on the columns, railings, windows, and stairs. The only difference being that there was a sign and a historical marker in front and the cemetery wasn't the only neighbor to the old hospital. Not far down the back loop road was the new high school.

It took years for me to finally put the terror of my experience of the terrible night at St. Mary's out of my mind, convincing myself it must have been a really vivid nightmare. I continued to keep my anxiety in check as we passed the hospital to head up the steep road to Main Street.

Our enormous extended family clacked with every step along the boardwalk taking in all the tourist sites, which was every business down Main Street. Not much had changed since my last visit years ago.

The Bucket of Blood Saloon was still there. Outside the door of the noisy saloon full of slot machines and people, was a rack filled with a variety of pamphlets of sites to visit, and things to do in and around Virginia City. A pamphlet on ghost tours had been tucked in the rack near the top. It caught my interest with a picture of St. Mary's Hospital as the featured haunted attraction on the front. I opened it up to see what the pamphlet had to say:

St. Mary's hospital was established in the early days when Virginia City was a booming gold mining town. Financed by the state, and run by nuns, it charitably cared for the sick, the wounded, and the insane.

Now a residency art center, St. Mary's is still a very active place for paranormal activity and draws ghost hunters from around the globe. One of the most distinctive happenings are sounds of rolling hospital beds that can be heard overhead, even though the rooms above are heavily carpeted.

A nun is the most frequent ghost seen by guests. Many have suspected she is still a caretaker since she can be seen roaming the halls and checking the rooms. She prefers one particular room and when that room is checked, the bed is unmade. Several times the nun has been seen rushing to the aid of a polio stricken boy in leg braces. It is suspected that the nun died when she came to the aid of one of the male patients during a fire. She was unable to convince him to depart and they both perished.

The top floor was where the clinically insane were locked up and cared for. Many guests have reported a wide variety of unexplainable paranormal experiences on that floor.

The most unusual report has been of the arrival of a carriage that is for carrying off the dead. The carriage has been seen arriving and departing on several occasions, complete with the sound of horses, even though none can be seen.

My heart was racing when I stopped reading and closed the pamphlet. I realized I needed to close my mouth as well.

"Are you okay?" my husband asked.

"What?" I shook my head to clear my mind of the fear that took hold of me as it twisted painfully in my chest.

"You're white as a ghost."

I gave him a push, coming back to the real world. "Don't say that unless you have ever seen one." I folded the pamphlet and shoved it into the side pocket of my purse.

I said to myself, "Now I can honestly say I have."

I stood on the boardwalk and gazed past where the side street separated the high fronted old west buildings. Nothing obscured my view of old St. Mary's Hospital, lonely the way it had always been. The white columns and porch railings gleamed in the desert sunlight. I was quite content to observe the old hospital from a distance. The place appeared benign, regal and well-maintained, but the ambiance it exuded was still haunting.

THE CASTLE ON THE HILL

Joseph A. Lapin

My senior year of high school, Mr. Crawley, my A.P. psychology teacher, brought our class on a field trip to visit the closed-down mental hospital called Mass State Insane Asylum. We had studied the asylum in class, and it was disgusting the way they had treated mental patients— placing them in chains, experimenting with dangerous medical procedures and psychotropic drugs, diagnosing them with illnesses that led to the glowing machinery of electric shock therapy. It was all nuts to me. Mr. Crawley wanted the class to understand the dramatic changes and fads in the mental health practices in the last 250 years. Somehow, Mr. Crawley told the class, our field trip would illuminate today's mental health climate.

I didn't want to be there, for obvious reasons, and I sat in the middle of the bus, staring at the seat in front of me that looked like the skin of a rhinoceros. My visions were getting more intense, and I was terrified they would come out today in front of the entire class. I didn't want to go, but I couldn't bullshit my way out of it. Mr. Crawley wanted to know why I couldn't attend the field trip, but I didn't want to tell him about my mother. (He probably knew anyway.) So I was stuck.

And the worst part, the absolute nail in the coffin, was that Vika Stillman would be on the field trip. I had successfully avoided her the entire beginning of the school year. But that day, I didn't have a choice. Vika wasn't good for me. She was just a false flame.

Through the bus, I could hear laughter and other students yelling. Someone was hurling rolled up pieces of paper at the 'nerds' in the front of the bus. I sat in the middle. I wasn't a nerd or a cool kid. I didn't want to belong to any of those ridiculous groups. I heard Mr. Crawley yelling, but it all seemed to be happening away from me, far away, as if from another universe, even though we were all contained neatly in this god damn freaking yellow school bus.

We were driving East on Route 2, what was once the Mohawk Trail. It was fall and the trees were on fire with warm colors—reds, yellows, oranges, and the infinite frequencies in between—the harmonic spaces amidst the frets on a guitar or the keys of a piano, places you need to bend to reach. I loved those places.

Mr. Crawley was talking about how the Indians used to trek on this path to meet other tribes and hunt. All in front of me, as if it was the most natural thing in the world, Indians were walking with their families, Mohawks, tomahawks, hair dresses, shamans—a lost and ancient world. The medicine man was begging and pleading from the side of the road, dancing and dancing, imploring me to understand something with the rhythm of his body, an archaic language that could transcend time.

"What do you want me to understand?" I asked towards the window.

"You say something?" Kovac asked, his chin hanging over the bus seat. Neal Kovac was a friend of mine. One of the few. Kovac didn't belong in Kilroy, Massachusetts either. Kilroy was a working-class mill town that was northwest of Worcester. We were in the Guinness Book of World Records for the most bars per capita, and our claim to fame was that one of the companies in town invented the spork. We both desperately wanted to find our way out of the town and discover something special, something real. We talked about it often. How we wanted to get the fuck out of Kilroy. But I still didn't want him to know about my visions.

"Nothing," I said.

Then Kovac sat back down. I would have to be more careful. Sometimes I found myself talking out loud.

I could smell cigarette smoke coming from the bus driver. At least she had the window down. She always smoked. Her name was Agnes. Agnes had been driving this same bus for twenty years. She smoked every day, and she made it clear to Mr. Crawley, when he got on the bus that morning, that she was sure as hell not going to change her habits 'for some big-shot teacher.' When I got on the bus that morning, listening to Agnes tell Mr. Crawley how things were going to be, I had noticed there were leaves underneath my seat—Agnes must have left the window open the night before. Now I was rotating one of those leaves by the stem, looking at the veins, infinitely small, and the sections of tissue, of skin, and I couldn't help but see the similarity to my body, the destiny of my flesh. That's when Vika Stillman sat down next to me. I tried not to look at her. I didn't want to see her brown hair with streaks of blond highlights. I didn't want to see her green eyes the color of ripe limes. I didn't want to see her body covered by her clothes—a leather jacket and jeans—knowing what a pleasure it was to take them off.

"You're quiet," Vika said.

"Nothing to talk about," I said.

"A lot on your mind?"

"Just want to get this over with."

She scooted closer and I could feel her body next to me. I was still trying not to look at her.

"Haven't talked to you in a while," Vika said.

"That's the way I planned it."

"Why do you have to be so hostile?" She started to pat her pockets in her leather jacket as if looking for something. "I know this must be tough for you."

"Why would this be tough for me?"

Then she found what she was looking for. "Smoke?" Vika asked.

"You crazy?"

"No pun intended?"

Vika reached into her leather jacket and pulled out a pack of cigarettes. They were 100's. She made me nervous and excited. That ocean was beginning to rage inside of me again. I couldn't think of anything to say. Now I was looking at her bomber jacket, the white stuffing on the top. Then I snuck a glance at her dark jeans wrapped tightly around her thighs.

"Crawley will smell it," I said.

"Not while Agnes the Terrible is smoking."

Lighting the cigarette, Vika took a deep inhale with her large and soft lips. She wore bright red lipstick. I could see the cracks in her lips like the veins running along the leaf.

Vika rolled down the window, reaching over me, her breast resting gently on my shoulder. She blew the smoke out the window. From outside arose a smell of leaves burning. The air was getting colder this time of the year, and it meant the days were getting shorter, shorter, shorter, until it felt that night was an inescapable prison.

"What you think about all this?" Vika exhaled smoke towards the window.

"You're going to get in trouble," I said.

"I don't care about trouble." The red tip of the cigarette glowed. "So what do you think about this place? I bet you're pretty scared."

"I'm not scared," I said.

"Not even with," she said, "you know?"

Kovac peered back over the seat. "You're smoking?"

"Shut up, Kovac," Vika said.

"You're about as nuts as the people who used to live here," Kovac said.

"Sit down," I said. "Crawley will see."

Kovac looked towards the front of the bus to check on Mr. Crawley. Then he looked back at us. "So what do you think about all these crazies?" Kovac asked. "All those insane people living in one place. You can't get rid of something like that."

From the front of the bus, Mr. Crawley said, "Sit down, Kovac."

Kovac sat down. I looked out the window again. The bus was getting off Route 2 and heading into a densely wooded area. The leaves were falling from every tree. Each one dying right in front of us. No one seemed to notice.

"Don't listen to him," Vika said, "it isn't so scary. It's just a building. I'm going to sneak off and explore." She blew smoke out the window, and this time I felt her black hair on my shoulder. It smelled like spring. "Come with me? Prove you're not scared. Maybe it will help you."

"Help me?" I asked. "We'll get in trouble."

"Oh," she said. "You worry too much about trouble. Trouble this. Trouble that. What are you so scared of?"

"I'm not scared of anything."

I had a problem back then. As soon as someone told me I was scared, I wanted to prove them wrong. Now I had something to prove to Vika. I wasn't scared of an abandoned mental hospital. I wasn't scared that this winter my mother could stop taking her medicine again and be sent back to another hospital. I wasn't scared of the thought that my own destiny, my genetics, my blood were hurdling towards insanity. At least that's what I told myself.

And that's when I noticed Mr. Crawley walking down the aisle of the bus, his hands resting on the top of each seat. He was a cool teacher, liked to really make you think, but he would never have tolerated a student smoking on the bus.

"Who is smoking?" Mr. Crawley asked. His voice ended all noise on the bus except for the tires going over the asphalt, the wind coming in from the open windows, and the bus gears shifting and chugging. The smoke would soon give Vika away. I didn't know why at the time, but I grabbed the cigarette and held it between my fingers. The smell made me want to puke. I put the cigarette in my mouth. A smile went across Vika's face, and I felt her hand on my knee.

"Who is smoking?" Mr. Crawley asked again.

I raised my hand.

"My. Tully?" Mr. Crawley stood in front of me now. "I would have never expected this from you. What do you have to say for yourself?"

I looked at Vika, and she smiled. All the students were watching me. I felt on a stage. "Want a drag?"

Everyone on the bus broke off into peals of laughter.

Mr. Crawley grabbed the cigarette and threw it out the window. "This isn't like you, Mr. Tully. I'll be watching you."

For some reason, either the laughter from the bus or Vika putting her hand on my knee, I wanted to be on my absolute worst behavior for the rest of the trip.

***

Mr. Crawley forced me to sit next to him in the front of the bus. He wanted to keep an eye on me. Kept asking me if I was feeling all right. I kept telling him that nothing was bothering me. That I was fine. But he kept telling me that he knew something was wrong, and if I ever needed someone to talk to, I could talk to him.

The bus took a sharp and sudden turn, and I could feel gravel crunching underneath the bus tires. We were climbing up a steep hill, oak and maple trees surrounded the road, every once in a while a birch tree for contrast. The bus approached a black gate, and a security guard, dressed in a green uniform, walked up to the bus. The bus driver opened the door, and it closed in on itself like an accordion.

When the security guard walked into the bus, I noticed he had a gun in a holster. Why the hell would he have a gun was beyond me. So I listened to what Mr. Crawley and the guard discussed.

"Jimmy," the security guard said. "Long time."

Mr. Crawley hugged the security guard. "Frank. Always a pleasure."

So they knew each other. I listened to their conversation, and I heard them talking about high school. Maybe grew up together. I didn't care. But the next part of their conversation really piqued my curiosity.

"Nobody leaves the group," the guard said. "We close down at three."

"I'll watch them carefully," Mr. Crawley said.

"I'm with you the entire time."

"I think we'll be safe."

"It's not safe," the guard said. "Homeless people break in all the time. Leave their little parties all over the place. Be careful, anyone gets lost in the tunnels they might be gone for days. Then it's my ass."

"Don't worry about my kids," Mr. Crawley said. "They're good." Then he looked at me. "I'll keep an eye on everyone."

From studying about the hospital, I knew there was a series of underground tunnels that connected the wards. The tunnels were a part of the original design and an attempt to provide safe passageways for doctors throughout the entire building, ensuring that each ward and facility was connected and could be reached instantly. They served as a means for transporting patients, so the doctors could move them from ward to ward without walking in the snow. The tunnels also allowed patients to be shuffled around the hospital without the threat of escape. It was a labyrinth, and when the hospital was functioning, the tunnels became a place for nurses and orderlies to abuse patients out of view. It became a place to use experimental procedures and practices. It became a place to cage patients who were considered uncontrollable and a danger to society.

The security guard stayed on the bus, and Mr. Crawley and the guard caught up on *old times*. We drove up a hill, the road curving through the trees, and it was impossible to tell where the road was heading. Then the woods started to clear, fewer and fewer trees, until we left the woods like coming out of a cave. The first thing I noticed was an old cemetery with pathetic looking gravestones—a cemetery that seemed as old as the Revolutionary War.

"There she blows," Mr. Crawley said. "Mass. State Insane Asylum. Opened in 1843 and closed in 1992 due to, allegedly, budget cuts, changing medical practices, and lawsuits claiming massive abuse."

All the other kids were hanging out of the windows, looking at the monolithic brick structure, spires stretching to the sky—a castle standing on a hill like a great bird of prey. A nightmare, really.

"The hospital is set on 180 acres of land. A real estate developer's dream."

I didn't even want to look at the hospital, but what struck me were the size and the sense that this was a city, a medieval town, not a hospital.

"This is where the crazies lived?" Kovac asked.

"That's exactly the type of attitude I'm trying to correct," Mr. Crawley said.

The bus came to a stop at the main entrance of the hospital. Graffiti covered the brick walls near the ground. Neon reds, greens, and blue, indecipherable words, my generation's cave paintings. "Remember," Mr. Crawley said, standing up now, "actual people lived here. People who were told they were sick."

The bus stopped and we filed out of the bus and into the entrance of Mass. State Insane Asylum.

"Mass. State Insane Asylum was the crowning achievement in the field of the clinically insane," Mr. Crawley said.

While Mr. Crawley lectured, all twenty of us were standing in the main entrance of the hospital. We peered around the room. The wallpaper was peeling as if it had been licked by time and decay. Kovac walked around the room, gazing down hallways. The security guard hovered around us, keeping watch so none of us crossed any imaginary lines. There was a large staircase towards the back of the main entrance, and some steps were gone like a mouth missing teeth. White trimming in floral patterns ran along the sides of the stairs. Kovac started to walk up them when Mr. Crawley and the security guard yelled at him, momentarily stopping his monologue.

Mr. Crawley picked up the lecture again: "The hospital was designed in a style called Kirkbride architecture, a revolutionary idea that patients need a rural setting, a connection to nature..." Mr. Crawley walked around the class, trying to find someone who wasn't paying attention. He used awkward silence to keep our focus. But I was just looking around the entrance, staring up into the dome ceiling, listening to the sounds of feet, which I was positive only I could hear, shuffling upstairs. Though if the other students actually listened, they could hear them, too.

"Mr. Tully," he said, catching me staring off. "The hospital extends from this main entrance here in two wings, stretching two hundred yards to the east and west." Mr. Crawley looked at me as if he thought I had an answer for him. "Know why?"

I knew why. I did the reading, but I didn't understand why he was riding me. So I just shook my head no.

"The opposite ends of each wing, the farthest back you can reach on the ground level of the complex, were used for the patients considered to be the most violent and deranged. So as the patients recovered, the idea was that they would be moved through the wards, eventually to leave the hospital through the main entrance. To be sent back into the world."

Mr. Crawley turned towards the west wing. The security guard opened a metal door with wire covering a small window. The door opened to a hallway with a metal divider. On the right side was a sign for patients. On the left was a sign for staff and doctors. Instinctively, the other students walked along the side for the doctors. I walked along the side for the patients, watching my class through the spaces in between the linked steel. The security guard tapped on the gate with a Billy Club, letting me know that he was watching.

"He can't be on that side," the guard said to Mr. Crawley. "This is how it starts."

"James," Mr. Crawley said, "You'll be staying after for the next week. Not another deviation or I'll talk to the principal about suspension." He began to continue his lecture. "Patients used to be committed for behavioral issues which, today," Mr. Crawley said, "would be considered eccentricity or even developmental challenges."

I walked through the gate, when I noticed Vika walk through the patient's side behind me. I turned around and she smiled. None of the students were talking, and the silence made it feel like we were walking through a church.

"I guess you'll be joining us after school, too, Vika." Mr. Crawley opened the door at the end of the hallway into the first patient ward. "Soon after the hospital opened, the rooms became overcrowded with beds." He swung open the doors. "Men and women, often naked and emaciated, sat on their beds waiting to be examined by the doctors and nurses. Each day, a doctor had to see over two hundred patients. An impossible task. Originally, the hospital was built to accommodate 500 patients, but a few years after inception, the hospital became the home to over 2,000 patients."

Except for the stains left from the spaces where beds and furniture used to be, the room was empty. From the ceiling, water was dripping into a puddle on the red cement floor. I looked into the puddle and saw my face. Then Vika's too. She was so close to me. I could smell her. "Patients were committed for diseases like Monomania with pride—a pauper or someone with lower-class status possessing the ideas of wealth and grandeur. Funny how dreaming of moving up in class status was an illness." Mr.

Crawley smiled at his buddy the security guard. "Religious Monomania—a person who perceives herself to be immortal. And then there was Depressive Monomania—a disease found especially in females, defined by grief over the loss of a loved one."

Vika stood next to me, and she whispered, "Let's sneak off."

The whole class walked into the next ward through another steel cage. Through the doors was the kitchen. Steel tubs like hollow timpani surrounded an open grill with a vent that was overhead, so large the oven could have cooked for an entire army. The class walked into the next ward, through another steel gate, and the walls of that ward were covered in graffiti. The windows were broken, spider webs hung in between panes of broken glass, and the hardwood floor looked like it had been stripped away by rotortillers. That's when I noticed the guard wasn't paying attention.

What I was about to do was a horrible idea. Vika was just a bright candle that only burned for a fleeting moment. But I was going to go through with it anyway. That's when I grabbed Vika by her hand and pulled her into an open doorway. We walked down a pair of stairs, stood in the dark stairwell, and listened to the voices of the class fade away. I could feel Vika's hand clutching mine, her breath on my neck, and I didn't want to move away. Then I heard a spark and saw the flame from Vika's red lighter. I saw her face, her lips.

"See a light switch?" She moved the flame around the stairwell. Hanging above the light switch was a headlamp. She flipped the light switch, but no lights turned on.

I picked up the headlamp and put it on Vika's head. It looked like a crown of thorns. I took the red lighter from her. "You take the light. I'll take the lighter."

"Nice work, hero," Vika said, and she kissed me quickly.

I wanted to grab her right there.

"You ready?" I asked.

"For what?"

"You wanted to explore." I titled her head so the light pointed further down the hallway, and it looked like we were staring into a bottomless well, the space where light and shadow met looked like a black ocean. "There's a bunch of tunnels that connect the entire hospital."

"What about trouble?"

"I've come to like it since talking to you again," I said.

We walked down the stairs, the light bouncing off the walls, revealing faded graffiti. The walls were sometimes brick. Sometimes cement. I could hear water dripping from a pipe.

"You're really not scared?" Vika asked.

The tunnel was descending, and on our right were steel cages that ran through the hallway. The aisles were musky. Vika ran the flashlight along the wall, and we saw words written in spray paint. I couldn't make out their meanings, but they looked sometimes like they could be names, other times messages from the dead.

"Maybe a little."

"I can tell you are," Vika said. "See it in your face. I'm not scared though. Nothing scares me."

"Everyone has their fears."

"Everything is an adventure, James." Vika reached into her pocket and pulled out her box of cigarettes. Because the light was on her head, every time she looked at me I was blinded. "Smoke?"

This time it wasn't a cigarette. She lit a joint and I smelled the sweetness. I didn't like to smoke. I got paranoid. "You brought weed on a field trip?"

"How many people can say they smoked in the tunnels of an insane asylum?" She took a drag and moved her light to the side so it didn't blind me. "You're not scared, are you?"

I took the joint and drew on it defiantly. I prayed that I wouldn't cough as I watched the smoke illuminated by the flashlight.

"You think they're looking for us yet?"

"Crawley and that security guard are probably flipping a shit."

We both laughed.

"So is it hard being here?" she asked.

"I hate hospitals," I said.

"It's just an old building."

"Not to me."

Vika sat down against the wall, and I sat against the wall opposite her. The wall was jagged and cold. But I didn't mind because Vika's legs were close to mine.

"I've missed you," she said.

"Give me a cigarette."

"I want to understand more about your mother." She reached up and put her hands on my temples. Then she kissed my forehead. "I wasn't very good to you before. Tell me something nobody else knows."

Handing me a cigarette, I opened the flame on the red lighter. I puffed and prayed, again, not to cough. She wanted another secret. She wanted all my secrets. "Why?" I asked.

"Because maybe I'll give you a kiss for sharing."

"You can give me one anyway." I looked around at the tunnel, darkness thick on both sides. "A secret for a kiss?"

She nodded yes and put her hand on my knee. "Tell me what you're so scared of?"

"Fine," I said. "But you have to tell me one too. I know you're full of secrets." I held the cigarette and watched the paper burn. "I'll tell you why I usually hate cigarettes."

"No risk there."

"Wait," I said. "When my mother was in one of the hospitals, smaller than this, the doctors wouldn't allow her outside often. In fact, they didn't allow many patients outside. So my mother noticed that people were allowed outside if they were smokers. So she started smoking. When I see cigarettes, I think of my mother watching them on breaks, as if watching a clock, hoping the fire would never burn out. There's just something about that image that scares me. I don't know how to say it really. It's terrifying to think we can waste our time just watching the tips of cigarettes burn. I'm terrified that one day I will wake up and realized that I was never alive."

Taking the cigarette out of my hand, Vika extinguished it on the wall. Then she leaned in towards me, as if sharing the secret was an aphrodisiac, and she kissed me with those big lips, her tongue slipping against mine, and I felt her hand rubbing my chest.

"Feel alive now?" Vika asked.

"Tell me your secret," I said.

She stopped touching. "If you can catch me."

Then Vika bolted, running down the sinuous avenue, the light fading down the tunnel like watching headlights drive away on an empty street. I ran after her, not wanting to be alone in the dark, not wanting to be away from her. We were heading into a part of the tunnels where no words were written on the walls.

Vika stopped around the next turn. She was staring at the ceiling. There was a grate, and a ray of muted light was coming into the tunnel. We walked in and out of the light—that commodity—and suddenly Vika ran down another random path. There were more and more paths now, and we ran down each, chasing after the other, without any care for direction, without any fear, running through the darkness without any idea of where to stop. We ran for the pleasure of it, for running together.

Trying to catch her breath, Vika stopped in front of me, allowing me to be nearer to her. That's when I noticed the flashlight was fading. I didn't want to make a big deal out of it and scare Vika. So I grabbed her hand and pulled her into an opening in the wall.

"I told you already," she said, "there's nothing to be scared of."

She turned around. There was a metal cage. On the wall in the cage were newspaper clippings taped to the wall and some black and white photographs. There was an empty chair with restraints on the arms. And that's when I heard the first scream.

"Know where we are?" Vika asked.

"You hear that?" I asked.

"Hear what?"

"I think we missed a turn."

"Oh no," Vika said. "We're lost."

"So you didn't hear that scream," I said.

"You didn't leave a trail?"

I walked over to the wall and sat down. The light started to flicker. "Shit," I said. Then the light went out.

For a few moments, we sat in the dark, listening to the water plunking into a puddle, slowly; with each drop, the water dripped in time and became, dramatically, stalactites and stalagmites. The puddle became a subterranean lake, which stretched into darkness.

"I had no fucking idea you weren't paying attention," Vika said. "How did we get so lost?"

"I'll get us out of here," I said like some cartoon adventurer. "Maybe we are nearer the end wings?"

"Closer to where they keep the violent patients?"

"Where they once kept the violent patients," I said. "We'll be fine."

The light flickered back on, illuminating a puddle and the shadow of something that appeared to be moving. I wasn't sure what it was at first, but then I realized it was the shadow of a man far down at the end of the hallway.

"Shit," I said.

"What's wrong?"

"You see something?"

"No!" Vika said. "Did you?"

Vika was holding onto me now. Fear, as well as secrets, seemed to be an aphrodisiac. That's when I heard the next scream, a lightning bolt in the darkness.

"Oh man," I said.

"What now?"

The light flickered off. I couldn't quite tell the gender of the scream. It reverberated as if the walls were made of ringing bells.

"You didn't hear?" I asked.

"Hear what?" Vika asked.

"The scream."

"Don't fuck with me right now."

"Nothing to be scared of."

"Now you say that."

The flashlight flickered on again, finding some life. And again, I saw the shadow, nearer now, maybe fifteen feet away, and with each flicker of the light, the shadow was closer, like someone walking through a strobe light.

"When I say go," I said, "get ready to run."

I felt her hand tighten. "You see something?"

"Ready?"

Then Vika took off running down the hallway, away from the shadow, the light flickering on her head as she ran. I ran after her, trying to follow her words, until I found myself completely in the dark, alone, without the sound of her voice. I still had the lighter, and I wished that she had it now with the headlamp going out. I ignited the flame and tried to find my surroundings.

That's when it started. A light appeared behind me. A white light so bright I felt pulled towards it like a magnet. I turned a corner and approached a room. A doctor walked in. A patient was sitting on a bed. I saw the doctor making motions for his patient to stick their fingers down their throat, inducing vomit.

"Keeping the bowels," the doctor said as if giving a demonstration, "in free action is indispensable in all cases of insanity. In melancholia, vomiting is decidedly more useful than in mania."

The doctor was talking to me. I kept telling myself that it was all an illusion. That it was just another vision. But it felt real. I could hear voices and smell bleach and human decay.

"The madness is in the patient's blood," the doctor said. "Removing the blood will help fix him. You start by abstracting blood by puncturing in frontal, nasal, or orbicular veins, or in the venae raninae under the tongue." Then the doctor laughed. "Bleeding from the feet or ankles is my favorite method."

Behind the doctor, the patient was bleeding from his ankles, his nose, and the space under his tongue with a look of terror as if he had become an animal, the doctor a great bird waiting to peck out his liver.

Then the vision vanished like a movie projector shutting down. I clicked the lighter back on. Water dripped from black pipes. I heard Vika scream. I moved down the hallway, using my hands to guide along the walls, trying to head towards the sound of her voice. "Vika!" I said. "Can you hear me?"

"James!"

Her voice sounded different. I saw the light again pronouncing another vision, that magnetic noise, coming from around a corner. The vision took over the hallway, and that strange white light illuminated it. Then I saw a tub in the middle of the room, and three orderlies dragged in a boy, kicking and screaming. The boy was about my age.

"As you can see, James," the doctor said, "the boy is being dunked into the water. Each time he is held under twenty seconds. An attempt to jolt his madness into submission."

Each time the boy came out of the water, he was too out of breath to scream. Then he was dunked in the water again.

A patient in a hospital gown was wheeled into the room on a gurney. The tubs disappeared but the room stayed. There was something in the back of the room, hidden in the shadows. The doctor walked over to the patient. He had a needle now in his hand and pressed down on the plunger: "Patient is being given thiopental, a temporary anesthetic."

The doctor stuck the patient with the needle and pushed down the plunger. The doctor placed electrodes on the patients' head. The power was turned on and the patient was sent into a seizure. The voltage threshold measured by age and sex. The electrodes stopped sending pulses and the patient came to a rest like a potato at the end of a microwave cycle. Attached to the patient's head were wires which glowed like nerve endings in the temporal lobe. The light grew and followed the wires, revealing that the wires were connected to a large black machine, throbbing like a heart. Men in gowns were recording numbers on paper from the dials on the machine. It was a perfect machine—quiet, still, but imposing.

I was frozen, in awe of the machine. It struck fear into me so intense I thought the blood running through my veins would just stop. I couldn't quite make out all the parts of the machine—it seemed infinitely complex—all the electrical work, the gauges, and the high definition computer screens. It was obvious that the machine could exist without the assistance of a human, but it could not work without the poor, poor patient. The machine had been feeding.

Another scream. The light in the room disappeared. The sound of the scream was close now. I turned around the corner when I saw the shadow again. This time, I didn't move, and I clicked on the lighter and waited for the shadow to step into the light. I wouldn't run away again. I wanted to define the shape—the thing that terrified me. Then the shadow walked into the light and, standing before me, was an image of myself. I was older and standing against the wall in a straitjacket. I rolled around the walls. Then the vision of myself became the geometry of innocent bones, a sun bleached skeleton, a jaw dropping and clenching, dropping and clenching as if controlled by a ventriloquist. Then the scream. All I could hear was the scream, pounding on my ears like bass drums. The scream. The scream. The scream.

"James!"

I could hear Vika now. Nothing was before me anymore. My body was still together. I was still breathing. Vika sounded near. "Keep calling my name," I said.

"Are you close?" Vika asked.

"Keep talking."

"I'm scared James."

"I'm about there."

I turned around a bend in the tunnel, and I could hear Vika's voice.

"James," Vika said, "I'm over here."

I clicked on the lighter, and I saw Vika crouching in the corner, her leather jacket draped over her shoulders. I grabbed her hand, and we walked together down the hallway.

***

It seemed like we had walked a couple miles when I saw the light again, glowing like headlights approaching from the opposite side of a desolate road. I thought it was another vision. I didn't think I could take another one. But when we got to the light, it suddenly opened to blue sky and the reds, yellow, oranges—the colors of autumn. Leaves were falling from trees onto the green grass, resting like splashes of paint. I was holding Vika's hand. She was holding mine, too. There was a steel gate that had been broken open. We walked out through the gate.

In front of us was the cemetery and the hospital was behind us. It was where the patients were buried. Instead of names, the tombstones had numbers on a cross. On the hill, overlooking the tombstones, I saw the same medicine man on Route 2, and he was dancing, his body moving to inaudible music. He was singing a song, standing next to a tree that was on fire with the autumn foliage. But the tree actually looked like it was engulfed in flames. His voice sounded deep and rough. The branches were crackling and falling to the ground. Vika wasn't looking at the Indian or the tree. She was just staring into the tombstones. She couldn't see the Indian or the tree. If only she would open her eyes.

Once again, the vision was gone, and I looked at all the trees and focused solely on the red leaves. I reached down and picked one of the red leaves off the ground. Holes were torn through them and they looked like they had been partially devoured. Now I understood what I was supposed to see. A red so dark that I knew that our country, our land, has been stained by a blood so deep it runs through our roots, the tissue in leaves, our skin, our veins. That our visionaries, our prophets, have been buried under logic and fear. And maybe visions, madness, and mental illness was a gift.

Behind us, Mr. Crawley and the other students were running towards us, screaming our names, asking us if we were all right. But I paid them no attention.

"What are you looking at?" Vika asked, still holding on to me.

"It's just a crazy world."

CORRIDORS

Brent Abell

Jason Howe awoke to a pounding sound in his ears echoing all the way through his skull and rattling his brain. His eyes opened a sliver, slowly letting in the dim light but it burned so he slammed them shut again. Cautiously, he lifted his lids a crack again. When his eyes adjusted to the light, he opened them fully and scanned the area surrounding him. The hallway he sat in suffered from a complete absence of color. Jason sat on a cold tile floor in alternating white and black checkered squares and the walls, furniture, and pictures were all gray. Even the flowers in the pot next to him were devoid of color. In his sixteen years of life, it was the dreariest place he'd ever seen.

Standing up, Jason turned his head from side to side, listening for anybody or anything that could tell him where he was. Nothing but silence answered back. He reached into his shorts and pulled out his iPod. After nestling the ear buds in, he tried to use the receiver to find a radio station, but all he heard was static on every station. Flipping through the artist list, he settled on shuffle and shoved the iPod back into his pocket. Focusing back on the hallway, he took note of doors on either side.

Maybe I can find someone in one of the rooms, he thought as his tall, lanky body started to walk towards the nearest door; Room 403.

Jason reached out and took hold of the closest door's knob and turned. The doorknob didn't budge and a cold chill radiated from it, sending an icy flash up his arm until he quickly pulled his hand free. Starting with his fingertips, he felt his arm grow numb. Jason violently shook his hand up and down, back and forth in a vain effort to get some feeling back. Glancing down at his fingers, he saw the tips start to darken and fade to black. It reminded him of the frostbite pictures he'd once seen on the Discovery Channel.

Jason stood stunned for a moment and as the fog cleared from his head, he wondered what he should do now. He looked back at his fingers, noting they started to return to their regular color as he felt the blood rush back through his arm. The tingle of it hurt, but he shook it off.

The silence really unsettled him. He walked down the corridor past a few rooms and stopped in front of Room 412. Jason took a deep breath and tried the doorknob. This time he heard the latch disengage and he slowly swung the door open. The dreary room suffered from the same gray motif the hallway was decorated in. Only a desk sat in the middle of the room, devoid of anything on top. Jason saw a window behind the desk with the blinds pulled down. Walking over to the window he stopped and looked at the desk more closely.

Photos were strewn all over its surface. Picking them up, he saw the images were blurry and he couldn't really make out anything in them. Some looked like they had a small black dot with a bright white aura around it. In others, the spot was bigger while some were just plain white. Tossing the pictures back down, he approached the window and took hold of the blinds. Pulling them up, he hoped to look out on a parking lot or something that would give him a clue to his location. When the blinds were fully drawn up, he found the world outside to be black.

Jason stared at his reflection in the window. His long brown hair had escaped from its ponytail and it looked like he hadn't washed it in a few days. A flicker of light flashed outside. The split second of light illuminated nothing; it was as if the dark consumed the quick sparkle. He stared at his reflected green eyes and sighed; for the first time in his life, he felt lost. Turning away from the window, he trudged toward the door with no answers, just more questions and a splitting headache. Jason opened the door and stepped back into the hallway.

Jason looked back and forth down the gray corridor again. The end of the hall looked to have an elevator and he wondered if it worked. Since there was some light in the building, he knew there was electricity. If the elevator failed to work, he hoped he could find some stairs close by. Turning to head toward the elevator he heard it for the first time - a low rumbling growl that echoed though the empty halls. Jason stopped in his tracks and cautiously turned around.

At the end of the corridor, the lights started to slowly flicker off. It continued like a wave of black washing toward him and then he heard it again. This time it was an ear-splitting roar that shook the drab pictures from the wall and shattered the gray pot, spilling the plain flowers all over the place. Jason noticed even the dirt lacked color of any kind. He tried to move, but his feet were stuck in a puddle of fear. Jason looked down and saw the floor had taken on the consistency of mud and his shoes were sinking. Pulling his legs with all his might, he broke free and ran to the elevator doors. The roaring approached him swiftly from the other end of the hall. He pounded the button, but the light never came on to indicate the elevator was coming for him. He spun around and saw a door marked 'stairs' off to his left. The sounds coming out of the encroaching darkness neared him as he bolted towards the stairs. The air changed around him as something lashed out at him from the black. It barely missed Jason as he dove to the floor and quickly bounced back to his feet. Opening the door, he slammed it shut as he felt the door buckle on its hinges from the blow it received from the other side.

Then as swiftly as it started, the building grew silent again.

***

Jason looked up and he was on the top floor; the only way to go was down. He leaned over the railing to see how many floors there were and he counted four. His breath came in short raspy bursts as he sat down on the stairs. Jason hung his head down between his knees and stared down at his shoes. The skulls on his canvas skate shoes stared back, each one frozen in the act of laughing. His iPod shuffled songs again and the sounds of heavy metal filled his head. Whatever that thing was, he knew it couldn't go up, so it must have backtracked to where it came from. The silence in the building was killing him.

"What was that thing and why are there no people? Why the hell am I talking to myself?" He asked nobody in particular as his voice echoed down the stairwell.

He stood back up and decided to try his luck on a different floor. The dilemma Jason found himself in was what floor would he go to? Did the creature go down one floor, two floors, none at all? Cracking his knuckles, he turned and faced the dented door that he had just passed through.

"I hope it moved on," he tried to reassure his self as he turned the knob and reentered the floor.

The first thing he looked at was the floor and was relieved to see it was solid again. He gingerly walked over the previously gooey spot and started to walk down the hall. Jason stopped before he reached the edge of the lights; the hallway from where the beast came was pitch black. Taking a step, he tried to move into the dark.

Jason slammed into the dark and fell backward like he walked straight into a brick wall. Letting out a loud cry of surprise, he quickly held his breath. The blackness of the hall remained silent; the roar he expected never came. He slowly got up off the floor and reached his hand out. His fingers came into contact with something in front of him he couldn't see and he pushed on it. The invisible barrier did not budge and his fingers bent back until the pain caused him to pull them away.

"Not going this way," he said as he turned back toward the door. He looked at it and shivered. Around where the beast hit the metal door, there was a dark viscous fluid dripping down. Jason bent down and lightly poked at it. It felt gelatinous and cold. He wiped it on his pants and backed down into the stairwell.

Maybe the thing hurt itself when it collided with the door, he thought and he sure hoped it did.

A hurt monster should be easier to escape from than a perfectly healthy one, Jason reasoned. He started down the stairs and decided to roll with whatever might be behind the door.

***

The door opened into another silent and gray hallway. He blinked and looked again, because it looked exactly like the previous floor, except he didn't see the dent in the door from his encounter with the thing in the hallway. Cautiously, he approached the first door and looked at the number, Room 307. Remembering the door handle from the first door he tried, he laid his finger on it and waited. His finger just sat there and it didn't get cold or turn black, so he gripped it and turned the handle.

The room was like the hall and the other room in every way, even the desk sat in the same location. He moved closer when he noticed that the stack of paper on top was a lot taller than the other desk. He picked up the pile and started to flip through the images. Unlike before, these had clear pictures he could see. The pictures were from Christmas at home, from school, and from vacation. They were pictures of him with Claire.

"What the..." he muttered as he tore through the photos.

Jason's grip slipped and the photos fell to the ground. He frantically shuffled through the rest of the pile on the desk and found they were all from about the same time period. He stopped when he heard a loud banging in the hall. Jason returned to the door and opened it just a crack. The lights were beginning to flicker again. He stuck his head out the doorway and looked both ways. The far end of the hall blinked into darkness, but it was silent, no noise accompanied the darkness.

He broke into a run as he flung the door open and took off back toward the stairway. The lights around him surged brighter and when they did, the creature made his presence known with a loud, painful, earsplitting roar. The lights surged again and Jason stopped. The darkness was being held at bay, it no longer advanced down the hallway. The roar of the thing faded to the whine of a kicked dog. Something in the lights wounded it and wounded it bad. The air around Jason felt as if it was being charged. The lights pulsed one last time and blew out, shattering all over the floor.

The other end of the floor remained silent. Jason reached out toward the dark and his fingers penetrated the gloom in front of him. Taking a small step forward, he walked forward toward the other end where the creature was waiting.

Jason was able to walk unhindered down toward the sounds of muffled cries. They were high-pitched and hurt his ears even though he had music blaring into his head.

When he got to the place where the blown out bulbs ended and the unnatural dark began, he hit the invisible barrier. This time he was feeling out in front of him so he didn't just hit it and fall. Jason squinted his eyes and tried to see if he could make anything out past the wall of darkness. He heard movement and backed away. Suddenly, he felt the temperature shift to freezing and a piercing cry rang out throughout the building. Jason could only stand in stunned silence as the beast made itself known.

As it crossed the barrier, the light bulbs began to shatter again, plunging the hall into an inky blackness. Jason finally got a good look at it before the lights were extinguished. It stood on four legs like a dog and was the color of the blackest night. It was covered in a coarse fur that stood out like quills on a porcupine. Jason broke free of his paralysis when it charged at him. The eight tentacles around its huge oval mouth frantically tried to grab hold of him as he backed away. It reminded him of something he read in an H.P. Lovecraft story, a monster with tentacles coming to earth to enslave it. The mouth came close to Jason's head as he ducked away, but he couldn't escape the smell of death and rot on its breath. The razor sharp teeth chomped down at him as he backed away even further. Before the thing could get its strength back, Jason turned and ran.

***

Jason's footfalls thundered down the hall as he sped toward the door. In a snap decision he decided to run back upstairs. He thought that the monster wouldn't think he would backtrack. Throwing open the door, he took the steps two at a time, reaching the top in a few short moments. The stairwell behind him remained silent. He stopped and listened and finally he heard a thumping sound. It sounded like a herd of elephants rushing toward the stairwell. When the thundering stopped at the door to the stairs it fell silent again. Jason put his hand over his mouth to try to stifle his panting.

Below, the beast stopped and listened. Jason could see it sniff the air. It licked the handrails and looked up. Jason dived back out of view, but his iPod fell out of pocket and clattered down the stairs, landing by the clawed feet of the beast. It glanced up and started to climb the stairs toward Jason.

Running back into the hallway, he slammed into the barrier and fell to the floor. He shook his head in disgust and started to rise. Once he was on his feet, he turned about the time that the lights started to blink out. On his right was a door. The barrier kept him from going down the hall, the beast kept him from using the stairs, so he guessed that the door was his last option. Jason rushed to the door and saw the room was 410, and turning the knob, he went inside.

***

The room was like all the rest, plain and cold. Like the other rooms he had been in, a single desk sat in the middle and two windows were centered on the wall behind it. A stack of papers sat perfectly in the middle. Jason picked up the pile and looked at the first pictures. They depicted him skating on a half-pipe in his friend Chase's yard. He flipped through and found that the next image was just a little later then the first and formed a flip book of him falling on his ass. Below were more blurry pictures that looked like Claire, but she had some sort of spot on her head. In each sequential shot, the spot in the middle of Claire's head grew. He shook his head and placed the papers back on the desk.

Jason stood there and stared, empty and vacant at the windows. The lightning that he witnessed earlier had returned and the storm raged outside. He found it odd that he didn't hear any thunder crashing. The room's silence unnerved him.

Oh, Claire where are you now? I need you, he thought and stared at the photos of her some more. His gaze lingered on one of them at prom. He sported a black tux and she wore a crimson red cocktail gown with a low top and a large slit up one leg.

She didn't wear red, she wore blue. She wore the color that matched her eyes.

The lightning flashed again and he wiped the sweat forming on his brow. The room grew warmer and a sweet aroma filled his nostrils.

The perfume I bought her for that night...

He picked up the picture and stared at her image. A large darker red spot appeared on her stomach. Black and blue lines wrapped around her neck and her bright blue eyes bulged out of their sockets. Her full red lips faded into a cold-looking blue hue and he could make out the dark veins in her cheeks and forehead.

She looked dead.

She was dead and he missed her.

Something slammed into the door and the picture slipped from his grasp. Spinning around, he saw the door to the room splinter from the force of the impact. Wood pieces showered into the room when the door gave way and exploded inward.

Jason stood stunned and watched the thing move slowly toward him, each clawed paw clicking on the tile floor. The tentacles waved at him and its teeth gleamed in the lightning glow from the windows. Its breath was labored and it swayed from side to side as it approached him. Jason never moved, even when the tentacles reached out to grab him, he stood his ground. The creature stooped lower and stared Jason into its eyes. Beneath its skin, he spied something sliding around. He watched as a hand shape pushed the skin trying to break free. A face pushed against the skin and stretched it out like a thin membrane. Each forward thrust brought the face closer to the surface. The creature hunched over and locked eyes with Jason. It exhaled heavily, blowing its rotted breath in his face. He winced as it burned his eyes, but he kept its gaze. Neither blinked and the raging storm blew outside the window.

Then it struck.

Jason was still staring into its eyes and trying to follow the writhing under its flesh when two of the tentacles snatched his arms and started to drag him closer to the thing's gaping maw. Lost in a building alone, Jason resigned himself to the fate before him. He closed his eyes and waited for the crushing of his bones by the large sharp teeth. Suddenly, the air in the room charged and a bright light exploded all around.

I miss her. I love her.

The blood…

The beast howled in agony and dropped Jason to the floor. He rolled away from the thing's claws and dove behind the desk while it thrashed around in agony.

I wish I could see Claire one last time.

Oh my god the blood…

The room exploded in light again. This time when Jason looked out, the creature had started to fade. It was no longer the inky black thing that was trying to devour him; it was the same gray color of the rest of the building.

It should have been me.

Why her?

My hands…

When Jason finished his thought, the light bulbs exploded around the room, plunging the room into total darkness. He could hear the labored breathing of the beast on his left and he made out its form when the lightning flashed outside the window. Then the breathing stopped. Jason said a silent prayer in his head. He moved along the wall to where he knew the thing laid. Feeling its hide with his foot, he prodded it harder. The lump under his foot remained quiet and still. He let out the breath he didn't realize he was holding and turned around.

A tentacle flew up into the air and wrapped around Jason's neck and started to choke him. It moved so fast that Jason was caught before he even realized what happened. The black appendage squeezed harder and he felt the wind leave his lungs. The beast let out a loud roar of victory and tightened its vice-like grip on Jason. His arms and legs flailed about as his vision blurred. The thing bit down on his hands. Sharp teeth tore through his wrists, severing tendons and shredding his muscles like paper. He heard his bones crunch in the dark and the mouth ripped the last of his hands free from his body. The remaining stumps sprayed blood on its face and it licked the red rain from its mouth. Shock began to set in, but he felt his tongue lop out of his mouth as it swelled. Before he gave in to the infinite black, he saw one last flash of light and then darkness swallowed him.

"I've waited for you my dear. I love you forever and ever," the beast whispered.

Claire?

***

"Nurse! Quick we need a doctor to Jason's room!" the orderly shouted and fumbled for his keys.

Inside the room, Jason screamed, "Claire", over and over again. The overweight orderly peeked inside the door's window and watched Jason thrash around uncontrollably.

"My hands! It was my hands! Oh God Claire I'm sorry!" Jason cried out and fell to the floor. Blood soaked through his straitjacket and pooled on the black and white checkered floor around him.

The orderly backed off when the on–duty doctor and three nurses rushed to the door. The doctor fished in his pockets for the keys and quickly unlocked the door to one of the solitary confinement rooms. The doctor dropped to the floor and tried to stop Jason from flailing around. "My hands! I know what my hands did!" he repeated over and over.

"Nurse, help me get this off him!" the doctor yelled to the closest one.

The nurse rushed to the restraint buckles and with her hands shaking, undid the arm loops behind Jason's back. His arms swung out and splattered blood on the gray wall. It dripped down the padding and gave the room its only color besides the white, black, and gray.

"She took them! She came for them!" Jason continued his episode, but the blood loss had begun to slow him.

The orderly swept in behind him and plunged the needle into his leg. Jason's thrashing slowed as the happy liquid coursed through his veins and calmed his system.

"Where is all the blood from?" the nurse asked and backed away.

"Help me get the bindings off," the doctor said and tugged on the crimson jacket.

The coppery smell sickened the orderly and he backed away, tasting the bile rise in the back of his throat.

The nurse screamed and covered her mouth.

The doctor stared at Jason in stunned silence. His arms slipped from the straightjacket and he fell back to the floor with the bloody stumps where his hands were waving in the air.

"I did it. With my own hands I did it... She took them from me..." Jason muttered in a drug induced haze. "I killed her..."

ROSE WING

Denzell Cooper

Cindy gripped the crowbar as she read the sign. It was small and simple: black lettering on a yellow background. No trespassing. It was attached to a seven foot fence that had been made from corrugated steel and topped with barbed wire.

Jason stared at her. "This is stupid. You're not going to do this so let's just get out of here." He kept the engine running.

Tall trees overhung the lane from the other side of the road. One in particular reached long branches over the fence. "Right where she said it would be," said Cindy. She breathed deeply to settle her nerves.

"Mum, this isn't you."

"I have to know what happened to her, Jason."

"And I said I'd help you to find out, but we've done that. We know she ended up here. Isn't that enough?"

Cindy shook her head. "No, it's not enough. Rachael was my mother."

"But breaking and entering?" He raised his eyebrows. Not disapproval, just shock.

283

The nurse hadn't recognised the name. There had been no Rachael Cavendish at the hospital when she worked there. What about Rachael Ainsworth? No, not a name she remembered, but the hospital kept meticulous records. It was possible that they were still inside.

"She just disappeared without a trace," Cindy said. "I need to know if she died here."

Jason let out a breath. "OK." He turned off the engine and nodded. "Let's go."

She shook her head. "No, you're staying here."

"I'm not letting you go in there alone."

"You can't come with me, it's too dangerous." If they got caught it would be her fault. Jason had been out of prison for a month and a half and he'd go straight back to serve the rest of his sentence.

She got out of the car.

So did Jason. "I can't let you go on your own," he said, opening the back door and taking a tow rope from the back seat. He pointed the keys at the car and set the alarm with a click. "You've never done anything like this before." He leaned over the bonnet and held out the rope.

Cindy ran her fingers through her hair. She looked at the fence and the sign. He was right, she had never done anything like this. Reluctantly, she nodded and took the rope from him, handing him the crowbar to throw over the fence.

The lane ran along the southern end of the hospital grounds, but the steep slope meant the patrolling guards never checked it. Cindy had always been a tomboy. She had spent her youth picking fights and climbing trees. Still holding the rope, she pulled herself up into the branches of the tree with practised ease and climbed out on the overhanging branch. She tied the rope to the other end and climbed down. Jason had spent six months in prison for breaking and entering, but he had always used brute force. By the time he had negotiated the climb over the fence, Cindy was at the top of the slope looking out over the grounds.

"To die here," she whispered, "all alone and without any family."

The main asylum hospital—three imposing, Victorian buildings—stood some five hundred yards away over open grass. They were built of red brick and iron. A guard exited a small prefab cabin that had been placed to one side. He lit a cigarette and started to walk around the building, a torch lighting his way as he checked doorways and windows for signs of forced entry.

At the edge of the grounds, just a short distance from where they lay hidden, the crumbling remains of a smaller building looked foreboding in the failing light. It, too, was made of red brick and iron, with boards over the windows and doors.

"That's it then," Jason said.

Cindy nodded. "The mortuary." According to the nurse, an underground tunnel connected it to the main buildings. When the hospital was operational, the tunnel had allowed corpses to be carried unseen across the grounds. Cindy turned to look at Jason. "Are you going to be OK in there?"

"We don't have any choice."

She sighed. "No, we don't."

***

The door hadn't been opened in eleven years, seven longer than the rest of the asylum. It was made of solid steel with no glass and a gap of only millimetres between it and the door frame. A chunky handle and a round keyhole were its only features.

Inside the hospital it wasn't dark, it was black, like being underground. It reminded Cindy of an open air museum where she had been taken into a mine shaft to experience what it was like. Jason had stayed above ground that day, so as they stood in the dark at the top of a stairwell, she knew what it cost him to accompany her here. He nervously turned his torch in every direction.

"You can stay here," she said. "You don't have to come with me."

The walk through the maze of connecting tunnels had been uneventful but slow. Coloured lines still remained to guide their way, as they had for the staff when the hospital was still operational. Cindy had watched as Jason swept the torch back and forth. Deep breaths and her constant reassurance kept him moving forward. She wondered how he had coped in prison; even as an adult he had to sleep with the lights on.

"I'll be fine."

He didn't look fine, but she didn't push the matter. He wouldn't thank her for making a fuss. She put her key in the lock and tried to turn it, not surprised to find it stiff.

The Rose Wing, the department that treated violent illnesses, had employed almost four hundred nurses during its seventy years of operation, with some handing in their notice after only a few weeks. The nurse Cindy had tracked down had put the high staff turnover down to the atmosphere rather than the patients. She was one of the two staff members who were at work on the last day, when the door to the Rose Wing was locked for the last time. She had cautioned Cindy against going in, even as she handed over the key.

"We'll be as quick as we can," Cindy said to Jason as she strained with effort against the lock. Finally the key turned and it clicked open.

She turned the handle and pushed but it wouldn't move. She put her shoulder to it and pushed hard, feeling it give a little, but still it didn't open. Standing back, she examined the door with the torch beam, looking for any other locks that she might have missed. There were none.

"Let me try," Jason said, handing her his torch. He gripped the handle, turned it, and put all his weight into the push. Grunting with effort, he pushed it open by a few inches, but struggled to move it any further. "Something must have fallen down behind the door," he said.

Cindy put one of the torches on the ground so that it would light the door and between them they pushed against it. It opened slowly. Her shoes slipped on the tiled floor and she had to walk to keep herself upright, but she kept pushing. A few more inches opened up and she reached around the side, hoping to move the obstruction. Cold air blew against her hand and she pulled it back.

"What is it?" Jason asked.

She looked at her hand. "Nothing," she said, shivering from the cold. "I can't find anything back there." Again she helped to push the door open.

Once there was space to get through, she squeezed around the side of the door. Without warning it flew wide, making her jump, and Jason sprawled on the ground. There was nothing blocking it.

He scrambled to his feet and grabbed his torch before returning to her side. They were in a long, narrow corridor. The floor was covered in dust and plaster that had lost its grip on the damp walls. A chair, made from wood with metal legs, had been abandoned at the other end of the corridor, which branched left and right. There were three doors to their left, and two to the right.

The nurse told her that there were two entrances to the Rose Wing. The main entrance would be difficult to approach without being seen by the patrolling guards, but there was a second door at the top of a stairwell that led to the treatment rooms.

None of the staff ever went there alone.

***

There were fluorescent strip lights along the ceiling that no longer worked, the electricity having been shut off when the asylum closed. Shining her torch into the first treatment room, Cindy saw fixtures and fittings that had simply been abandoned and forgotten, relics that would probably still be there in another thirty or forty years. A machine with several valves and wires stood threateningly alongside what appeared to be a dentist's chair. An empty frame was all that remained of a window that had been broken and boarded up long ago.

Cindy stopped when she reached the middle door on the left. The others were made of wood with reinforced glass windows. They stood open. This one was more like the door at the entrance to the Rose Wing: solid steel and windowless. She pressed her hand against the cold metal and took a deep breath.

"Mum?"

"Rachael was scared of this room," she said. "She was afraid of all these rooms, but especially this one."

Jason walked back to her, keeping his eye on the abandoned chair. "Maybe," he said.

"Why was she so afraid? Why didn't she want to go into this room?"

"How can you know that?"

"I just know."

Jason studied the door, shining the torchlight over it. "Come on." He took her arm.

"I need to look." She pushed the door open. "I'll be quick, I promise."

The room was the smallest of all, barely six feet wide by eight long. Her footsteps made no sound as she walked in and when she shone the torch around she saw that it, and all four walls, had been covered with a thin layer of padding that was now crumbling from damp and neglect. The room was empty. Not just devoid of furniture but entirely clear and plain. There wasn't even a window.

"There's nothing here," Jason said as he followed her in.

She didn't answer for a moment. She examined the other side of the door and found that was padded too. "I think that's the point."

"What do you mean?"

Cindy walked to the middle of the room and stood there, arms outstretched. She couldn't reach both walls at once. "Sensory deprivation," she said, looking up to find that there was no light and no fitting.

Jason walked to the far end of the room, where the window should have been, and picked at the crumbling padding. He wandered around the room, his hand pressed against the wall.

"They were locked in here and left," she said. "No light. No sound." She imagined how afraid she would be in that room alone. How long, she wondered? A night? Twenty-four hours?

"Can we go now?" Jason stood by the door, holding it open for her.

She nodded. She didn't want to be here anymore. She walked to the door and stepped outside. It thudded closed, trapping Jason on the other side. "Jason?"

"What happened?" His voice was quiet, muffled.

It had happened so fast. Had she pulled the door closed? She half remembered doing it, but it didn't make any sense. "I don't know, the door just closed." She hesitated. "It must have been a draught." She pushed against the door. "Are you leaning on the door? It won't open."

"No. What's going on?"

"I don't know." She pushed but it wouldn't budge. "Try to find a handle. Help me open it."

"There's nothing on this side of the door. Oh God, it's too dark in here! I need to get out."

There was a crash as something heavy hit the other side of the door. "Are you OK?"

"I need to get out!" Another bang.

"OK, it's just jammed." She pressed her whole body against it. Something made the hair stand up on her neck. She shone the torch down the corridor. There was nothing, just the abandoned chair. "I'll get it open in a moment."

"I need to get out now." Another bang against the door. "Oh God," he said, "the torch has gone out!"

Cindy pushed against the door but it didn't even move. It was like it had locked itself shut. She started to panic. The room had no other way in and she didn't have a key.

"There's someone in here."

"What?" She considered running to fetch the security guards. They'd probably be prosecuted for breaking and entering, but Jason was starting to panic and might hurt himself.

"I think there's someone in here with me. God, no, go away." He cried out. "Go away!"

"There's nobody there, Jason." Cindy listened against the door. She could hear Jason shouting at someone to go away. Was there a reply? She shook her head. "It's just your imagination playing tricks on you."

"Leave me alone," he shouted, and the door opened by a crack.

Cindy pushed it back, grabbed Jason's arm and pulled him out of the room. His cheeks were wet with tears and his forehead with sweat. He scrambled away from the door and sat against the wall opposite, burying his face in his hands as his torch flickered back to life. He flinched as she put a hand on his shoulder.

"There's someone in there," he said.

She shook her head. "We were both in there, Jason, the room was too small for anyone to be hiding."

"I know what I heard."

She wanted to go into the room to prove it to him, to make it all better like she would have done when he was a child, but she didn't want to look. There was certainty in his voice. "Are you going to be OK?"

He shook his head. "I don't think I can do it."

"OK," she said, rubbing his arm. "OK. We'll go back."

She helped him to his feet and they started back toward the door. He was shaking. Her own heart skipped a beat. She was leaving. Falling at the first hurdle.

"I can't do this," she said, extricating herself from his arm.

"What?"

"Just wait here. I won't be long." She turned back down the corridor. "Sorry," she said, without looking back.

***

Cindy's footsteps tapped as she walked along a metal walkway. She hadn't told Jason what the nurse had said about the Rose Wing: the stories she'd heard when she worked here; the things she claimed to have seen. Cindy had tried to push them out of her mind but suddenly they seemed very believable. The nurse had urged her not to go in. Taking deep breaths, Cindy silently begged to be allowed to pass.

Iron staircases spiralled down to her left while open rooms passed by on the right. She didn't shine her torch inside. Her ears were pricked, listening for any sound other than that of her own feet as they tapped along the walkway with a measured pace.

Tap, tap, tap came a sound from behind her. It was like an echo, except an echo should have been more like the original sound. This was hollower, somehow, like it had echoes of its own. Cindy stopped and listened but it didn't come again. She walked on and after a few steps it started again. She stopped and breathed out through her nose.

Though every fibre of her being screamed for her to run, either onward or back, she didn't. She took a deep breath and turned, shining the torch back the way she had come. There was nothing, just a dark and empty walk. She shivered. The silence was so complete, she imagined that Jason could still hear her breathing. She turned back and shone the torch in the other direction. Still there was nothing.

There was another tap.

It was almost imperceptibly quiet, but it was there, right above her head. She turned the torch up to the ceiling but found nothing, just dirty ceiling tiles. She took a deep breath to calm her nerves and started forward again.

As her feet tapped on the metal walkway, again she heard the tapping above her head. "It's nothing," she told herself, but wasn't convinced. She picked up her pace and after a delay the tapping noise did too. Finally, she broke into a run and fled the last few paces to the end of the walkway where a stone corridor with a tiled floor turned left. A stairway led down from there to the ground floor. Cindy stopped, panting, and leaned against the wall. "Go away," she said.

To her surprise, the sound retreated back down the walkway.

***

Jason's stepdad always called him a girl. *Go back to your room, stop being such a girl. Men aren't afraid of the dark.* Jason would lie awake and yearn for the days before Richard came to live with them, when his mum would keep him safe and dry his tears.

He was angry when he went to school: punching other boys just to make himself feel like less of a coward, taking risks, smoking and shoplifting. If anyone suspected he was scared then they didn't say so. They didn't think he was afraid of anything. But he was.

Jason leaned against the door to the Rose Wing as if it might slam shut at any moment and lock him out. He gripped the torch and shone it down the corridor, wishing that his mum would hurry back and wondering about the chair. Why had it been left there? Who had brought it? He shivered and wiped his hands on his face, embarrassed by his reaction to being locked in the dark. But the voice. There was someone in the room with him, speaking when he took a breath. Or was it just the sound of his own breathing? He felt the heat rise to his face. When he used to lie alone in the dark he would imagine that he could hear something in the room. Someone at the foot of his bed, whispering.

He knew where she was heading. They had both studied the map that the nurse had drawn so that they wouldn't get lost in the dark when they only had torchlight to guide them. It was a simple route: turn left, turn right, continue to the end of the walkway, down the stairs and along to the end of the hall. All the records were inside the doctor's office. If there was any trace of what happened to Rachael, it would be in there.

He turned the torch in the other direction. The stairwell seemed comforting in comparison. It was the way home, to places that had lighting and heating. Stop being such a girl, Richard would have said. He tightened his grip on the torch. He hated that man. He hated him for how he had been treated. He hated him for how he had treated his mum, for the drinking, the gambling and the one night stands. He hated him for the fact he had left her. Jason had only been in prison for a day when the man walked out. A single day. He couldn't even stick around to help her through that.

Clenching his fists, he took a step away from the door and walked to the other end of the corridor, turning the torchlight up the left and right passages when he reached the chair. It was all empty and quiet. He grabbed the chair and turned, carrying it back to the door and using it to prop it open.

"That was easy enough," he said to himself. Nothing to be afraid of.

He turned the torch on the door to the sensory deprivation room. It was ajar, as he had left it. He felt sweat break out under his arms but he started walking anyway. As he passed the door he heard it swing open, but he didn't look at it. He kept walking.

When he reached the junction where the chair had been he paused. There was a draught from above his head.

Examining it with the torch he found that one of the ceiling tiles had been removed. "A draught." He laughed. "Just a draught." He turned the torch on the door to the sensory deprivation room. It was wide open. He blew out his breath. "Just a draught."

"Girl."

Jason couldn't be sure whether the voice was real or inside his head. It sounded like Richard, except not quite like Richard, more like someone doing an impression. "I'm not afraid of you," he whispered to himself. He turned left to follow her but hesitated, shining the light back the way he had come.

So the door was open, it didn't mean anything. It was just the breeze from the open hole in the ceiling. He started back down the corridor and stopped by the sensory deprivation room. Breathing deeply, he shone the torch inside the room and caught his breath.

Writing was scorched into the opposite wall. It wasn't neat but it was clear: **I won't let her go**. Jason kept the torch pointed at it, illuminating the final word with the torch beam. "Mum," he said quietly, his legs feeling suddenly very weak.

He turned and felt cold breath by his ear, paralysing him. There was a giggle and he heard a woman's voice. "I won't let her go, Jason," she whispered, her cold breath making his skin prickle. "Run away, girl," the voice said, impersonating Richard. The muscles in his shoulders tightened. He wanted to turn, but he dared not see her.

The cold breath retreated and again he heard a woman giggle, then there was nothing.

He stood, paralysed for a moment, but the message was clear. For a breath he considered running away, back down the tunnel to safety, but he couldn't. He whirled, shining the torch in the direction the voice had come from, but there was nobody there.

***

The doctor's office stood at the end of the hall, a faded blue door with a slightly less faded square where a plaque had been removed. Cindy was relieved to be there, desperate now to return to Jason and get away from the hospital as soon as she could. She had heard no more tapping as she walked through the lower floor.

She opened the door and stepped inside, shining the torch around a comfortable looking room with a large desk, shelves and a leather armchair, all covered with a thick layer of dust. A map on the wall showed the layout of the Rose Wing, putting the doctor's office on the eastern corner of the building. There were two expansive windows. Cindy imagined them before they were boarded up, looking out over the grounds in the summer; blue sky and an unrestricted view all the way to the woods.

The shelves were stacked with folders and notebooks, all with thick spines labelled in red felt-tip pen. She went to them and ran her finger along the labels in the torchlight, looking for the patient log. When she found a black notebook labelled 'Sensory Deprivation' she paused. Jason was waiting upstairs. She shook her head and continued to search.

After three more folders she changed her mind, deciding that she would just take a quick look. She took the sensory deprivation notebook from the shelf.

Cautiously, she opened it. Names were listed along with details of the treatment and notes of the effects. Two days, resulting in auditory hallucinations. Four days, resulting in a marked improvement in mood - patient quieter than usual. She flicked through page after page of records and names until she came to her mother's: Ainsworth, Rachael. The name had been crossed out and a single word written underneath.

"Missing," Cindy read aloud. She looked at the date in the margin and closed the book, dropping it on the desk.

Going back to the shelves, she continued her search. When she found the patient log she went straight to the same date. Her mother's name was there. Missing had been written alongside the name. The log didn't give any details; it was clinical and detached. Corridor B, room 3: a double cell with only one occupant.

"Why were you there alone?" Cindy said to herself, and flicked back through the book.

In an entry from the previous week she found what she was looking for. Gwendolyn Hill, Rachael's roommate, committed suicide in room 3 after seventy-two hours in sensory deprivation.

"Oh, Rachael," Cindy said, putting the book aside. "Did you find her? Is that why you were so afraid?" She sat down on the edge of the doctor's desk and thought about the situation Rachael had found herself in. How terrified she must have been when she knew she was going to the same place. "She didn't want to die," she said to herself.

She knew that Jason was waiting for her upstairs. She thought of him alone in the dark. She hated herself for leaving him like that, but she needed to see where Rachael had lived before she could say goodbye.

She turned to the map on the wall and searched it for the patient accommodation.

***

The metal walkway was dark and quiet. Jason walked quickly, breathing deeply and keeping the torch beam focused on his goal at the opposite end, where a stone corridor turned left. He ignored the open rooms and spiral staircases to either side of the walkway, concentrating on the dull clang of his feet on the metal. In his mind he replayed what had happened, imagining that there was someone following behind him. He turned around but there was nobody there.

She needed him. He opened his mouth and tried to speak, but it came out as a croak. Clearing his throat, he tried again. "Mum, we have to get out of here!" Jason imagined that she was just around the corner and would hear him shouting. There was no reply.

The torch went out.

He tried to keep walking, breathing steadily, but with no light his coordination left him. His shoulder hit the wall and he jerked away, into the railing. With both hands on the cold metal, he slowly felt his way along the railing to the next gap, then reached out for the next railing but found nothing in the dark. He didn't want to release his grip and end up falling down a staircase. Jason shook the torch. "Come on."

Taking deep breaths, he turned so that his back was against the railing and stepped forward with his hands out in the dark. They touched rough brick as they found the wall. He took a step to the left, keeping his hands against it. Another step and again he found himself reaching out into space. It was one of the open rooms.

Jason felt in the darkness for the other side of the doorway. His fingers brushed soft material and he cried out, pulling them back. There was heavy breathing in the dark, a hissing sound. It came closer. Crying out, he took a step back, putting his hands out behind him to find the railing.

Something pressed firmly against his chest and knocked him off balance. He fell back into darkness, still gripping the unlit torch as his head and back hit the stairs hard. The momentum of his feet carried them over his head and as he rolled the torch came back on. When his head hit the metal for a second time he lost consciousness.

***

The torchlight caught the shapes of wheelchairs and gurneys that lined the corridors, now rusted, rotten and covered in crumbling plaster. They cast shadows that moved along the walls as Cindy followed the map in her head to the patient accommodation rooms: two corridors, each with six rooms and a nurses' station at the near end.

As she entered corridor B, she imagined the place as it would have been when Rachael was there. She tried to convince herself that it wouldn't have been depressing, but it was difficult. The white walls and tiled floor were cold and clinical. Constant monitoring by the nurses would have taken away any pretence of privacy or freedom.

The nurses' station was partitioned from the rest of the corridor with a brick wall and thick, shatterproof glass. The door was locked so she peered through the window. She saw lists of patients still pinned to the walls.

The corridor was wide with a high roof. Debris from the crumbling walls and ceiling covered the floor. She walked to room 1 and shone the torch inside. Two single beds. The mattresses were collapsing. The floor was carpeted, and the only comforting thing in the room. There was nothing homely, no curtain rail at the window or pictures on the walls. Just those two beds. Bare, like a jail cell. Nothing that the patients could use to hurt themselves or anyone else.

The lights above her head flickered into life, lighting the corridor in yellow. Cindy turned and squinted against the light. She searched the open space but there was nobody there.

"Hello?"

By the exit was an abandoned wheelchair, its back resting against the wall. The light at that end of the corridor went out, plunging it back into darkness. Cindy pointed the torch in that direction, but it died as she did so. She backed away, catching her breath as she noticed her own reflection in the glass of the nurses' station.

"It's an old building," she said.

Cindy continued backing away, breathing deeply as she tried to keep calm. Somehow the light made the darkness more frightening. She jumped as she felt something solid behind her and turned to find the door to room 3. Nothing moved in the darkness. It was quiet except for the hum of the lights. She peered through the window in the door, but the room was dark. All she could see were shapes. Two cots, just like the first room, but there were other shapes here as well, dimly lit by the overhead lights. Smaller shapes littered the floor; cylindrical objects like baked bean tins. She pushed the door open and stepped inside, leaning down to pick up one of the cylinders, and was surprised to find that her assumption was right: it was a food tin. Cindy held it up to the light and dropped it. Whatever had been inside had rotted long ago, leaving a film of black mould that had spread to the outside.

She turned and kicked another with her foot so that she wouldn't have to touch it. This one was heavy, as if it was unopened.

Cindy leaned down and picked it up, again turning to hold it to the light in the doorway of the room. It was a tin of peach slices. "What are these doing here?" She said to herself.

When she stepped out of the room she felt a breath by her ear. Goose pimples rose along her shoulders and she shivered. Her hands were shaking but she forced herself to speak. "I'm not going to hurt you." She turned in the direction of the breath, looking into the darkness of the room, but nobody was there.

Cindy stepped backwards into the corridor, keeping her eyes on the darkened room.

"Get out," whispered a voice from inside the room.

Cindy stared. It was a woman's voice. She knew that there was nobody in there, which left only one possibility. Forcing herself to take a step forward, she spoke to the darkness "Rachael, is that you? I'm your daughter."

The light above her went out, leaving the corridor in darkness except a single flickering fluorescent strip at the far end. She saw a movement as the door to room 3 swung closed. Cindy backed away. "Don't be afraid, Rachael," she said, "I'm not here to hurt you."

There was a cold breath by her ear. She gasped and there was a breathy giggle in response. "I'm not Rachael," whispered the voice. Cindy felt each word as it was breathed into her ear.

The final light went out and the torch came back to life at the same time, making her jump back. She shone the torchlight desperately around the corridor, flinching at every shape. There was nobody there. She backed away from room 3 until her back was against the opposite wall, and then finally allowed herself to cry. "I have to get away," she said. Forcing herself to stand up straight, she started walking toward the exit. Jason would be waiting. She would get to the top of the stairs and then shout for him. He would come to help her.

The torchlight caught the abandoned wheelchair and she hesitated. On the seat was something black. Wiping at her face she approached a little closer, still breathing heavily. It was a metal grille. She ran her fingers through her hair, blinking away the tears.

Cindy turned the torch up above the wheelchair, illuminating the wall, and found an open ventilation shaft.

***

A bright light stung Jason's eyes. His back ached. He turned his head away from the light and pain shot through his neck and the bridge of his nose, making his head throb. He took a sharp breath and screwed up his eyes. When he finally opened them again he found himself looking at the bottom step of the stairs. Dust motes swam in the light from the torch. The room was silent.

He turned onto his stomach, groaning as he stretched his back, making it ache. He had no idea how long he'd been lying there and knew that he had to start moving. The way out was up, he knew, but his mum was still somewhere inside the hospital. He vaguely remembered being pushed down the stairs.

He pushed himself up from the floor, stretching and closing his eyes against the dizziness that threatened to bring him back down. He put out his hand and steadied himself against the stairs for a moment until the dizziness passed.

Still holding on, he leaned down and picked up the torch. He swept it over his surroundings, finding himself in a large hall with a wooden floor. Dust and grime were everywhere. Against the walls, folding tables and chairs had been neatly stacked after the last meal before the Rose Wing closed. A large serving hatch had metal shutters pulled down across it. They were blue in patches where the paint still remained. Jason hesitantly walked toward the opposite end of the hall where a pair of swinging doors stood closed.

His footsteps echoed in such a large, empty space, ringing through his aching head. He stumbled but kept his balance and pushed his way through double doors into a short corridor that turned to the right. A door stood closed on the left, with a sign on the wall above. It was the chapel.

"Mum," he shouted as he started forward. "Mum," he tried again when he reached the turn in the corridor, leaning around the corner and shining the torch into the empty darkness.

There was a scratching sound from behind. Jason turned and shone the torch at the hall doors but there was nothing there. The scratching sound started again. It was coming from the chapel, and as he lit it with the torchlight Jason could see the door vibrating back and forth. His mouth went dry and the hairs stood up on the back of his neck.

"It's a rat," he told himself as he backed away around the corner. "Just a rat." He turned and walked away, listening intently to the scratching sound. It stopped and he paused. A door slammed. He took a few more steps and heard the scratching noise again. Turning slowly, he shone the torch back down the corridor toward the corner. There was nothing, but the scratching noise continued. It wasn't a constant sound. Rather, it came in short bursts.

"Just a rat," he repeated as he looked down the corridor. The torchlight showed nothing there, but the sound was closer than before, he was sure of it.

Jason could feel his heart beating. He took a step back, and then held his breath as fingers reached around the corner and scratched at the wall. They were gnarled and old, with long, broken nails. They scratched again. Jason backed away, feeling light headed. The top of a head poked around the corner; an old head with white hair and grey skin. It was a woman's head and it glared at him through eyes that held an uncanny resemblance to his mum's.

"Doctor," it hissed, and disappeared behind the corner, the hand being pulled back as well.

Jason turned and ran.

***

Cindy stood on the back of the wheelchair and shone her torch into the open vent. It was an aperture of a couple of square feet, and inside it stretched away for a few feet before turning skyward. There were scuff marks along the floor and food had been dropped in the corners. The smell of rotting meat and vegetables was overpowering. She climbed down, stepping from the back of the wheelchair to the seat and from there to the floor. She sat down on it to think.

Jason's distressed cries interrupted her thoughts. "Mum, where are you?" He sounded close to tears. "Mum?"

"I'm in here, what's wrong?"

He came to the entrance to the corridor and shone the torch into her face, forcing her to cover her eyes. "We have to go."

"What's happened?"

He grabbed her arm, turning the torch toward the exit and scanning the darkness. "I'll explain on the way. You have to get out of here."

"OK, calm down. I just want to check something and then we can go."

He shook his head. "We have to go right now. I think she's going to hurt you."

"Who?"

"Rachael. She told me she wouldn't let you go."

"She told you?"

He was breathing hard. "We have to go. Please, mum, just get out before she gets here." He kept the torch pointed in the direction he had come from.

"OK." She walked with him to the entrance to the corridor and shone her torch in the same direction. There was nothing there but more abandoned furniture and crumbling plaster. She started to walk but Jason stopped her.

"No, this way." He tried to pull her in the other direction, toward the doctor's office.

"What did you see down here, Jason?"

His lip quivered as he turned. He shook his head. "I don't," he said. "I mean, I can't."

"Did you see Rachael?"

"She locked me in there," he said. "She told me she wouldn't let you go. Now she's coming this way." He shone the torch back down the corridor as if she might appear at any moment. "We have to go."

Something just didn't add up. The food tins and the open vent; the voice in the dark and the miraculous lights. They seemed connected but separate. Cindy connected the dots, but it didn't seem possible. She spoke hesitantly. "What if she's still alive?"

***

"Mum, please, I don't want to see her again."

"She's alive. I'm sure of it."

Cindy walked quickly. Her footsteps tapped on the floor and Jason followed reluctantly behind. She heard him sniff back tears. The torchlight was little comfort. She slowed her pace and turned. His eyes implored her not to go any further.

"You go," she said, "I'll catch up."

"I can't leave you."

"I'll be fine. Just go."

He shook his head, taking deep breaths.

"I have to do this," she said, "I think she's still here. But you don't have to come with me."

"Yes I do," he said. "I can't leave you here on your own."

She knew he was afraid. She was afraid too. But she couldn't leave, not now. "Then you know why I have to find her."

"No. She said she wouldn't let you go."

Cindy turned and started walking again. "That wasn't her. It was someone else," she said. "Something else." She rounded the corner and saw the double doors ahead. "It was here that you saw her, wasn't it?" She turned to look at him.

He nodded. "I think she came out of the chapel."

Cindy turned the torch and shone it at the chapel door. It was plain wood, painted white with gloss paint that had gone grey with dust and age. The corridor was quiet. There was no scratching sound.

She blew out her breath. This was it. She walked to the door and pushed it open, holding up her torch to illuminate the room.

In the beam she saw rows of chairs. It was a small chapel; three rows of four chairs on either side of a central aisle. The door was at the back of the room and there was a stage at the front that was raised by a single small step.

Cindy stepped inside. It was quiet. She shone the torch over the stage. A large wooden cross was attached to the wall and a lectern had been placed to one side. A glass vase, covered in cobwebs, held faded and moth-eaten silk flowers on the window ledge beside the stage. She walked into the room and the door swung closed behind her.

Above the wooden cross was an open ventilation shaft.

"Jason, come in here."

She walked to the stage. The vent was smaller here than in the accommodation corridor, but it was still big enough to squeeze into if you were small.

"She's not here," Jason said.

Cindy shook her head. "No. She's in there." She pointed at the vent.

"What?"

"She's using the ventilation shafts to move around. I think she has been since she first went missing. I found rotten food inside the one by her room and I heard someone moving above my head upstairs."

Jason turned his torch to the vent. "Even if that's true, how are you going to find her?"

She shook her head.

"OK, so let's say Rachael is alive and using the vents to move around. We go home, call the police and let them deal with it. They'll find her."

Cindy had to admit that he had a good point. There had to be miles of shafts running through the hospital, with countless ways to climb inside. She nodded. He was right. "OK."

She turned and started toward the door, then stopped. Crouched behind the door was a woman. She wore a green cotton dress in a style that might have been fashionable twenty years ago.

"Hello," Cindy said. "Are you Rachael?"

The woman scowled and bared her teeth. She started scratching at the wall beside her. "Doctors," she said, accusingly.

Cindy realised that she wasn't just crouched, she was coiled. Her eyes said that she was afraid, but though her white hair was long and matted and her pale skin was a road map of crisscrossing lines, she was ready to attack them if she needed to.

"I won't hurt you," Cindy said. "I'm a friend."

The woman didn't say a word. Cindy took a step forward and she hissed, stopping her in her tracks.

"Jason, we have to get her out of here."

"OK." He took a step forward and the woman's eyes went wide. She growled and Jason stopped. "It's OK."

"We're here to help you, Rachael. You are Rachael, aren't you?"

"Leave me alone. You won't take me there." She turned to the door. "Gwen," she shouted. "Take them away."

Jason turned to Cindy. "Who's Gwen?"

"She was Rachael's roommate. She died, but I think she's still here."

There was a scratching sound from the door. This time Rachael wasn't touching it.

Cindy took a careful step forward, keeping her eyes on Rachael.

Rachael stared back. "There are doctors here," she whispered.

"Rachael, we're not doctors." Cindy took another step forward. "I'm your daughter." She heard Jason walking behind. When they were within reach she paused and put her hand out to stop him. "I want to take you away from here." She crouched and held her hand out to Rachael. "I'm going to take you home."

She could see Rachael's chest move up and down. Her lips were drawn back in an animalistic snarl. The scratching sound from the door continued as Rachael backed away as far as she could from Cindy's outstretched hand. She scratched at the door.

"It's OK," Cindy said.

Like a spring, Rachael launched herself at Cindy, knocking her off balance so that she fell onto her back and hit her head hard, knocking her teeth together. She cried out as Rachael climbed over her like she was just an obstacle.

"Jason, stop her."

Scrambling to her feet, she saw Rachael, illuminated by Jason's torch, dive over a chair away from him and run for the front of the chapel. She was heading for the open air vent. Cindy ran for the front of the room, hoping to get there before Rachael. "Don't let her out," she shouted as she pushed past Jason. "Go that way." She pointed the torch at the door.

She got to the front of the room just after Rachael, who immediately started scrambling up the wooden cross. She grabbed her and Rachael screeched in frustration as she was pulled away. Cindy held tight as Rachael fought to break free from her grip.

"I won't go there," Rachael screamed. "I won't! Gwen, help me."

Cindy's torchlight spun as she fought to hold onto Rachael. She saw the door fly open and knock Jason back. He swung around, shining the torch at the door but nobody was there.

She pulled Rachael to Jason's side. He shone his torch at the door as it slammed shut. Rachael screamed and struggled, but Cindy had her arms pinioned to her sides and without the element of surprise she wasn't strong enough to break free.

"Go," she said to Jason. "I can hold her."

He walked cautiously to the door and pulled it open. Faint light flickered on the wall opposite. He paused for a moment but leaned out into the corridor and shone his torch around. "Oh no," he said.

"What?"

He turned back, holding the door open. "There's a fire in the hall. I don't think we can get through."

"Go the other way." She followed as Jason turned in the opposite direction, heading toward the patient accommodation. "We'll get out through the windows," she said.

***

The fire spread unnaturally quickly, chasing them, or so it seemed. When they came to the accommodation rooms, flames blocked their way in and ruined any hope they had of reaching the windows. "Keep going," Cindy said, still wrestling with Rachael, who was shouting for Gwen. "I think the doctor's office will be clear."

Every door they passed along the way had flames behind it, but in the end she was right. Though the fire was at their backs and still spreading fast, when Jason pushed the door open he found no fire in the doctor's office. Cindy hauled Rachael through the doorway and Jason closed the door behind them.

"Hold it closed," Cindy said as she let go of Rachael, who went straight to the door and fell against it, calling Gwen's name as she sobbed.

"How did you know there wouldn't be any fire here?" Jason said.

Cindy shone her torch across the room at the larger of the two windows. The glass was intact and it had been boarded up from the outside. "I don't think they ever came in here." She walked across the room and stood to one side of the window. "But that won't stop the fire." She lifted her torch over her shoulder and smashed it against the glass.

The window cracked but it didn't break. The door rattled loudly and Jason's torchlight spun as he fought to stop it from opening.

"Keep the door closed, Jason, don't let her get out."

"There's someone out there."

"I know." She lifted the torch a second time and screamed with effort as she hit the window with all her strength. It shattered, showering the window ledge and the floor beneath with broken glass.

The middle had broken but it had left sharp edges all around. She smashed at the remaining glass with the torch, clearing the window to get at the board. Hitting it with the torch did nothing; it was heavy and had been fixed securely to the outside of the window.

She ran her hand through her hair and looked at Jason and Rachael. The door had frosted glass in it and the light of the fire was visible through it. It vibrated hard but Jason was holding it closed. She turned back to the window. "Help," she shouted. "Help!" She hoped that the guards would be investigating the fire. She banged against the board with her palm. "Help."

Jason joined in. "Help," they shouted together as Cindy banged her palm on the board. Rachael seemed not to have noticed. She placed her hand against the window and called to Gwen.

Someone knocked hard on the other side of the board. "Help," Cindy screamed. "Please help us."

"Stand back," said a man's voice. "Get away from the window."

Cindy went to Jason and helped to hold the door closed. There was a scratching sound from the other side as Rachael continued to call Gwen's name. "OK," she called to the guard, coughing from the smoke that seeped under the door, "please get us out of here."

A moment later something hit the board with a crash. It cracked in the middle but held. A second crash and the board caved in. A third and it broke. Fingers reached into the gap and pulled at the board, cracking it and opening it up before ripping part of the board away. The gap was large enough to squeeze through.

"Jason, take Rachael," Cindy said. "Get her out."

A man shone a torch through the gap in the board. "Come on," he said. "Quickly now."

Cindy held the door closed as Jason grabbed Rachael. She tried to pull away from him but he held her tight and dragged her across the room.

"You won't take her," whispered a woman's voice from the other side of the door. Cindy didn't respond. There was a scratching noise and it felt like something hit the door hard, trying to force it open.

Jason pushed Rachael through the window, assisted by the man outside. She screamed and shouted for Gwen, but they manhandled her through the gap. Jason turned to Cindy, shining his torch at her. "Mum?"

"Just go, Jason, I'll follow you."

He turned and climbed through the gap, with the guard's assistance. She could hear Rachael screaming. The scratching continued but Cindy held the door closed.

Finally she let go and ran across the room as she heard the door fly open behind her. She felt the heat at her back but she didn't turn. She flung her hands through the gap and the guard took hold of them, helping her to climb through. She gasped the fresh air gratefully.

A second man held Rachael back as she screamed for Gwen and tried to break free.

"Who's Gwen?" He held onto her as she fought to cough the smoke out of her lungs. "Is there someone else in there?"

She shook her head. "No." She turned to look at the building. "There's nobody else." Flames leapt from the windows.

"You do know this is private property?"

She nodded. "My mother was in there." She looked across at Rachael. She still reached toward the building, tears streaming down her face. Suddenly she looked very old and frail. "We didn't start the fire."

He shook his head.

From behind her, carrying on the cold wind, she could hear the sound of distant sirens.

ABOUT THE AUTHORS

Brent Abell

Brent Abell haunts Southern Indiana and is joined by his wife, sons, and pug who devours the souls of the guilty. His work has been published or has upcoming stories from numerous presses and his debut novella, *In Memoriam,* was released in late 2012 by Rymfire Books. He is a cool cat to drink rum, smoke cigars, and debate the state of heavy metal music with. Stop by and join the blog party at http://brentabell.wordpress.com.

Chad P. Brown

Chad P. Brown was born in Huntington, WV. Once he outgrew his childhood fears of haunted houses, clowns, and toy monkeys with cymbals (although the monkeys still creep him out a little bit), he discovered a dark love for writing and an affinity for macabre and eldritch matters. He is an Affiliate member of the Horror Writers Association and holds a Master's in Latin from Marshall University. He has appeared in such anthologies as *SPIDERS*, *Gothic Blue Book 2: Revenge Edition*, and *Fifty Shades of Decay*.

Twitter: @chadbrown72
Facebook: Chad P. Brown

Sarah Cass

Sarah Cass is mom of 3, wife to 1, living in a place she fondly refers to as 'Hickville'. Writing is an escape from a life of Midwest humdrum and family chaos. While her tales span from romance to creep – one central theme runs throughout – mental disorders. Psychological distress fascinates and entices – the darkness of the mind opens a realm of story possibilities at every triggered synapse. When she's not torturing her characters, she can be found sharing her life and writing at her blog, Redefining Perfect (http://redefiningperfect.com).

Twitter: @sadiecass

Alex Chase

Alex Chase is an American author of over a dozen short stories, appearing in anthologies such as *50 Shades of Decay* and *Mental Ward: Stories from the Asylum.* A prose writer, poet and routine conference presenter, he is a proud member of the Horror Writer's Association and Mensa. He attended the Chautauqua Writer's Festival this past year and is currently pursuing a bachelor's degree in English. When not at his computer, he can be found running, meditating and spoiling his loved ones.

Twitter: @AlexChaseWriter
Facebook: Alex Chase Writer

Denzell Cooper

I live in Cornwall, England. When I'm not working as a maths specialist tutor or writing weird horror/fantasy stories I can often be found wandering around old mortuaries, castles and graveyards late at night in the hope of catching a glimpse of the lingering dead.

Rose Wing will be my first professionally published story, and is an idea that I had kicking around in my cluttered cranium for about 7 years before I wrote it down. It also represents one of very few attempts to write ghost stories, despite my fascination with the subject.

Twitter: @DenzellCooper
Facebook: Denzell Cooper Writer

Jason Cordova

Jason Cordova is a California transplant currently living in Kentucky. His first novel, "Corruptor", was published in 2010 and since then has been featured in numerous anthologies. A military veteran and former teacher, he has seen enough to make the darkest of souls quiver. To purge these past horrors, he writes.

Yes, he taught at a middle school. Pity him.

Twitter: @warpcordova
Facebook: Jason M. Moondragon

Lindsey Beth Goddard

Lindsey Beth Goddard lives in the suburbs of St. Louis, MO. Most recently, her work has appeared in the anthologies: *Night Terrors* (Kayelle Press), *Welcome To Hell* (E-volve Books), and *Mistresses Of The Macabre* (Dark Moon Books) and the e-zines/ magazines: *Sirens Call*, *Flashes In The Dark*, *Hogglepot*, *Dark Fire Fiction*, *Infernal Ink*, *Twisted Dreams*, and *Yellow Mama*. More of her stories are scheduled to appear in: *Fresh Fear: Contemporary Horror*, *Quixotic: Not Everyday Love Stories*, and *Dark Moon Digest*. When not writing, she enjoys interviewing fellow authors, playing with her three children, and watching horror movies.

Twitter: @LindseyBethGodd
Facebook: Lindsey Beth Goddard

Sharon L. Higa

At six years old, Sharon L. Higa became obsessed with the supernatural, compliments of an older cousin who fascinated her with stories of hauntings and horror. Travelling the world with her family, the fascination grew, resulting in creating and telling her own stories. She wrote intermittently for a number of years, but it was after she and her husband moved to East Tennessee that her family and friends convinced her to write and publish her works. She now writes full time. She resides with eleven cats, one dog and Mark, her patient and loving husband of twenty two years.

Facebook: Sharon Higa
LinkedIN: Sharon Higa

Lockett Hollis

Lockett Hollis lives and writes in the USA. He is an eclectic enthusiast of all things dark or near-forgotten, and a collector and devourer of weird fiction, history, comparative religion, esotericism, philosophy and philology. He is currently working on the second book in a presently unpublished supernatural/medical thriller novel series.

Twitter: @LockettHollis
Facebook: Lockett Hollis

K. Trap Jones

K. Trap Jones is an award winning author of horror novels and short stories. With a strong inspiration from Dante Alighieri and Edgar Allan Poe, his passion for folklore, classic literary fiction and obscure segments within society lead to his creative writing style of "filling in the gaps" and walking the line between reality and fiction. His debut novel THE SINNER (Blood Bound Books) won first place in the Royal Palm Literary Award within the Horror/Dark Fantasy category. His latest novel THE HARVESTER will be released in Fall 2013 from Blood Bound Books. He is also a member of the Horror Writer's Association.

Twitter: @ktrapjones
Facebook: K. Trap Jones

Joseph Lapin

Joseph Lapin is a journalist, author, and poet living in Los Angeles, California. He is a contributing writer at the *LA Weekly*, and his work has appeared in *Salon*, *The Rattling Wall*, *Pacific Standard*, *OC Weekly*, *Sliver of Stone Magazine*, *The Village Voice*, and *Literary Orphans*. Originally, he's from Clinton, Massachusetts. He graduated from the MFA program at Florida International University.

Twitter: @josephalapin
Blog: josephalapin.com

Kimberly Lay

Kimberly Lay is a mother to five spirited daughters and lives in a house full of animals she often refers to as the zoo. Whether that is a reference to the girls or the pets, depends on the day. After a gypsy-like childhood traveling across the country, and living in 33 places by the time she turned 18, she has called Boise, Idaho home for over 16 years. When not surrounded by Young Adults, she writes stories about them with plenty of her crazy life experiences to draw from. Oddly enough, she is deathly afraid of ghosts.

Twitter: @Laycrew

Facebook: Kimberly Kennedy Lay

68853425R10186